Tahsha,

RaeAnne Thayne

The CAFE *at* BEACH END

CANARY STREET PRESS

made it this far. Come on. Only another few miles to go. We're almost there, baby. You've got this."

Though she knew it was irrational, even delusional, she thought the car seemed to pick up a little energy, like an old horse that smelled the familiar stable of home. A moment later, Meredith chugged onto Main Street on fumes and prayer.

Miraculously, she found a parking space not far from the historic brick building that housed the Beach End Café.

As she gazed at the building, with its cupola and planters spilling over with red and purple flowers, a flood of memories washed over her. Most of them were good, but a few made her throat ache and her eyes burn.

She had adored this place, once upon a time. During her childhood, the café had been her happy place. Whenever she had been feeling lonely or sad or frightened, she would come here in her mind.

Here, she had found love and acceptance. Her grandmother hadn't cared if she had a B in French literature or if she couldn't remember how to conjugate "to plunder." Frances and Tori had loved her just as she was.

If she closed her eyes, she could still picture herself and her cousin as they had been back then. One blond and fair, the other dark, but with the same hazel eyes they had inherited from Frances through their respective parents.

They had been as close as sisters. Closer, even. Sharing laughter and dreams and secrets during those halcyon summer months when Meredith would stay with her grandmother.

She could picture them now in a time-lapse age-progression that played across her mind. They were young girls, stopping at the candy store down the street to fill their pockets with sweets purchased using Meredith's spending money. Then preteens, riding cruiser bikes through town and giggling at all the cute boys hanging out at the skate park at Driftwood Beach. Then teenagers, sitting around a bonfire and talking and laughing with those same cute boys while stars glittered overhead and the sea murmured its endless song.

Had that really been her? The memories seemed vague and undefined. Hazy and not quite real, as if it had all happened to someone else.

Probably because it had. Meredith was a different person than that lonely girl, yearning for affection.

She once had a nanny who used to tell her that all the cells in her body replaced themselves every three months, so she really did become a new person, like a snake shedding its skin.

She had learned as an adult that wasn't wholly true—that some cells regenerated every few days, others had much longer life spans into the decades and others never regenerated. Still, so many moments in her life had that ethereal, distant feeling, as if they had happened to someone else.

Certainly the past eighteen months seemed a nightmare from which she couldn't quite wake up.

All of those things had happened to her, though. She couldn't wish away her history.

She tightened her fingers around the steering wheel as she finished parking and turned off the engine.

Like it or not, she owned it and would have to figure out now how to take the broken pieces of that history and rebuild herself into something better.

Reaching beside her for her umbrella, Meredith climbed out of the car and extended it, every muscle in her body aching from the long drive and the uncomfortable seat that offered zero lumbar support.

Sharp yearning washed over her for the leather luxury of her Mercedes, complete with both heating and cooling properties. She pushed it away. That was part of her *Before* life. This was her *Now*.

With rain clicking against the nylon of the umbrella, she arched her back and inhaled a few deep breaths, for courage as well as calm.

The mingled scent of sea and storm washed through her, smells that immediately took her back to long rainy afternoons in Frances's old cottage on Starfish Beach, playing board games and watching old movies.

Even in the rain, Cape Sanctuary seemed warm and welcoming, with flowers hanging from streetlamps and more in baskets in windows. Outside the café, a bench with peeling red paint beckoned visitors and their tired feet to stop and enjoy the view.

Did it also apply to those with tired spirits? Because her spirit was at low ebb right about now.

Other disheartened travelers might be welcome to rest here. Not her. Meredith knew she would not be greeted with the typical warmth and comfort the café usually exuded.

The people inside would not be thrilled to see her. Or at least one person wouldn't be, anyway. Her cousin and once best friend, Tori Ayala, would probably slam the door in her face and send her straight back out into the rain.

Grow a spine, she chided herself.

Tori couldn't send her packing. Not when Meredith owned half of the café.

She walked to the front door, lowering her umbrella once she was under the shelter of the entry. Heart pounding, she pulled open the door.

At the chime of bells from the front door, the low hum of conversation and clink of glasses inside seemed to die away and everyone turned to see the newcomer.

It was midafternoon, past the busiest hour of lunch. Still, the café seemed to be enjoying a healthy business, more than Meredith might have expected for the off-hour.

"Be with you in a moment," a cheerful voice rang out. Nerves fluttered through Meredith. She knew that voice, entirely too well.

That voice had once been on the other end of all those secrets, sharing her own and taking Meredith's too.

12

The last thing she wanted was a confrontation with Tori the moment she rolled into town, but she knew this one was unavoidable.

She straightened, hitching her last designer purse a little more securely on her shoulder. All she had left was a wreck of a vehicle and the three hundred dollars contained in a Louis Vuitton bag worth about six times that much.

Conscious of the patrons of the restaurant giving her sidelong, curious looks, Meredith shoved her hands into the pockets of her jacket, fighting with everything inside her against the urge to grab her bag tightly, push her way out the door and flee back into the rain.

And then what?

She couldn't leave. Not when she had nowhere else to go.

A moment later, the person she most dreaded seeing came out of the kitchen. Her cousin Tori wore a trim black apron with the Beach End Café embroidered across the front in white, and her arms competently hefted a tray of at least three or four orders.

Her brown hair was caught atop her head in a messy bun, and she had a pencil tucked behind one ear.

She looked as beautiful as ever, bright and vibrant and so dear that the sight of her made emotions rise up in Meredith's throat.

The sentiment was obviously not reciprocated. As Meredith might have predicted, Tori stopped dead the moment she spotted her. The tray in her arms wobbled slightly, but she maintained control with the ease of long practice.

Meredith's stomach rumbled as the smell of sizzling meat mingled with coffee and fried potatoes, scents she would forever associate with the café.

Meredith suddenly remembered she hadn't eaten since a hurried meal the night before, an inexpensive frozen dinner she had bought at the convenience store next to her questionable hotel in Sacramento and cooked in the microwave of her room.

She pushed away the hunger pangs as something to deal with later. Which was becoming the mantra of her life.

"Hello," she said, not sure what else to say.

Her tentative greeting was met by a wall of fury that seemed as tangible as those storm-tossed waves at Driftwood Park.

"Get out," Tori snarled. "Get the hell out."

Meredith could feel herself shrink. She hated confrontation. It made her want to disappear, to curl up around herself in the fetal position with her hands over her head.

At the anger in Tori's voice, Meredith wanted to slink out the door, climb back into her car and drive away through the rain-spattered streets.

She couldn't do that. She had come too far, literally and figuratively, to give up now.

She drew in a deep, café-scented breath and faced her cousin. "You want me to leave my own café? Why would I do that?"

"It is not your café," Tori snapped, flushing.

"Not all of it. But half of it is."

Tori's mouth tightened and she hefted her tray higher. "Forty-nine percent. I'm still the controlling owner."

"I know that," Meredith said quietly.

She felt lucky to have any stake at all in the café, especially when she didn't deserve so much as a box of straws.

Frances had clearly stipulated in her will that Tori would always have final say in all the café operations, given that she had spent her entire life working here whereas Meredith had only spent a few weeks every summer.

"I don't have time for this right now," Tori hissed. "I have customers. Some of us work for a living instead of existing on money we stole from gullible senior citizens."

As she no doubt intended, her words cut deeper than any chef's knife.

Before Meredith could muster a response, Tori gripped her tray and headed for a table in the corner where a group that looked like construction workers must have decided to take a break, probably because of the rain.

They, like everyone else in the café, were giving her surreptitious looks. Meredith wanted to disappear. Instead, she again straightened her spine.

She should be used to the whispers and stares by now. She was, in Chicago, but she had hoped for some respite here in Cape Sanctuary, thousands of miles away from the scene of the crime.

She stood gripping her damp umbrella, not sure what to do.

She had faced worse than this, she reminded herself. Tori couldn't kick her out, and she couldn't call the police on her. Meredith had as much right to be here as her cousin did.

When Tori was done delivering the meals, she headed back with the empty tray. The polite smile she had donned for the customers slid back into a glare.

"I thought you were leaving," she snapped. "Don't let the door hit you on the way out. Or do let it hit you. I don't care either way, as long as you go."

Meredith let out a breath, wishing she could find amid the animosity some trace of the cousin who had once been her dearest friend in the world, the one she knew she could always count on. The one who invariably cried when Meredith had to leave every summer to return to her real life.

She knew she wouldn't find what she wanted here. She had burned that relationship to the ground long ago.

"I'm afraid I'm not leaving," she said, fighting for calm. "Not this time. Grandma Frances left me half of the café—yes, I know, forty-nine percent. The only way I'll leave is if you can buy me out."

She had hoped they could have politeness between them, if nothing else, but she didn't blame Tori for her anger. Meredith knew she had earned all of it and more.

"Can you?"

Her cousin's features tightened. "Buy you out? You know I can't."

Meredith shrugged, trying for a placating smile. "Then I'm afraid you're stuck with me until I figure out what to do next."

"What do you mean, stuck with you?"

She shrugged. "I might only have a half stake in the café, but Frances left me all of Spindrift Cottage. I'll stay there while I start to learn the ropes of things here."

"Learn the ropes," Tori echoed, as if she couldn't quite make sense of the words.

"Yes. I'll move into the cottage today and then report for duty tomorrow."

Tori made a low sound of frustration in her throat. "So typical. You show up out of the blue and expect the whole world to start revolving around you."

"I'm sorry you see it that way," Meredith said with a calmness she didn't feel. "I only want to help. Since Frances died, I've left the entire burden of running the café to you, which isn't fair. I'm here to do my part now. I would have come earlier but I had…a few things going on."

Meredith was aware her fingers were trembling, and she had to hope Tori couldn't see.

"You're not welcome here," her cousin snapped again.

The impulse to escape overwhelmed her. She could always live in her car, since that was about all the shelter she could afford now.

When had she become such a coward?

She unfortunately knew the answer to that entirely too well.

As much as she didn't like confrontation, she couldn't avoid this one. Tori couldn't make her leave. Despite everything, even though Meredith knew how little she deserved it, Frances had loved her. Her grandmother had given her a cherished legacy, part of the café Frances had loved as well as ownership of a small two-bedroom cottage on the beach.

That cottage was hers. No angry creditors could take it away.

"Do you have the key to Spindrift Cottage, or would you prefer I reach out to the attorney handling Frances's estate?"

"I hate to break it to you but Spindrift Cottage is a mess. It's barely habitable. The previous tenants trashed it before their lease expired last fall and then the roof leaked during the winter. I had it fixed, which I'll bill you for, but I haven't done anything else to it."

Meredith swallowed, feeling vaguely queasy. Maybe she would end up sleeping in Posy after all.

"Thank you for that, anyway."

"I was too busy to do anything more, even if I were so inclined, since I had to clean out Frances's cottage entirely on my own."

Tori, Meredith knew, had inherited their grandmother's house, Seafoam Cottage. She also lived in a third cottage, Sandpiper Cottage, on the same strip of beach, one that Tori and her late husband had purchased from Frances and remodeled shortly after they married.

All of the houses were small clapboard beach cottages built at the same time. Her grandmother had inherited them from her own father and used to live in one and rent the other two out, until Tori and Javier bought Sandpiper Cottage from her.

Meredith fought her growing dismay. Tori was probably only trying to scare her away. How bad could the house really be?

"I'll be fine," she said. "I don't need much."

Tori's huff of disbelief and disdain burned.

"Is it furnished, at least?"

"Technically, yes. There's a bed, a sofa and a kitchen table with one chair. Certainly not up to your usual gold-coated standards."

"I'll be fine," she said again, with a confidence she was far from feeling. Even if it was a tent in the middle of a swamp, she wouldn't say a word to Tori.

No matter what shape Spindrift Cottage might be, it couldn't be worthless. It was on the beach, after all, and this was California, where the real estate market was one of the most expensive in the country.

This would work. It had to. She would fix up her legacy, sell the cottage and use the proceeds to rebuild her life somewhere far away.

She wasn't serious about Tori buying out her share of the café. It had been a total bluff, though she wasn't about to admit that to her cousin.

Once she sold the cottage, she planned to deed her share of the café over to Tori. It would be small recompense for all that Meredith had put Frances—and by default Tori—through, but something was better than nothing.

Meredith had exactly three hundred dollars to her name, which was hardly enough to even buy paint to spruce up the cottage. The bald truth was, she needed cash and the most obvious source of cash to help her flip the cottage would have to come from working at the Beach End Café.

"What time should I be here tomorrow? I saw the Help Wanted sign out front. I was thinking I could fill that opening."

Tori gave her a disbelieving look. "You want to bus tables for the morning shift."

Bus tables. That seemed about right for her skill level, when it came to working in a restaurant.

"Sounds perfect. So what time would that be?"

"We open at six thirty. The crew arrives at six."

Six a.m. Meredith gave an inward shudder.

"I'll be here. Go ahead and take the sign down."

Tori gave her a look that plainly told Meredith exactly what her cousin would like to do with the sign. Meredith chose to ignore that as well.

"Where can I find the key to Spindrift Cottage? Do you have it or do I need to find that attorney?"

Tori gazed at her wordlessly for a long moment, then reached into her apron pocket, pulled out a ring of several keys attached together with a purple carabiner and extracted one. She held it out.

Half afraid Tori would change her mind and shove it back into her pocket, Meredith snatched it up. Her fingers closed around the cold metal and she pulled it into her own pocket.

Her stomach rumbled again, loud enough that Tori must have heard. While Meredith would have liked nothing more than to slide into one of those dearly familiar booths and order one of the famous Beach End burgers—or at least a slice of Dutch apple pie to go—she decided she had better not press her luck.

"Thanks. I guess I'll see you in the morning. If not before, since we'll be living on the same beach."

She gripped the key like a lifeline and hurried out of the café. In her haste, she forgot all about the rain and the umbrella she still held in her hand. She opened it too late, after she was already drenched.

Surely there was some kind of metaphor in that to describe the mess of her life, but she had neither the energy nor the creative juices to figure it out.

She was here, in Cape Sanctuary. She had a place to sleep and a job. It might not be the ideal situation, but Meredith was desperate enough that she didn't care.

2

Tori

The door to the café shut with its customary chime of bells, a cheery, musical sound at odds with Tori's suddenly sour mood.

Meredith. Here.

Her day had been going so well too.

The café had been busy since they opened, all deliveries had come on time and the cooks were both relatively cheerful, which didn't always happen.

She had been thrilled to wake up to rain pounding the roof of the cottage, rain that the area desperately needed. The air had smelled delicious, damp with growth and spring, and everything had looked clean and new in the saturated light.

For the past three or four days, Tori hadn't been able to shake the strange feeling that something wonderful was headed her way. She couldn't have put her finger on why, she just had a little niggle of anticipation between her shoulder blades.

Boy, that was the last time she trusted her own intuition.

Could she have been more wrong?

Meredith. Here.

What did she want? She surely couldn't expect to be welcomed back with open arms. If she did, she was in for a rude awakening. Tori would have liked to greet her with a head-spinning roundhouse kick to the chest instead.

And wouldn't that have gone over well in a café full of customers? Not to mention get her arrested. Good thing she wasn't a violent person, though having Meredith living on Starfish Beach might just turn her into one.

"Who's the princess?" Ty Kemp, one of the two line cooks, looked curiously out the window, where Meredith walked through the rain toward a car parked down the street.

Princess was an accurate description. Meredith had been the spoiled, pampered child of ridiculously wealthy parents. Even dripping wet, she walked like she balanced a stack of books on her head, with a smooth, graceful glide.

"My cousin. No one important," Tori answered shortly.

She returned to the empty booth in the corner she had been using as a makeshift office while she caught up on paperwork in between her other responsibilities.

Try as she might, she couldn't focus. She kept seeing Meredith, thin, almost fragile, dressed in a jacket that seemed a size too large.

Why did she have to come back to Cape Sanctuary?

After everything that had happened the past few years—okay, more like the past fifteen—Meredith couldn't seriously expect Tori to be thrilled to see her.

Could she be either arrogant or obtuse enough to think she could waltz in, announce what she wanted, and Tori would simply smile and hand her an apron?

Yes. That was probably exactly what she expected.

She did own half of the café and one of the cottages, thanks to Frances. Their grandmother had loved Meredith up to the end, despite everything.

"None of what's happened is Meri's fault, honey," Tori could remember Frances saying in her soft voice, frail and breathless after her heart began to fail. "How can I blame her for her husband's mistakes?"

"She had to know," Tori had argued. "Meredith is not a stupid woman. How could she not know Carter was stealing from his clients to fund his own lifestyle?"

"Maybe. Maybe not. We don't know what went on between them. I know she's had a hard time of it and needs our understanding."

"She's not getting mine," Tori had snapped.

"I only know that I certainly don't want to be on the hook for everything your grandfather did before he died. If I was accountable for his sins, half the town would refuse to come to the café."

Tori had tried to argue that Meredith had to have participated in Carter Rowland's Ponzi scheme, or at the very least had certainly benefited from the lavish lifestyle it afforded.

Frances wouldn't listen at first. Then she had become too sick for more arguments between them.

Frances might have been willing to look only at the good. But Tori was not her grandmother and never could be. She was not willing to forgive and forget the havoc Meredith and her thieving bastard of a husband had caused in their lives.

She wanted to send her cousin packing. Sam Ayala, her brother-in-law, worked for the Cape Sanctuary police department. Surely he could find some reason to tell Meredith to get out of town before sundown, like something out of an old Western.

The last thing Tori wanted was to let Meredith start working at the Beach End Café.

But how could she possibly say no? Like it or not, the woman had every right to be in Cape Sanctuary and just as much right to start working at the café if she wanted.

"Ty says the pretty lady with the fancy purse who was in here a bit ago is your cousin."

Denise Arnold, plump and cheerful, gave her an inquisitive look as she plated a BLT and fries.

If Tori had her way, she would deny any association with her. "Yes. Her father and my mother were brother and sister."

"So that's Meredith. After all this time. I wasn't sure she really existed. Frances used to talk about her like she was royalty or something."

"Nope." Though Meredith's late husband had been considered king of the swindlers.

Denise looked around to make sure none of the other staff was in earshot. Since business had slowed, Ty had gone outside, probably to vape, though he was working to quit.

"I wasn't trying to eavesdrop but did I really hear something about her owning half of the Beach End?"

She couldn't deny it. What would be the point? "I'm afraid so. You know how Frances was. Generous to a fault but not always the best judge of character. She always saw only good in the people she loved."

Whether they deserved it or not.

Tori tended to err on the other side of that equation. Frances used to tell Tori she was far too young to be so cynical.

Tori didn't know if that was from having a mother who popped in and out of her life on a whim or from losing her husband tragically when she was only twenty-five.

"Well, this should be interesting," Denise said, shaking her head. "I hope she doesn't want to come in and change everything."

Tori picked up a large package of napkins from beneath one of the counters and headed for the swinging door of the kitchen.

"Too bad for her, if she does. The café is absolutely fine the way it is. Our customers like things as they are. Classic food, decent prices, good service. They know exactly what they'll find when they come here to eat. If Meredith thinks she can march in and change things, she's in for a rude awakening."

"Awakening or not, that one is going to be trouble, mark my words," Denise lamented.

Unfortunately, Tori didn't need Denise or her unusually dire tone to convince her of that. The moment Meredith had walked through the door, Tori had been hit by a wave of foreboding as fierce as a tsunami.

She couldn't buy Meredith out. Tori simply didn't have the liquid assets, and she couldn't risk taking out a loan she might not be able to repay.

For the past seven years, since Javier died, she had barely scraped by as a single mom, with the small salary she made managing the café for Frances.

She had used his small life insurance policy to pay off their mortgage to Frances, though her grandmother hadn't wanted her to.

Her grandmother had in turn used that money to pay off a loan she had taken out when times had been tough several years earlier and the café had slipped into the red.

Basically, Meredith owned forty-nine percent of a business that was barely profitable. If her cousin thought she was going to rebuild her fortune here in Cape Sanctuary, she was sadly mistaken.

Which begged the question, Tori thought. Why hadn't Meredith's mother bailed her out when Carter's legal troubles began? The family was rolling in money.

She immediately knew the answer. Because Cilla Collins must have hated the scandal her son-in-law had caused and would have done everything possible to distance herself from it, and by default from her own daughter. Cilla was the very definition of narcissistic.

She hadn't gone to Meredith's prep school graduation because she was recovering from a bad face-lift and hadn't wanted anyone to see the scars.

The chime of the door distracted her from both her thoughts and from the mundane busywork so necessary to running a café.

She looked up and felt an instant's alarm when she saw her

daughter, Emilia, and Em's cousin Cristina pushing open the door, laughing as they shook off a shared umbrella.

They seemed to bring sunshine along with them to push away the gloom of the day, two pretty, brown-eyed girls who could be sisters.

"Em! What up? School's not out for another hour!"

Her daughter gave her an innocent look that didn't fool Tori for a second. "We had a pep assembly for the baseball team during last hour because they're going to the state tournament. Coach Jordan said we didn't have to stay."

She frowned in disbelief. Did Emilia really think her mother was that gullible? Yes. Probably.

"Taylor and Josh are part of the team. You didn't want to stay to cheer on your friends?"

Both girls shrugged. "They know we love them, even if we don't make it to some lame pep assembly," Cristina said.

"We're just going to hang out at our place to do homework. But we stopped by to see if we could get a plate of french fries or something," Em said. "Neither of us ate lunch today and we're starving."

"Why?"

"Because we're growing girls?"

"No. Why didn't you have lunch?"

Emilia shrugged again, her favorite gesture. "We weren't hungry at lunchtime. Anyway, the main line in the cafeteria was spaghetti, and the school spaghetti is disgusting!"

"So nasty," Cristina confirmed. "It's like eating dead worms."

"Everybody hates it, which meant the à la carte line was epic. We didn't want to wait that long."

Naturally. Why eat disgusting spaghetti, when they knew they could always stop at the café after school—or during, for that matter—and Em's mom would set them up with a decent meal?

"We can find something for you. Do you want a grilled cheese to go with your fries?"

"That would be cool, Aunt Tori." Cristina beamed at her.

"Can we also have a couple of Diet Cokes?"

"Sure. I'll put it on your tab. You can work it off Saturday when you come in to help me organize the deliveries."

Em didn't look thrilled at that reminder that her Saturday morning would be spent working, but Cristina dragged her over to a booth in the corner and soon their heads were close together and they were both laughing at something.

Probably at Tori and how lame she was to make Em help around the café in return for fries and pop.

She shook that off. She used to be her daughter's best friend. Since Javi's death when Emilia was six, they had been a team. The two of them against the world.

Then Frances began to struggle with her heart and Tori took on more and more responsibilities here. As a result, Emilia had grown up either here, playing dolls at a table in the corner, or at Frances's place, keeping her grandmother company while Frances gardened, beachcombed or knit on the porch overlooking the ocean.

Everything changed again at the beginning of the school year, when Em turned thirteen.

People had warned her about the teenage years, how some children start testing boundaries, pushing limits. Tori had always been certain she and Emilia were different, that nothing would ever get in the way of their tight bond.

She had been wrong.

Even before Cristina moved back to Cape Sanctuary along with her father, Sam, Javier's brother, Em had begun to change. She was no longer the sweet, easy, eager-to-please child. Instead, as her own opinions grew and matured, she began to become more defiant and oppositional.

Tori felt as if she couldn't do anything right these days. With a physical ache, she yearned to have those earlier days back, when Em couldn't wait to come into the café after school to tell her mother all about her day. These days, Tori felt lucky if Em shared *anything* with her.

She couldn't worry about that now. While her daughter would always be her greatest concern, she had more urgent things to stress about today, like how she was going to cope with Meredith Freaking Rowland blowing back to Cape Sanctuary like a human hurricane.

She headed for the kitchen to put the order in with Denise.

"Girls are here early, aren't they?" The cook, hands busy slicing tomatoes, gestured with her head out the door toward Emilia and Cristina. "School's still not out for a bit, unless they're having some holiday my grandkids didn't tell me about."

"No holiday. A pep assembly, apparently, which they decided to forgo. They're hungry. Could you cook them up a couple of cheese sandwiches and an order of fries?"

"You've got it. Aspen left, by the way. Said she wasn't feeling well."

That left Tori alone to work the dining room, she realized. Where was Meredith when she needed her? At least it was the slow time between lunch and dinner.

But when she left the kitchen, she found a large group was waiting to be seated, with a couple of regulars behind them.

She moved two four tops together, seated both groups, handed out menus and then stopped at Em and Cristina's table.

"I'm short-staffed, Em. Can you grab your own drinks?"

Emilia huffed out a breath.

"Fine," she said in an aggrieved tone that conveyed the exact opposite of her single choppy word.

Tori frowned, but she didn't have time to call her daughter on her attitude right now.

Between the other diners and a phone call she received from another Chamber of Commerce board member about the agenda for an upcoming meeting, Tori didn't have time to check on the girls, other than to deliver their sandwiches when they were ready.

When she hung up the phone from the board member, she saw the girls had finished their food and were sliding out of the booth.

Tori managed to catch them before they headed out the door.

"Where are you two off to now?" she asked, in what she hoped was a mildly curious tone instead of an interrogation.

"We're going to hang out at our place for a while," Tori said. "We, um, have some homework."

More likely, they wanted to practice some dance moves for their favorite social media app.

"I'll be home in about an hour," she said. "Let me know if you need anything. I can stop at the store on my way home."

"I should be good."

As they walked outside, they didn't bother to lift their umbrella and Tori saw the rain had stopped. The sun was even peeking out of the clouds.

May could be fickle on the northern California coast. Some days felt like summer, others were more like January. And then there were the not uncommon days that somehow managed both.

On impulse, Tori followed the girls out into the afternoon and stood outside the café, inhaling the clean, fresh scent of flowers and ocean and spring. Only a moment, she told herself, lifting her face to the sun. After the day she had already been through, she needed a little self-care.

She was basking in the warmth, eyes closed, when she heard a vehicle pull up and park in one of the few slots in front of the café. She opened one eye, pasting on a smile for a potential customer.

It froze when she saw Sam Ayala climbing out of a small SUV with the logo for the Cape Sanctuary Police Department on the side.

She opened both eyes, bracing herself for the odd tension she felt around Sam since he and Cristina moved back.

"You barely missed the girls. They left about ten minutes ago, heading to Starfish Beach."

He glanced at his watch. "That's fast. School has only been out five minutes."

"Apparently, the middle school had a pep assembly they both chose to miss."

He didn't look as if he believed that excuse any more than Tori had. "With only three weeks left of the school year, I think most of the students think they're done learning."

"Unfortunately."

He held up a large insulated thermos. "I stopped by to see if I can bum some coffee from you. I'm working a double shift today and could use a little more rocket fuel."

She was proud that the café served the best coffee in town, something the locals tried to keep a closely guarded secret.

"Sure. Come in."

Sam headed to the counter and made small talk with a couple of the locals while Tori dumped out the dregs of what remained in his thermos, rinsed it out and refilled it with fresh coffee.

Sam had been part of her life, at least on the periphery, since she was seventeen and started dating his younger brother. He had been a distant figure, though, already married to Joni and living in Los Angeles County.

After she married Javier, they saw Joni and Sam for the occasional family holiday and visits back to Cape Sanctuary. Theirs had always been a friendly, polite relationship.

She wasn't sure what changed since his divorce three years earlier, especially since he and Cristina moved back. She found herself always feeling…unsettled around Sam.

"What are the girls up to now?" he asked when she returned his coffee to him. "You said they were heading to Starfish Beach?"

"That's what they said. They claim they're doing homework.

I'm leaving here shortly and I'll keep an eye on them, but if you don't want them to be alone until I can get there, I can always send them to their grandparents."

Sam's parents, Pablo and Teresa, lived only a few blocks inland from her place on Starfish Beach and had been a steady, warm presence in Em's life since she was born.

"They should be fine. How much trouble can they get into?"

"I'm not sure we really want to know the answer to that," she answered tartly.

Sam's smile made her feel as jittery and unsettled as if she had just chugged his whole thermos.

"Thanks for this," he said, setting far too much money on the counter.

"Sam. You don't have to pay me for coffee. I've told you that a dozen times. The least I can do for Cape Sanctuary's finest is keep you in coffee. Besides that, you're family. I'm happy to cover you."

"I appreciate that, but I just came from a department where graft was the norm. I'm trying to avoid even the perception of wrongdoing. Which means I'll keep paying for my brew."

She wanted to argue, but she had learned since his return to Cape Sanctuary that Sam could be as stubborn as his brother had been.

She nodded, telling herself she would simply try to drop off a pie for him and Cristina one of these days as a sign of her appreciation. He wouldn't say no to pie, would he?

"I almost forgot to tell you," Sam said on his way toward the door. "About an hour ago I spotted a car I didn't recognize pulling up to Spindrift Cottage. Do you have someone staying there?"

The reminder of Meredith was more than enough to sour her mood again. "Not by choice," she muttered.

"Do you need me to evict a squatter?" he asked, his tone only half joking.

"I wish you could. Unfortunately, she owns the cottage. There's nothing I can do. It's my cousin, Meredith."

"The one…"

"Yes. That one."

Unlike Sam, who came from a large, boisterous extended family, Tori only had one cousin, at least as far as she knew. She didn't know her father's identity and her mother had had only one sibling, Meredith's father.

Since both of their parents and now Frances were gone, Tori and Meredith—and of course Emilia—were all that was left of their line.

She would have loved a big family full of cousins. Instead, she was stuck with one she couldn't stand.

"I have no idea why she's really here in town. I suspect she wants to flip the cottage."

"What do you think about that?"

"It's hers. Frances left it to her. She can do what she wants with it."

She hesitated, then decided to tell him the rest of it. "Frances also left her half ownership of the café. Almost half, anyway. I got fifty-one percent, Meredith forty-nine."

He raised an eyebrow. "Does she want to be a partner?"

It was comforting, somehow, to share this with Sam. Now that Frances was gone, Tori didn't have very many confidantes. She had a few close friends and a few more she would consider good friends, but she had never been one to vent about her frustrations for hours on end.

"Who knows what Meredith really wants? I don't have any idea. I do know she plans to start work tomorrow here, busing tables, of all things."

"That should be fun."

"Sure. That's one word for it." She could think of about a dozen more, most of which she couldn't repeat.

"I have never hated anyone in my life before. It's a strange feel-

31

ing," she admitted. "But after what she and her husband have done, I think it's safe to say that if Meredith were caught in a riptide, I would stand on the shore and tell her *bon voyage.*"

"Wow. I wouldn't have guessed you could be so vindictive."

She sighed, feeling small and punitive. It wasn't true, anyway. If Meredith were drowning, Tori would probably jump in to rescue her. She wouldn't be happy about it but she would still do it, for Frances if not her own conscience.

"If not a riptide, she deserves to be stung by a hundred jellyfish," she muttered.

Sam's brown eyes crinkled with his smile. He was obviously not convinced she meant her words. "Careful. I'm still a police detective. You had better hope nothing happens to her while she's back in Cape Sanctuary or I'll know exactly where to turn to find my prime suspect."

"Not if I make it look like an accident," she said with a scowl that only made him laugh more.

That was the problem with Sam. He knew her too well. He was also so honorable; she knew he wouldn't hesitate for a moment to arrest his widowed sister-in-law if he suspected her of a crime.

"I should probably tell you Spindrift Cottage isn't the only one that will be occupied. I have rented out Frances's cottage for the next few weeks, as well. If you see someone there you don't recognize, don't automatically assume they're trespassing."

"Good to know. Do you have a family coming in?"

"No. A writer coming to town for a little solitude. He booked as soon as I listed the cottage. He's staying all through June."

"Has he written anything I might have read?"

"Doubtful. He said he's trying to finish his first book and needs solitude."

"Should make for an interesting few weeks on your little stretch of beach. In a blink, you went from having it all to yourself to sharing it with a reclusive writer and a cousin you can't stand."

"Yippee," she muttered, which only made him smile more.

"I've got to run. Thanks again for the brew. Don't go throwing your cousin into any riptides, okay?"

"I refuse to make promises I can't keep," she answered.

Sam's smile stayed with her for the rest of the afternoon.

3

Meredith

As she looked around the interior of Spindrift Cottage again, Meredith felt panic rise up in her throat like bile.

Tori had told her it was a mess, trashed by the previous tenant. If anything, her cousin had downplayed the reality. It wasn't simply a mess, more like a full-on disaster, with peeling wallpaper, water damage to the ceiling and two broken windows that would have to be replaced before birds moved in and decided to make a nest.

It smelled musty enough that she worried there was mold growing everywhere she couldn't see.

At least Tori had been right about furniture, with a saggy ripped sofa and a wobbly chair and table in this room and a dingy mattress she was almost afraid to touch in one of the bedrooms.

She couldn't possibly live here. Sleeping in her car would be preferable to this.

She straightened her shoulders, a gesture that was becoming almost habitual. Yes. She could. The place only needed a little bit of elbow grease and some paint, she told herself. She could do this.

For someone desperate and in a housing crisis, Spindrift Cottage was a palace. It had four sturdy walls, a roof that had been repaired and would now keep out the rain, and best of all it was hers. No one could take it away.

What would her friends say about how far she had fallen? For a moment, she had an almost painful ache to talk to Isabel Johnson and Diego Muñoz, her assistants at the gallery and two of only a handful of friends who had stuck by her.

Oh, how she missed them both. Her friends *and* the gallery she had loved so passionately.

She didn't care about anything else that had been seized after Carter had been arrested. The penthouse had never felt like home, with its gleaming furniture and priceless antiques. It had felt more like a prison for most of her marriage.

All of the cars but her Mercedes SUV had been Carter's. He had purchased all the jewelry in the bank deposit box, most of it probably for his mistresses.

The gallery, on the other hand. That loss still burned beneath her skin.

For five years, she had poured her heart and soul into it, channeling all her sorrow and pain and loss. She had loved fostering new artists, helping older, more established ones find new audiences, and connecting novice and expert art lovers alike to work that resonated with them.

The gallery had become her refuge from the ugly maw her marriage had become, the one place she truly could be herself instead of Carter Rowland's wife.

In the end, even that had been taken from her. The gallery and her small but growing personal art collection had been sold, the money all going to the meager victims' compensation fund.

She had lost everything.

Most of it had only been hollow trappings of a life she had never wanted. The gallery, on the other hand, had been her heart.

She pushed away the familiar ache of despair. Who had time

for that? She had to focus on survival now, on making this mess livable.

It still seemed like a miracle that the courts couldn't seize this house, as it was an inheritance that had come to her after her divorce had been final and after Carter's subsequent death in prison.

A cloud moved over the sun outside again, creating new shadows in the room. She flipped a light switch, which triggered a small floor lamp. Another switch next to the first turned on a single light bulb without a fixture in the middle of the living room.

At least she wouldn't have to sleep in the dark, though she would have to have the power switched over to her name as soon as possible. She didn't want to be beholden to Tori for anything.

She would have to spend some of her remaining nest egg on cleaning supplies, a few groceries and a mattress cover.

The prospect of spending the night here before she could make sure she didn't share the space with anything else, rodent or spider or otherwise, wasn't at all appealing.

She walked through and made a quick inventory on her phone of what she would need to survive for a few days, until she started making a little money by working at the café.

It was a huge, daunting list that would make serious inroads in her savings, but she wasn't going to worry about that now.

First things first. She could try to do something about the smell.

She opened the window that looked out onto the covered front porch. That would at least allow fresh air to blow through without any of the rain that had started up again.

The breeze was cool but smelled of the sea and the overgrown climbing flowers outside the porch.

She stood by the window, breathing in the sweet air as she listened to waves brushing the sand and raindrops pattering on leaves.

The tension that had become as much a part of her as her skin slowly began to seep away, drip by drip.

She closed her eyes. This wasn't so bad. Calming, even.

Maybe after months of crushing stress and insomnia she would finally be able to sleep at night here, comforted by the lullaby of the sea.

The magnitude of the task ahead of her threatened to overwhelm her, but Meredith calmed herself with the reminder that she didn't have to tackle the whole thing at once. One step at a time.

The cottage was livable, barely. The rest could be fixed with elbow grease, time and the money she would earn working at the café.

She had never had her own living space before, she realized with some degree of shock. Something she could decorate as she wanted, without having some supercilious designer tell her what didn't work.

Even her apartment in college had been purchased and decorated by her parents.

How would she make Spindrift Cottage her own for the time she would live here, especially when she didn't have any money?

She would have to be creative. She could picture shells, driftwood, maybe a few inexpensive houseplants and yard sale furniture.

She spent an enjoyable few moments breathing the fresh air and envisioning what she could do to make the cottage more comfortable when whispers drifted to her through the open window.

"We should call my dad, if nobody is supposed to be here. He can send an officer out."

It sounded like a youngish teenage girl.

"Not yet," another girl whispered. "Don't you think we'd feel pretty stupid if we called your dad out here for nothing, Crissy? We should check it out first. Who knows? It might be a Realtor or something. Or maybe my mom hired somebody to clean up. This place is a sty."

This must be Tori's daughter, Emilia, she realized. She had seen pictures of her that Frances had sent, of a girl with dark curly hair and a mischievous smile. Meredith had never met her in person, though. She had to be at least eleven or twelve now.

"What if it's a drug dealer picking up his stash?" the other girl said.

"Driving that piece of crap car?" Emilia said. "Drug dealers have much nicer rides."

"You can't just go bursting in and ask what they're doing here."

"Relax. You can go back to my house if you want. I'm just going to peek in the window. Nobody will see me. And if they do, I have pepper spray."

Meredith really didn't feel like being pepper sprayed. Wouldn't that just make the day perfect?

She carefully opened the door and was rewarded by a flurry of movement as the girls dived into the bushes out front. She had to hope they were wise enough to avoid the prickly climbing roses.

"I know you're there. Don't pepper spray me, though. I'm unarmed. Is that you, Emilia?"

A shocked silence met that question. "Yes," one of the girls said slowly. She popped her head up from the foliage with wide eyes. She still had curls, thick and dark and lovely.

She was shortly followed by another girl with long, smooth dark hair parted in the middle.

Older than eleven, then, Meredith corrected herself. These lovely young women with their dark eyes had to be at least a few years older than that.

"Who are you and how do you know my name?" Emilia asked suspiciously.

"I'm your mother's cousin. My father was your great-grandma

Frances's son, Michael. I'm not trespassing. Since Frances left me Spindrift Cottage in her will, technically the place belongs to me and *you're* trespassing."

If anything, the girl's eyes widened even further. "You're Meredith? Seriously?"

She looked as if she expected Meredith to start sacrificing baby goats right there on the porch.

"That's right."

"Oh man. Does my mom know you're here? She's going to be *pissed*."

"I stopped at the café first to get the keys from her. So yes. She does know. And yes. She isn't happy about it."

She also probably wouldn't be happy with you for consorting with the enemy.

She almost said the words but decided not to. After that initial shock, Emilia seemed to accept her presence here with far more equanimity than her mother had.

"Hello," she said to the other girl when Emilia made no move to introduce her. "I'm Meredith Collins."

She had legally changed her name back after the divorce and had been seriously tempted to change it completely to something totally new. Anything would have been preferable to her own name.

In the end she had chickened out, as she had been doing most of her adult life.

"Oh, yeah. This is my cousin Cristina."

"Nice to meet you, Cristina. I like your earrings."

"Thanks."

"How old are you now, Emilia?"

"Almost fourteen. My birthday is October 15. Cristina will be fourteen in July."

She supposed a date nearly five months away qualified as *almost* when you were a teenager.

Both girls were looking her over carefully, and Meredith had to wonder what she saw. She knew she had lost weight over the past year, that she had deep circles under her eyes, that her hair hadn't been cut or styled in months.

"You can't seriously be thinking about staying here," Emilia said with certainty.

I hope you never have to know what it's like to be desperate and have housing uncertainty.

"Yes, actually."

"It's nasty."

"For now. I can't argue with you there. I'm going to work on cleaning it up, and then I'm going to be doing some renovations over the summer to fix it up. You girls wouldn't want to earn a little extra cash, would you? I could use some hired help."

"How much?" Emilia asked.

"I don't know. We'll have to negotiate, job by job."

They exchanged looks.

"Maybe. We're saving up so we can buy cars when we're both sixteen."

"Sounds like a worthy goal."

"My mom hates you, you know."

Meredith's smile faded, remembering joyful summers when she and Tori would hang out all day, playing in the ocean, building sand castles, laying out on towels in the sand, sharing secrets and dreams.

"Yes. I'm aware. Not completely without reason."

"Seriously? What did you do?"

Meredith wasn't about to get into the whole ugly past with two young girls.

"Long story," she said, forcing a smile. "I'm hoping we can put the past behind us and move forward from here."

Emilia looked skeptical. "Good luck with that. She *really* hates you."

At the girl's words, the hopelessness of the situation pressed in. Maybe it had been a mistake to come here. Maybe she should

have simply sold the cottage as-is, sight unseen. She didn't want
to spend weeks or possibly months living only a few houses down
from someone who despised her.

Cape Sanctuary had called to her, though. This place had
been a bright, shining oasis during her childhood. With her
world in tatters, Meredith had clung to the idea that she might
find some measure of peace here.

She wasn't willing to give up that dream yet.

"Can you tell me the best place in town to pick up some
cleaning supplies?" she asked, trying to change the subject. "I
need just about everything."

"Probably the grocery store at the north end of town," Emilia
said. "It's not very big, though."

"If you want bigger stores, you'll have to go somewhere else,"
Cristina informed her. "We don't even have a mall. The shopping in Cape Sanctuary is seriously pathetic. Not like I used to
have."

"Oh, are you new to town too?"

"Kind of. I mean, my grandma and grandpa have always been
here so we visited a lot, but my dad and I moved here last fall
after he got shot."

She blinked at the casual way the girl said this. "He got shot?"

Cristina gave a nonchalant shrug. "He's a cop and he got shot
by a guy he was trying to arrest last summer."

"My goodness."

Her life might be a mess but at least no one had tried to shoot
her. Yet.

"He was okay. It only hit him in the shoulder. Anyway, I
was supposed to move in with my dad right after that, since
my mom and stepdad were moving to Germany for his work. I
didn't really want to go with them, but then my dad took a job
here in Cape Sanctuary near my grandma and grandpa and we
moved here instead."

"With no mall. How have you survived?"

"It's not easy. But at least I have Em."

The two girls beamed at each other, clearly BFFs, making Meredith's throat ache again.

Tori had always said she would name her first daughter Emilia, she suddenly remembered.

As an only child raised by her widowed grandmother, Tori used to talk about having a big family. She had wanted at least three or four children.

How tragic that Javier had died so young, before that dream could come true.

Emilia's phone buzzed with an incoming text. She pulled it out, looked at it, then groaned. "My mom's coming home early. We better go back and pretend we've been working on homework the whole time."

"Nice to meet you both."

The girls waved and left, leaving Meredith to face the disaster of her cottage on her own.

4

Meredith

The next morning at ten minutes to six, Meredith walked through the darkness on her way to the café. It was only a few blocks from Starfish Beach, and she figured walking would be better than having to pay for gas and for parking all day.

While she was living in Cape Sanctuary, she might have to look around for a secondhand bike, which would be better for the planet and her wallet.

If things were different, she could always carpool with Tori, she supposed, though that idea was likely to go over as well as veal parmesan at a vegan wedding.

Anyway, walking wasn't bad. The café wasn't far and it felt good to move and stretch her muscles, sore from driving for two days straight and then scrubbing dust and dirt and mold for hours the evening before.

The only establishment open yet along the whole block, apparently, the café provided a warm, welcoming light against the predawn darkness and tendrils of sea fog curling through the streets.

Inside, she could see a sturdy woman in an apron bustling about in the kitchen, and a moment later, the woman was joined by a hipster-looking guy with a man bun and carefully groomed beard, both covered in netting.

Meredith approached the front door, which still sported a Closed sign. As she half expected, it was locked. The two people inside didn't appear to notice her. They made no move to open the door, anyway.

Feeling awkward and conspicuous, she made her way to the back of the café, suddenly remembering the employee entrance from her summers spent running in and out with Tori.

She rounded the corner of the building just as her cousin rode up on a beach cruiser sporting a wicker basket loaded with produce.

Meredith emerged from the shadow of the building as Tori started lifting produce out of the basket.

"Can I help you carry something?" Meredith asked.

With a little shriek, her cousin jumped and whirled around. "You scared the daylights out of me. What are you doing hiding back here like a creepster?"

"I wasn't hiding," Meredith said, striving for dignity. "The front door was locked. I tried to get the attention of the kitchen staff, but they didn't appear to hear me so I was coming around to the back door when you rode up."

"First of all, I don't have a *kitchen staff*. This isn't some fancy Chicago rooftop restaurant. I have two excellent day shift cooks, Denise Arnold and Tyler Kemp. Second of all, I don't need your help."

She picked up the bags and headed for the door.

"Is that all from your garden?" Meredith asked. "That's amazing. I got a little look yesterday when I arrived. It was beautiful."

This seemed to slightly mollify Tori. Or at least she dropped her outright antagonism.

"It's too early for most things to grow, but I started some things early inside. Now I have some early peas, baby potatoes and strawberries. I'm sure the cooks will put them to good use."

Without waiting for an answer, she opened the door and headed into the restaurant. Meredith followed, feeling awkward and out of place.

The café smelled delicious, of fresh-baked bread and fried potatoes. The two cooks she had seen from outside greeted Tori, then turned to study Meredith, almost as if they had rehearsed it in advance.

The woman gave her an appraising look. "This must be the cousin you were telling us about. Not much to her, is there?"

"Isn't that the truth?" Tori muttered, half under her breath. Meredith knew her cousin wasn't referring to her weight, which had dropped recently, but from what Tori likely considered her general lack of character.

"This is Meredith," Tori said. "She owns a part share of the café and thinks that entitles her to have an automatic job here."

Did Tori have to turn everything into a dig? Meredith could feel her face heat, but she didn't rise to the bait.

"This is Denise Arnold and Ty Kemp. They're the best cooks in town. I wish I had about six more of them to work the other shifts."

"Nice to meet you," Meredith said. "I'm looking forward to learning the ropes here."

"You know how to cook?" the young hipster asked.

She shook her head quickly. "I can make macarons and a very good velouté. But I don't imagine you have much call for that."

"Not much. No," Denise Arnold agreed. Her dark eyes looked amused.

"These two have the kitchen covered during the morning shift. They certainly don't need your help."

Meredith was quite sure the two cooks couldn't miss the emphasis Tori put on the word *your*.

"Your job will be busing tables and washing dishes. You will be helping Brandon Trevino and Josef Kovalenko. Josef should be here shortly to show you the ropes. Brandon comes about midmorning, when his job coach from the vocational rehab program brings him."

"Sounds good," Meredith said. "Is there anything I can do to help while I wait for Josef?"

"Know how to make coffee in a decanter brewer?"

Meredith didn't have the first idea what she was talking about. Something told her she was in for a long day of humbling ignorance.

"I don't think so," she said.

"You can watch Ty do it today and then tomorrow you can take over that job first thing."

She nodded, even as the prospect seemed daunting. She suddenly felt stupid and helpless. She had a degree in art history and had run a successful art gallery for four years, but none of that would be at all useful here.

Other than the summers when she used to occasionally help out Frances here at the café, she hadn't worked in the food service industry. She had certainly never made coffee in a decanter brewer.

She hadn't done much, actually, except own an art gallery.

She wasn't completely new to busing tables, she reminded herself. That was one of the jobs she had helped do during those summers spent in Cape Sanctuary. It would probably come back to her soon enough.

"I'm about to open for the day," Tori said. "Buckle up."

She crossed the café to the front door, where she turned the Closed sign around and then unlocked the door.

She had barely stepped inside when the door opened with a chime and a couple of older men came in together.

"You're two minutes late this morning, Tori," one of the two chided her.

"Sorry about that," her cousin said, greeting both men with the sort of warm smile that told Meredith they were regulars to the café. "You're here early."

"I have to drive down to see my cardiologist in Davis and need some fuel for the journey."

Meredith couldn't help thinking that perhaps the man shouldn't be eating at a greasy spoon diner right before heading to a cardiologist appointment.

"Do you want your regular, KC?"

"Sounds good. Greek yogurt and an egg white omelet."

"I have fresh strawberries from my garden for the yogurt, if you want."

"Sounds delicious. How'd you get strawberries to grow already?"

"I started them early inside and use soil warmers."

They started talking gardening, all things that were as confusing to Meredith as coffee makers, until more people came in for breakfast.

Tori greeted every new customer to the café with that same warm smile. She seemed to know most of them, though Meredith heard her welcome two groups of visitors to the area and ask how they were enjoying their stay.

Josef came in about twenty minutes after the café opened, a tall, stooped man who looked to be in his early thirties. He had thin, almost gaunt features and serious dark eyes, but he greeted Meredith with courtesy when Tori introduced her and told him Meredith would be helping him.

"What we do?" he said in a heavily accented voice that sounded eastern European. "People do not even notice. They notice if we do not do our jobs. Any restaurant, even the best places with the Michelin stars and the gourmet chefs, cannot function without those who keep the tables cleared and the dishes clean."

She watched him through the morning. He worked hard, quickly and efficiently, taking pride in his work. He seemed to be very good at his job.

The café did a steady business all morning. Tori served as

both hostess and server, along with a thin, nervous-looking young woman with several piercings and a tattoo who introduced herself as Aspen.

Meredith found the operations of the café fascinating.

Most of the customers seemed to be locals. They gave her curious looks, and she overheard a few ask Tori about her.

Her cousin glowered. "That's Meredith. She's a family member of my grandmother's, down on her luck."

She had to hope no one here would recognize her as the despised Chicago socialite Meredith Rowland. Why would they, though? She was far from the glamorous art gallery owner she once had been.

While she might be a household name in Chicago, spoken of in the same tone one would use when talking about scabies, stories of her infamy-by-association had probably not reached the left coast.

By the time the breakfast rush was over, her feet pinched and her biceps ached. Apparently, the flats she wore didn't cut it, walking back and forth from the dining room to the kitchen a hundred times. And apparently missing Pilates class for fourteen months in a row resulted in a loss of muscle tone. Who knew?

Tori left around eleven. She didn't tell Meredith where she was going, but she heard her tell Denise she had an errand.

Meredith carried another tray of dirty dishes from a group of four and set them down at the sink, where Josef was rinsing and loading them into the commercial dishwasher.

She bent to tie her shoe. When she rose, the room spun and she saw little sparkles at the corner of her vision.

"You're looking a mite peaky, Meredith," Denise said, giving her a concerned look. "Have you eaten anything today?"

She had grabbed a banana when she first woke up, which felt like ages ago now. While she had purchased a few groceries, buying cleaning supplies had taken a big bite out of her budget. She was trying to save money where she could and planned to make a peanut butter sandwich when she returned to the cottage. And maybe every day until she got paid.

"I'm fine," she lied, forcing a smile.

"Sit down," the cook ordered. "I can't have you falling over on one of the customers. How about some of my chicken noodle soup. That's the soup of the day and always brings the boys to the yard."

That must be what smelled so delicious. Meredith's mouth watered at the comforting, familiar scent that suddenly reminded her of her grandmother, with painful clarity.

Oh, she wanted some of that soup.

"I can't eat the café's profits," she protested.

Denise's apron bounced when she laughed. "We got any profits, Ty?"

"Not many," he answered as he flipped a ham-and-cheese sandwich on the grill.

"I always make extra. Much more than we go through in a day, especially now that the weather's warming up. Sit down and have a bowl. Josef and Aspen will, won't you both?"

"Yes. Yes, of course," Josef said. Aspen nodded and slid into a chair. Without waiting for Meredith to answer, Denise ladled three bowls and handed them out as if she were dealing cards at a blackjack table in Vegas.

Meredith spooned up some of the soup, which tasted as hearty and comforting as it had smelled. She found it so delicious, she felt ridiculously emotional.

It was from the cook's kindness, more than the soup, she realized.

"Now," Denise said after Meredith had enjoyed a few more tastes, "tell us about yourself. I've worked here six years now and never met you before. Tori has never even said a word about having a cousin. Far as I can remember, you didn't make it back for the funeral."

She had wanted to, desperately, but had been sick at the time and couldn't travel. She had watched the memorial online and had cried bitter, painful tears by herself in the tiny studio she had moved to when their penthouse and all its contents had been seized.

"Though I did keep in touch with Frances, Tori and I...don't exactly get along."

This made Denise laugh again, a belly laugh that rolled out of her and somehow seemed to warm Meredith almost as much as the soup.

"You don't say?"

"What did you do?" Aspen asked, crunching a saltine cracker into her bowl.

"How do you know I did something to her?" Meredith countered. "Maybe it was Tori who did something to me."

"Wouldn't surprise me," Ty said.

"Our Victoria does have strong opinions about the way people should act, and she's not afraid to let you know," Denise agreed. "Still, it's too bad you let a wedge between you and your cousin keep you away from Frances too."

How did she explain to these kind people what a mess her life had been, long before her husband had been arrested and charged with a lengthy list of financial crimes?

She had been weak and frightened. That was the real reason.

She had wanted to come back to Cape Sanctuary to visit Frances so many times after the one and only time she had visited after her marriage.

Carter wouldn't allow it. At first, he would claim he needed her help with some social event or other, had claimed he couldn't manage without her there.

Eventually, he hadn't bothered with the pretext. He hadn't needed to. By then, she had been too afraid to dare defy his wishes by buying a plane ticket.

She couldn't count the number of times she had started to book a plane ticket using the gallery credit card. He would have come after her, though. She had no doubt. And then things would be much, much worse.

She had stayed away because it seemed easier at the time. She hated thinking about what a coward she had become.

"It was totally my fault," she said. "Not Tori's. I should have tried to make things right a long time ago."

"Well, maybe it's not too late," Denise said. "Tori could use some family if you ask me."

"She has family," Josef said stoutly. "We are her family."

Denise smiled. "True enough. True enough."

They chatted for a few more moments. Aspen finished her soup, then headed for the bathroom. She had only been gone a moment when the chime out front alerted them to a new customer.

Denise looked out of the kitchen toward the newcomer. Her eyes widened with appreciation. "I wouldn't mind sharing soup with that guy," she muttered.

Meredith couldn't refrain from following her gaze, to find a tall, dark-haired man with lean features standing inside, waiting to be seated. He had a little dark stubble brushing his jawline and his blue eyes looked tired, as if he were at the tail end of a long journey.

To her shock, Meredith felt a little tug of awareness.

Where did *that* come from?

She blinked in shock. No. Definitely no. She needed to nip that right in the bud before it had any chance of taking root.

She was nowhere *close* to ready to find herself tangled up with any man, especially not a sexy, disreputable-looking stranger.

"You should take care of him."

For a ridiculous moment, with her mind already full of that uncomfortable and unwanted awareness, she could only stare at Denise as her imagination went wild. "Excuse me?"

"The sexy guy out there. He's waiting to be seated. Aspen's in the ladies' and Tori isn't back yet. Put him in one of the booths by the window. It can only be good for business to have eye candy like that out on display for the whole town to see."

Oh. Right. The man was a customer and needed to be seated. That was all. She rose and smoothed down her apron, feeling awkward and foolish.

She headed for the front door, heart pounding. She picked up one of the tattered menus and pasted on a polite smile.

"Hello. Er. Welcome to the Beach End Café. Are you...waiting for someone else to join you?"

His gaze seemed to sharpen on her. His eyes weren't only blue. They were a vivid, unearthly hue that reminded her of an Yves Klein abstract.

The intensity of his gaze left her unsettled. Was that a hint of recognition she saw there or was she imagining it? She searched his gaze for some hint that he was about to out her to the restaurant staff, but his expression passed so quickly, she wondered if she had imagined it.

"No. Just me." His voice was low, slightly raspy, as if he had just rolled out of bed.

"Would you prefer a booth or a table?"

"A booth is fine. Away from the window, if possible."

So much for Denise's plan to use him as window dressing.

"You don't like the view here?"

"The view is fine. Lovely, actually. But I need to do some work on my laptop and could do without the glare and the distraction."

"Oh. Of course."

She looked around the café and found a quiet corner with a booth against the inside wall. Gripping the menu tightly, she led the way to it. "Will this work for you?"

He looked around at the mostly empty café. "It should be good."

He slid into the booth, setting a battered-looking leather messenger bag on the table. She placed the menu next to it. "Can I start you off with something to drink?"

"Coffee. Black. And water. Tap," he said. "I'm ready to order too."

Let me guess, she thought. *Food. Hot.*

She wasn't at all prepared to take his order. That was way past her pay grade. "If you can give me a minute, I'll grab your server."

"You're not on the waitstaff?"

She shook her head. "No. And I'm not a hostess either, really, only filling in. I bus tables and help wash dishes. But I'll go find your server. Her name is Aspen, and she should be here momentarily."

She rushed away as fast as she dared. Aspen was just coming out of the ladies' room. The young woman shoved her cell phone into her back pocket and straightened her shoulders.

Her eyes were red and puffy, and she had clearly been crying.

"Is everything okay?" Meredith asked.

The server glowered at her. "Fine. Why wouldn't it be?" she snapped.

"You just looked upset."

"I'm fine." Her tone plainly said *mind your own damn business.*

Meredith blinked. "Okay. Sorry," she said. "I just seated a customer for you." She gestured toward the corner where the sexy newcomer had pulled out his laptop. "He says he's ready to order."

Aspen turned without answering and headed toward the new customer while Meredith went to get him the black coffee and tap water he had requested.

The door chimed again, this time with a group of six requesting a large booth.

Over the next half hour as the café grew busier with lunchtime, Meredith went about her duties with a tingly awareness of the man in the corner booth working on his laptop.

Tori returned from her errand, put on her apron and washed her hands before heading out to the dining room. Meredith saw her go over and talk to the man. She couldn't hear what they said, but she saw the man gesture to his laptop with a question in his eyes. Tori nodded and answered him with a smile.

He seemed to settle in after that, and she assumed he must have asked Tori for permission to occupy the booth while working.

For the next hour as Meredith cleared tables and delivered beverages, she was aware of the good-looking guy with the laptop. She had the oddest feeling that he was as aware of her as she was him. Every so often, she thought she could feel his gaze and would look up from whatever she was doing, only to find him buried once more in his computer.

Worry tangled through her and she had to fight the urge to flee. Had she been right earlier? Was it possible he recognized her?

The story of Carter's crimes had been huge in Chicago, where most of his victims were, but perhaps his infamy, and hers by association, had spread to Cape Sanctuary because of her connection to Frances.

He couldn't recognize her, she told herself. How could he? She had looked like a different woman there, with long blond hair, designer clothing, diamonds and pearls.

Here, she wore jeans, a plain red shirt and the black Beach End Café apron she had been assigned. Hardly fashionable attire. Gone were the costly hair treatments, the carefully applied makeup she had never really enjoyed but had considered part of her job.

She had hardly taken time for mascara that morning, and she had finally chopped her own hair on the road somewhere when she couldn't stand it another minute. It was barely long enough for a ponytail now, which she wore at the nape of her neck.

If he didn't recognize her, why else would he be sneaking those looks, though? It certainly couldn't be male interest.

What difference did it make? None. She still had nowhere else to go and needed to stay in Cape Sanctuary until she could sell the cottage.

She managed to avoid visiting the table again, handing it off to Josef for coffee refills. Still, as she went about her other responsibilities, she was aware when the man finished his sandwich and salad, then turned back to his laptop.

She could only hope he wasn't doing an internet search of her right now. Finally, after about an hour with this finely wrought tension in her shoulders, he began to put away his electronics.

She breathed a sigh of relief and finished clearing a table near the door. She didn't linger, wanting distance between her and this stranger who left her so uneasy.

Later, she wasn't sure exactly what happened, but as she picked up the tray and turned to carry it into the kitchen, the man was there, in front of her.

She stumbled in surprise and tried to hold on to the tray. She managed to right it, but one half-empty bowl of salsa was already too close to the edge of the tray. It toppled to the floor, splashing salsa all over him as it fell.

It was one inglorious moment of a hard day in a difficult week in a horrible year, and Meredith suddenly wanted to cry.

"I'm so sorry!" she exclaimed. "I don't know what happened. Are you all right?"

"Yes. Fine. No harm done. Just a little salsa. I didn't like this shirt anyway."

"Oh! Your shirt." Tori was going to be so angry.

"It was totally my fault. I was in the wrong place at the wrong time. Which might end up the title of my autobiography."

"It's ruined. I'm so, so sorry."

She set the tray back on the table and started wiping at his shirt with the cloth in her hand, only realizing after a few seconds that she was only making things worse, spreading toma-toes and peppers and onions across his chest.

He stepped back, gripping his laptop case more tightly. "Re-ally, it's fine. My own fault. I should have been watching where I was going. I'm afraid my head was somewhere else."

Where? She had to wonder. It also occurred to her that he might not be a local, as she had been assuming. Denise hadn't known him, anyway.

"I'm Liam. Liam Byrne."

She didn't have a name tag yet, considering it was her first day. Tori hadn't said anything about a name tag, probably be-cause she was hoping Meredith would go away.

"Meredith," she finally said. "Meredith Collins."

She never wanted to use her married surname again.

His smile widened and she felt light-headed all over again. "Hi, Meredith. Nice to meet you."

"Is it? Salsa and all? I can pay to have your shirt cleaned." She had no idea how, but she would figure out a way.

He looked down at the blotch on his shirt. "It's no big deal. Really. I'll grab some stain remover and throw it in the wash. It will be good as new."

"If it's not, let me know."

"I'll do that." He paused. "I'm sure I'll see you around. The food here is delicious. Exactly what I needed today. I'll defi-nitely be back. Next time I'll try to be more aware of my sur-roundings."

"As will I."

She managed a smile, picked up the tray again and carried it to the kitchen, feeling as if meeting Liam Byrne was the one bright spot in her difficult first day.

5

Liam

Liam Byrne walked out of the Beach End Café, elation bubbling through him like a good head on a pint of lager.

He had found her.

Meredith Collins Rowland, widow of the late and unlamented Carter Rowland.

His hunch had paid off. The few people on the official task force he had talked to off the record said that since she was no longer under investigation, she was free to do what she wanted.

When she left Illinois, none of Liam's contacts claimed to know where she was or where she was going. The rumor was that the task force expected her to show up eventually with her mother.

Liam didn't buy it. From his own extensive research, he knew her mother had cut her off after the scandal broke. He got the impression that Cilla Collins-Meyer was far more concerned about her social standing and her second husband's political career to care much about her daughter's financial crisis.

Liam was a forensic accountant with an expertise in lifestyle analysis.

It was his job to study patterns of behavior. He had guessed correctly that Meredith would come to Cape Sanctuary, where she had spent several weeks every summer with her grandmother until she was a teenager.

As far as the FBI was concerned, the case against Meredith Rowland was done. Months of deep investigative research hadn't unearthed any evidence that she was part of her husband's misdeeds.

Liam wasn't at all convinced. Which was exactly why he was here.

How could she not have known?

Yeah, he was just a data analyst and this wasn't his case. That wouldn't stop him. His specialty was digging through financial records, bank accounts, investments, to find details others missed. He wanted the same chance with this case.

He had found Meredith Rowland.

A week earlier, he had picked up a faint trail when he discovered she had bought a used car in Evanston, Illinois, and registered it in her maiden name. After digging around, he found she had been living in a run-down studio apartment and was pawning furniture and clothing.

She was on the move, but he wasn't sure where.

He had asked permission to track her movements, but the permission had been refused.

Liam couldn't let it go.

Whether she had been in on her husband's flagrant pilfering of several Illinois public employee retirement plans, Meredith was the single strongest link to recovering the nearly half a billion dollars still unaccounted for, for all those victims.

She had to be.

When it became clear the multiagency task force didn't intend to prosecute Meredith or expend additional resources by digging further, Liam had decided to take matters into his own hands.

He had several weeks of leave coming to him. Why couldn't he launch his own investigation?

So he had followed the bread crumbs and guessed that she would come to Cape Sanctuary. From there, it had been easy enough for him to find a place to rent here, at the cottage his research had revealed was owned by her cousin. He hopped into his own car and drove up from Los Angeles, devising a cover story as he went.

If he hadn't studied her file so intently, he would never have guessed the meek, nervous-looking woman busing tables at a tired-looking café called the Beach End could be the wife of one of the worst white-collar criminals in years.

Now that he was here, in the same town, the same café, Liam wasn't sure where to start. How could he persuade Meredith Rowland to start divulging her secrets?

He was a numbers guy, not exactly the cloak-and-dagger type. The woman wasn't simply going to hand over all her secrets to him.

He had to convince her to trust him somehow.

How the hell was he going to do that?

He had a sneaking suspicion that finding out Meredith's location would be the easiest part of the whole half-baked idea.

6

Tori

"You can't be serious."

Tori stared at Corinne Selby, the principal of Cape Sanctuary Middle School, sudden nerves knotting her stomach as she tried to absorb the shocking news.

"I'm sorry. I'm very serious." The principal spoke in a low, steady voice she probably intended to be calming. It sure wasn't working on Tori.

"How can she be flunking history and have a D minus in geometry? She was doing fine at the midterm, at least the last time I spoke with her teachers at parent-teacher conferences. I mean, I knew she probably wasn't going to be student of the year for the eighth grade, but she was holding her own."

Dr. Selby looked at her notes. "You're correct. It appears Emilia had solid Bs in both classes at the midterm. But unfortunately, she has missed the deadline to turn in several major projects in history, and she hasn't turned in any geometry homework for the last half of the trimester. She had a D on the last test."

Okay, Tori felt like the world's worst parent right now. How could she have been so oblivious, standing by casually waving as her daughter headed off the rails?

"Wow. I'm sorry. This is such a shock. I had no idea. I guess I should have been monitoring her grades online a little better, but she assured me she was doing fine."

She tried not to glare at Em, who sat slouched beside her, arms folded across her chest and a bored look in her kohl-lined eyes that certainly hadn't been so made up when she left for school that morning.

"Unfortunately, that isn't the case, at least in those two classes. She is not doing fine. In addition to her academic performance, Emilia also has a total of five unexcused absences, seven for the afternoon classes. That's why I'm handling this instead of the individual teachers involved."

This couldn't be happening. Tori fought what felt like a dozen different emotions. Anger, guilt, disappointment and that over-whelming sense of failure.

At times like this, she missed Javier so badly, it burned through her like battery acid. It would have been so comforting to have someone else on the parental team with her to help shoulder the burden.

"You said it's not too late to fix this?" She grasped tightly to the slim lifeline the principal had held out.

"Yes, but I'm afraid it won't be easy. Not easy at all, in fact."

"That doesn't matter. We'll do whatever it takes."

"It will take a firm commitment from Emilia and a great deal of work on her part, but she can still pass both classes. We have nearly three weeks until summer vacation. Mr. Cefalo and Ms. Summers have each given me packets of the missing work for their respective classes. If Emilia can finish all the homework that's missing in geometry and turn in the three missing history projects, the teachers are willing to adjust her grades accord-ingly, even though the assignments will be docked some points for being turned in late."

"Of course. That's only fair." Tori shifted in her chair, feel-ing like she was the one in the hot seat at the principal's office.

When Tori had gone to this school, she would have been mortified if Frances ever had been called into the principal's office because of her, but Em seemed wholly unconcerned.

"That's very gracious of the teachers," Tori went on. "I will make sure she finishes the work. Thank you."

"That does still leave the matter of the unexcused absences."

Dr. Selby leaned back in her chair, fingers tapping the edge of her desk. "It might interest you to know that we have a second student who has missed those exact same classes."

Tori closed her eyes. She should have known. "Let me guess. Her cousin Cristina."

Dr. Selby only raised an eyebrow. "When I asked the girls why they've missed so many classes, I can't really get a satisfactory answer. You and Cristina's father might have better luck getting to the bottom of things."

A year ago, she might have agreed with Corinne. Emilia used to tell her everything. Team Ayala. That's what they were.

Since Cristina and Sam moved to Cape Sanctuary, that dynamic had shifted.

She looked over at Emilia, this daughter she loved with every piece of her heart. As dramatic as it seemed, Tori felt like Em's entire future teetered on the edge here.

It was only one trimester in eighth grade, she told herself. And only two classes out of that trimester. She was passing the others.

This wasn't the end of the world, though it felt like it.

"I'm sorry this happened. I should have kept a better eye on her progress."

"You're not responsible for Emilia's decisions," Corinne said gently. "She is thirteen. She's going to high school next year. Assuming she passes these classes, anyway. She has to be accountable for her own choices. But let's all work together to see if we can help her make some better decisions for the rest of the school year."

Since that was clearly a dismissal, Tori rose. Dr. Selby held out two thick manila envelopes. Tori started to reach for them, then checked herself and gave Emilia a speaking look. Her daughter sighed as if no other teenager had ever been as put-upon and took the packets.

"Thank you, Dr. Selby. And I'm sorry it's come to this," Tori said, then nudged her daughter.

"Sorry," Em mumbled, though she didn't look or sound at all repentant.

Tori walked out of Corinne's office with Emilia, who moseyed along behind, without a care in the world.

When Tori spotted a familiar duo seated across from the school secretaries in the office visitor chairs, obviously waiting their turn with Dr. Selby, Tori fought a wild urge to go to Sam and cry against his broad chest.

She refrained. While they had always been friendly, they certainly didn't have that kind of relationship.

Em immediately went to her cousin, though, and hugged her as if they hadn't just seen each other an hour ago.

"Uh-oh," Sam said with a frown. "You look like you just faced the gauntlet. What have they done?"

It was what the girls *hadn't* done that was the problem. Namely their schoolwork and attending classes. "I can't say for Cristina, only Em. But she's in serious trouble with her grades. I guess you'll find out soon enough."

The girls were giggling about something on Em's phone and seemed unconcerned about the whole thing. Tori didn't know what infuriated her more, that Emilia had blown off the last half of the trimester or that she apparently didn't really care.

"I'll give you a call later for a debriefing," he said.

She nodded, somehow comforted by the prospect. Maybe she wasn't in this completely on her own. If Cristina was struggling like Emilia was, maybe she and Sam could team up to make things right.

She and her daughter walked out into the hall just as a bell rang.

"That's fourth hour. I've got to go. I don't want to be late."

She wanted to have this out right now but knew now wasn't the right time with students spilling out into the hallway, jostling each other, chattering, staring at their phones.

"This isn't over. You're on house arrest until further notice. No more sleepovers, no more hanging out after school. The only thing you're doing from now to the end of term is homework. I'll pick you up as soon as school is out."

"You don't have to. I can walk."

"I'll pick you up," she said firmly, leaving no room for argument. "You can work on homework in a booth at the café."

"You know I don't like to do homework at the café. I like peace and quiet."

Somehow she managed not to snort too loudly at that particular assertion. Usually Em did homework with the TV tuned to whatever latest binge she was streaming or with her headphones on and music blaring.

"I'll pick you up in the circle drive. Don't make me wait for you."

Em glared and stormed off. Tori was quite certain that if they were in a different era, her daughter would have flounced her petticoats at her.

Feeling like a solitary island in a sea of milling young people, Tori drew in a breath, trying to calm herself. She didn't want to fight the tide so she waited a moment for the hallway to clear when she spotted Vanessa Chan walking down the hallway, her arms loaded with boxes.

"Hey, Ness," Tori said. Vanessa, the school media specialist, was in her book group and had a sharp sense of humor and diverse reading tastes.

Vanessa's distracted features brightened. "Hey, Tori. What brings you to the halls of academia?"

She made a face. "A meeting with Dr. Selby."

"Uh-oh. Everything okay?"

Sure, other than I'm a terrible mom and my daughter has checked out for the school year.

She shrugged. "Em is struggling in a few of her classes. We're trying to get her back on track before the end of the year."

"Oh man. I'm sorry to hear that but she's so bright, I'm sure she can turn things around."

"It's not a question of ability but motivation."

"Trust me, I'm a middle school librarian. I totally get it. That's the age-old conflict."

She suddenly felt guilty for standing there when Vanessa was clearly struggling under the weight she juggled.

"Sorry. Can I give you a hand?"

"That would actually be great. I wasn't expecting so many packages or I would have brought a cart."

Tori took several boxes from her friend, then followed her down the hallway toward the media center.

"Hey, any chance your new vacation rental might be available a few weeks from now?" Vanessa asked as they walked. "My parents are coming to town to visit me and the kids once school gets out. I have an extra bedroom but I figured all of us would be more comfortable if they had their own place. I love them to pieces, but they get on my last nerve. My mom is always trying to do my laundry and clean my toilets, and my dad will potter around trying to fix every leaky drain and clean out every rain gutter."

That sounded like a dream to Tori. She had been cleaning her own rain gutters *and* Frances's for years. What were the chances she could talk Vanessa's mom into coming to clean *her* toilets?

"No. I'm so sorry. I wish I could help you, but I just rented it to a guy who wants to stay for a month. Every other rental in town was booked for at least some of that time, but since my place is new to the market and I don't have any other bookings yet, he grabbed it."

"Wow! That's great. And you were worried you wouldn't

be able to rent it at all! I guess it's nice to know you'll have a steady renter."

After much consideration, she had decided to use Frances's cottage as a vacation rental instead of finding a long-term tenant. She had planned to put away the extra cash for Emilia's college expenses but at this rate, Tori might be using it herself for a world cruise instead.

"Do you know of anywhere else in town that might be available?" Vanessa asked.

"You might want to check with Kathy Holt. She was talking about renting out their guesthouse."

"Oh, that's a good idea. I'll give her a ring."

"Where do you want the boxes?" she asked when they reached the media center.

"My desk is fine. Thanks."

The two of them chatted about the book they were reading that month and how Vanessa was doing since she had separated from her husband a few months earlier, until a student came over to ask the media specialist where to find a biography about Harriet Tubman for a report. She led the student to the section, then returned to Tori.

"Sorry about that."

"Don't be sorry. It's your job. Anyway, I have to get back to the café."

"Listen, does Em need tutoring or something? I know a couple of students who are great at that kind of thing."

"She needs something but I don't think it's tutoring," she muttered. A kick in the backside, maybe.

"I'll see you next week. We're at Stella's house, aren't we?"

"That's right. She picked the book so it's at her house."

"Good. My favorite. She always has the *best* wine."

She laughed. "Better not let your impressionable students hear you say that."

Vanessa grinned and waved as Tori left the media center. She walked out to the bike rack where she had locked up her beach cruiser just in time to see Sam sliding into his vehicle. When he spotted her, he climbed back out and headed toward her.

He wore khakis and a blue dress shirt, his standard police detective attire, and her heart gave a little kick, as it seemed to do lately every time she saw him.

He frowned, his lean features twisted with frustration. "I'm going to assume your news is as grim as mine. Cristina is failing two classes and she's been ditching school."

She unlocked her bike from the rack. "Not quite as grim, I guess. Em is only failing one class and has a D in one more. But, yes. She's ditching too."

"What are they thinking?"

"They're not. That's the problem. I think when they're together, they automatically start losing brain cells."

He sighed. *"Folie à deux."*

"Excuse me?"

"The madness of two. It's a psychological term that usually refers to a shared psychosis but in crime circles it's come to mean two people who might be harmless on their own but throw them together and, boom. The results are incendiary."

"My daughter is not a criminal. This is all new behavior. She had great grades before…"

She couldn't finish the sentence but she didn't need to. His gaze narrowed. "Before Cristina and I moved back to town."

She refused to feel guilty. "Well, it's true. Em was a model student who would never have dreamed of skipping school and not turning in her homework. I'm not saying Cristina is to blame. Like you said, the two of them are just incendiary together."

"Folie à deux."

"Sure. Whatever. The real question is, what are we going to do about it? They're starting high school next year. These grades matter to their future."

"I agree."

"I don't want to split them up. It's been great for Em to have Cristina here. Almost like having a sister."

She felt a sudden pang, thinking of Meredith and how they used to share everything, back when she had considered Meredith the sister of her heart. They were both only siblings and had reveled in having a confidante and best friend.

That was a long time ago. Before Meredith outgrew Cape Sanctuary, Frances and her.

"Em has been good for Cristina too. She's helped make this transition to small-town living much easier for Cris. I'm not sure it would have been bearable for her, without her cousin."

"I'm glad they're close, but we can't let their social lives take over their academic work. We obviously need to take charge or who knows what kind of havoc they're going to cause during summer vacation."

She shuddered, imagining it.

"Agreed."

"It's not too late to make changes. I've told Em she's on house arrest until her missing work is done and no more hanging out after school or sleepovers on the weekend."

"I gave Cristina the same speech."

"Good. I'm glad we're on the same page here."

"They're going to kick up a fuss," he warned.

"I know." She wasn't looking forward to that part of it, separating Emilia from her partner in crime.

"What if we combined forces? We might see better results if we attack this as a team."

"What did you have in mind?" she asked, suddenly wary.

His phone rang before he could answer. He looked at the display with a frustrated look. "I've been waiting for that call. It's a confidential informant on a robbery I've been working. I've got to take it. Are you going to be around tonight? I can drop by later and we can hash out a game plan."

"What time?"

"I work until around nine. I'll give you a call as soon as I get off. I was thinking it would be better if we could talk without the girls around to come up with our strategy."

She was usually up at five for the morning shift at the café before breaking quickly to get Emilia off to school. It made for a long day.

"Sure. That works. I might have to throw cold water on my face to keep awake, but I'll make it. This is important."

He gave her a distracted smile that shouldn't have left her insides tingly, then picked up his phone and slid back into his unmarked police vehicle.

Could she work as a team with Sam, given this unwanted attraction she had only started to recognize?

She had to get control of it. Even if he shared her attraction, which he obviously didn't, nothing could ever come of it. He was Javier's brother, for heaven's sake. Emilia's uncle. It was completely inappropriate to even think about those things.

He didn't look at all like Javier, other than sharing dark hair and eyes. Javi had been short, only a few inches taller than she was, with a compact, wiry frame and eyes that always seemed to be laughing at something.

Sam was just over six foot, lean but muscled, with a strong jawline and long, lovely eyelashes.

She pedaled harder, heading through a residential shortcut on the way to the Beach End. Right now, any attraction she might be unwise enough to feel for her brother-in-law had to be shoved back into the lockbox where it belonged.

Their daughters faced a crisis, a pivotal moment in their young lives when their futures teetered on a knife's edge.

Melodramatic much? She shook her head at herself as she rode up to the café, braked to a stop and climbed off.

She would do much better to focus on the girls and their academic problems than on this attraction to her brother-in-law that could never come to anything.

7

Meredith

After only a few days working at the café, Meredith was completely exhausted.

All she wanted to do was stretch out on the bench out front and take a nap.

A small one. That's all she needed.

Instead, she waved goodbye to Josef, who she had learned would never chatter up a storm but was quietly kind, and walked out into a glorious afternoon.

The day was sunny but a cool breeze blew off the water, light and refreshing. Gulls cried overhead and she could see a few people on the beach near the café, though she knew the real tourist season wouldn't kick in until after Memorial Day.

Her muscles ached as she walked through town back toward Starfish Beach. She wanted to say it was the pleasant ache of a job well done, but she knew that wasn't true. She wasn't doing anything right. She still didn't feel like she knew what she was doing, though she was beginning to figure out the complicated coffee maker.

She wasn't sure any of the other restaurant staff would say she was handling her job with particular skill.

But to her surprise, the work was actually more enjoyable than she had expected. She liked watching as customers tucked into their meals with enthusiasm as well as the sound of laughter and conversation and the clink of silverware on china as friends chatted over food.

She found something soothing in the routine. It wasn't busy-work by any stretch of the imagination. Josef had been right; the café couldn't function without the work they did. The servers didn't have time to clear the tables, to wipe them down, to load the dishes into the dishwasher. They wouldn't be able do their jobs if not for her and Josef and the very sweet Brendan, who had a gentle smile and an earnest heart.

Under other circumstances, Meredith thought she could actually enjoy working at the Beach End Café. How could she, though, with Tori's simmering resentment of her presence always there, like a toothache she couldn't ignore?

Her cousin had run an errand that day, something at Emilia's school, and returned in an even more sour mood. With Tori barely speaking to her, Meredith wouldn't have dared ask what was wrong, but she overheard her telling the cooks something about Emilia missing homework and skipping classes.

She hadn't seen Emilia since that first day when she had talked to her and her friend. Something told her school wasn't really a priority for those two.

By the time she walked the few blocks to her cottage, some of the kinks in her muscles had worked themselves out. She was still tired, though, so tired she wanted to curl up on the lumpy mattress and take a nap.

She couldn't, though. She had too much to do.

She summoned the last of her energy and walked out to the small overgrown garden bordering the sand.

Meredith knew about as much about gardening as she did working in a café.

What *did* she know about? Over the past eighteen months, she had come to the grim realization that her practical skills were basically nonexistent. Oh, she could explore in depth about pointillism vs. stippling or philosophical perspectives of art but had no idea how to keep a bean plant alive.

Still, one thing she had learned in a lifetime as Cilla Collins-Meyer's daughter was that appearances mattered. Right now, her cottage was a junk heap. If she could improve her surroundings, she knew it would help her state of mind.

Clearing out the weeds in the yard was a good first step. She decided not to change. What was the point? The clothes she wore were already sweaty from a long day at work. Wishing she had a cute floppy beach hat to protect against the sun, she threw on her sunglasses and wrapped a Dior scarf around her head like she was Grace Kelly driving a convertible down the Amalfi Coast.

She headed out to the mess of the yard and went to work pulling weeds as shadows lengthened and the sun shifted toward the horizon.

This wasn't so bad. Yes, the work was hard, especially after a full day on her feet, but Meredith found something comforting and soothing about working with her hands to the sound of the waves nearby.

Tori and Emilia came home about an hour after she started work. The teenager waved at her and started to come over, but her mother said something curt.

Emilia answered her with a frown and the two exchanged words that ended with Emilia flouncing up the stairs to their front porch.

Meredith had no idea what Tori said but could guess it wasn't anything flattering about her.

She sighed, guilty again at all the choices she had made that had led them to this point.

The first fissure in their relationship had come right after high school. For years, she and Tori had talked about what they would do when they graduated. Tori wanted to see the world beyond Cape Sanctuary. While that hadn't necessarily been Meredith's dream, she did love the idea of spending a month or six weeks traveling across Europe and showing her beloved cousin Venice, Paris, the Alps.

That dream had not happened. Because of her, as it turned out. Tori had been ready. She had bought a plane ticket and rail pass, saving all the money she made in tips for a year of working at the café in order to afford the trip.

A month before they were to leave, Meredith had finally texted to tell her she wouldn't be able to go after all.

At the time, she hadn't seen a choice. Cilla had pulled strings and cashed in favors in order to inveigle a summer internship for Meredith at The Met. Her mother had considered it a coup, especially considering her frenemy Eloisa St. Cloud had been trying to get her daughter the same internship.

Meredith hadn't dared explain to her mother that she had made clandestine plans with her cousin for a senior trip to Europe. Cilla would not have approved. She didn't like Tori—or Frances, for that matter, Cilla's own mother-in-law.

So in the end, Meredith had been too weak to go against her mother and had instead let her cousin down.

She pulled weeds harder, wishing she could pull out all the bad memories from her mind as concisely.

She worked until the sun began to slide into the sea, a magnificent display of orange and gold and amber. Finally she had to stop to eat something or she might end up sleeping here in the warm dirt.

She was admiring the pile of weeds with a great sense of accomplishment when she suddenly heard loud breathing behind her.

Definitely an animal of some kind, she realized, afraid to turn around. Did they have rabid coyotes in this part of the country? She had no idea. She held her breath, feeling hot breath against her hair, and finally turned, ready to be shredded by sharp teeth. Instead, a friendly looking black dog dropped a drool-covered ball on her lap.

Okay. She probably wasn't about to be ripped from limb to limb.

"Hey there," she said, her voice calm though her heart was beating rapidly in her ears.

She wasn't a fan of big dogs. She had been bitten by one of the guard dogs at a friend's estate when she was about twelve and had a fear of canines ever since.

This looked to be a Lab. The dog had a friendly, eager face and was obviously waiting expectantly for Meredith to throw the ball.

"Where did you come from?" she asked. She looked up and down the beach but couldn't see anybody. "Are you lost?"

Maybe she wouldn't be eating any time soon, if she had to reunite a lost dog with its owner.

The dog had a braided green collar with a metal ID tag facing the wrong way. As tentatively as if she were diffusing a bomb, she reached to twist the tag around so she could see it.

"Jasper. Is that your name?"

The dog's ears perked up and, tongue lolling, he looked down at the ball, then back at her.

Meredith had to smile. If only some people were as clear about what they wanted from life.

She picked up the ball and threw it with ludicrously weak aim. It landed in the sand a few dozen feet away. The dog had taken off after it before the ball even hit the ground. He picked it up and raced back to Meredith, dropping the ball at her side.

She obediently picked it up and threw it, this time a little farther, to the baby breakers licking at the sand.

The dog raced down gleefully, scooped up the ball and was back in seconds.

"You're not going to stop, are you?"

The dog just watched her, eagerness in his dark eyes and with a sigh, she gave in again.

"Where are your people?" she asked when the dog came back for another round. He just looked at her, head cocked and tongue out.

They had to be nearby, she thought. Maybe the dog had simply raced ahead of someone walking along the beach from Driftwood Park, closer to downtown.

She would wait a few more moments and then call the number on the tag.

The dog showed no sign of tiring but just as she was about to start walking in that direction, she saw a man come out of the cottage next door.

"Jasper," he called. "Come on, bud. Home."

The dog gave her a reluctant look and then picked up his ball and trotted toward the cottage.

She saw only the silhouette of the man, tall and lean, until he turned and then her breath caught.

It was Hot Guy from the café. The one Denise said could butter her grill anytime.

He had come into the café every day since she started working, though Meredith hadn't interacted with him at all past that first day. Brendan had been taking care of the tables in that area.

He must have recognized her at the same moment. To her great dismay, he moved down the steps and headed toward her.

"Sorry about that. The gate doesn't close tightly, and apparently he's figured out how to open it. He loves to play ball and will seek out any willing partner, whether I'm busy working or not. Thanks for entertaining him."

"No problem," she lied.

His gaze sharpened and she suddenly wished she were a little more presentable instead of dirt-spattered and sweaty, with flyaway hair after she had discarded her scarf some time ago.

"I know you. Meredith, right? You work at the Beach End Café."

"Sort of."

"How does somebody *sort of* work somewhere? Sounds intriguing. I'd love to know your secret since I tend to go all-in with everything I do."

At his words, her mind flashed with steamy images she didn't necessarily want, and an unexpected shiver chased down her spine.

Her reaction to him annoyed her. Yes, he was extraordinarily good-looking, but what did that matter? Carter had been gorgeous, with blond hair, blue eyes and a smile that charmed her from the very first time they met.

And hadn't that turned out swell?

"This is my first week. Technically, I own part of the café. Long story, but it was my grandmother's place and she left it jointly to me and my cousin."

"So you're new to management."

"Oh, I'm not managing the café. We build to that, apparently. I'm busing tables and washing dishes. My cousin is quite clearly in charge."

He looked surprised at her tart tone, then smiled. "That must mean your cousin is my landlady. Tori, right?"

She had been so shocked to see him suddenly appear next door that she hadn't realized the implications until now. "Your landlady. I heard Tori tell someone you've rented Seafoam Cottage for several weeks."

"Yes, that makes us temporary neighbors, I guess."

"I heard her say you're a writer."

His mouth tightened almost imperceptibly. "Yes," he said after a moment. "I'm trying to be, anyway. I don't have anything published yet. I received a small inheritance from a relative, so I've decided to use it to take a sabbatical from my day job and finally try to finish my novel."

He didn't look like a writer. He looked far too tanned and athletic to spend all day at a computer. He looked like he worked outside doing something physical. Wrangling horses or leading river rafting expeditions or something.

Then again, she had watched a PBS documentary about Ernest Hemingway and no one could ever call him soft.

"That's great," she finally said. "Everyone should take the chance to follow his dreams. Good for you."

Again, surprise flickered in his expression, so briefly she almost wondered if she had imagined it.

"Thanks. I need it. My book is a mess."

While she didn't know how to deal with overtly sexy men, she did understand the self-doubt so inherent among many creatives, especially after years of working with young, struggling artists at the gallery.

"What kind of book are you writing?" she asked. Her best tactic to put nervous artists at ease was to ask them to tell her about their work. She imagined it would work with writers too.

He waited a beat, as if trying to formulate an answer. "It's, um, an art heist thriller. The hero is an FBI agent on the trail of an art thief."

"Really? If you need research help, let me know."

"Are you an expert on art heists?"

"Not at all. But I have a degree in art history and some experience working in an art gallery. I also did an internship at The Met and was there when a Van Gogh was stolen."

"Is that a confession?"

She could feel her face heat. No. Of all the things that had happened in her past, she could honestly say she had been innocent of that particular crime.

"I'm just teasing," he said when she couldn't come up with an answer. "Thanks, though. I might take you up on that."

"I can also help out if you need a beta reader. A friend of mine where I used to live was writing a book that had a subplot involving an art gallery and I helped her. I enjoyed the process."

"That's very kind of you. Thank you. I'm Liam, by the way. Liam Byrne."

He smiled and she could feel her face heat further. Nerves jumped inside her. What was wrong with her? She was in no position to be attracted to anyone right now.

She fought the frantic impulse to run away into her house. She had no reason to fear this man, whether she was attracted to him or not. There were good men out there, even though she hadn't had the good fortune to marry one.

"I remember," she said.

"And you're Meredith… Collins, right?"

She frowned at his slight hesitation, then pushed it away. He couldn't know.

"Yes. That's right."

"It's nice to officially meet you. Thanks for being so understanding about Jasper here. He loves new friends."

"It's fine. He's very sweet."

"I guess I'll see you around. I'm not much of a cook, so I have a feeling I'll be eating most of my meals at the café."

"That will make Tori very happy, I'm sure."

"Not you? You're part owner now. You have to focus on the bottom line."

Right now she was too busy focusing on her own survival to worry about the café, though she imagined that would change when she began to feel more at ease in Cape Sanctuary.

He whistled to the dog and the two of them walked toward an open area of the beach. Liam threw the ball for the dog, who chased after it with obvious glee.

She watched them for a moment, then forced herself to go into the cottage.

She had to put her attractive neighbor completely out of her mind. How ridiculous that she could be so stirred up after their brief interaction. She wasn't in the market for any man, sexy or not.

Right now, her priorities had to involve trying to figure out how she could make her meager savings last until she started to earn a few dollars in tips.

She had too much work to do rehabbing this house, learning the ropes at the café and trying to convince Tori not to hate her too much.

8

Liam

He walked down the beach, fighting the urge to throw a fist into the air.

Meredith Collins—also known as Meredith Freaking Rowland—seemed to have bought his cover, that he was an eager, struggling writer with a head full of dreams, trying to finish a book.

He couldn't believe she hadn't immediately grown suspicious and told him to leave her alone. After she had endured eighteen months of constant scrutiny from investigators, he might have thought she would be a little more wary about a stranger moving in next door with an elaborate story.

She hadn't been. In fact, she had even gone so far as to offer to help him with research.

That he had set his fictional work of fiction in an art setting, knowing she had a background in art history and had once owned a gallery, seemed to be a mark in his favor.

This might actually work.

He hooked Jasper's leash on his collar and headed down the beach away from the trio of cottages, enjoying the cry of the gulls and the constant murmur of the Pacific.

The peaceful setting seemed to calm him somehow, quieting a restlessness he had only begun to acknowledge.

He hadn't taken a vacation in years, driven to excel and prove himself. After more than a decade with the Bureau, he knew he was considered among the best in the entire agency, trusted by his superiors as a steady, dogged analyst who had helped break some of the most challenging and complicated antitrust and racketeering cases. He had even been seconded to the Los Angeles Police Department to work a few cases with them.

His mother often said how proud his father would have been of him.

Liam wasn't so sure.

He gazed out at sea, feeling that familiar ache of loss. What would his life have been like if his father hadn't been a New York City firefighter on September 11, if Tommy Byrne hadn't run into the Twin Towers and been among the many who hadn't come back out?

Liam had been thirteen that grim day, the second oldest of his mother's three children but the one Moira had leaned on most after her husband's death.

He had stepped up to help his mother with Patrick and their younger sister as she figured out their next steps, went back to school, moved them all to Chicago to be closer to her family.

That was the entire reason he was here. Investigators couldn't seem to find the missing funds Carter Rowland had pilfered, including his mother's entire savings left from the settlement she had received after Tommy's death and set aside for Patrick's care.

Liam was not willing to give up. This felt like the most important case of his career, even though he was here completely off the books.

What did it matter if he had been instrumental in convicting international drug smugglers or breaking up several criminal conspiracies? If he couldn't help all the people who had lost their life savings to Carter Rowland, especially his own mother, what the hell use was the past ten years of public service?

Meredith Collins knew something. He was positive of it. She couldn't be that impossibly naive. No one was.

He had watched every moment of the trial and remembered how she always had this deer-in-headlights look. He had thought it an act, and not a particularly convincing one.

She knew something. He had a month to insert himself into her life and to convince her to trust him with the information she must have.

For the first time since he had come up with the plan to pursue her on his own, Liam felt a flicker of misgiving...until he thought of all the thousands upon thousands who had been bamboozled by Carter Rowland.

His phone rang, as if on cue.

He smiled when he saw who it was. "Patrick. Hey, man. How are you?"

"Good. Where are you? Where's Jasper?"

His older brother adored the dog and loved when Liam brought him on to their video calls. "He's right here with me. He says hi."

Patrick's response was gleeful and lifted Liam's spirits more than anything else ever could. His brother was two years older than he was but had autism as well as significant developmental delays from a brain injury suffered before birth.

"He's a dog," Patrick said with a chortle. "He can't talk."

"Yeah, but you know Jasper is the smartest dog around."

"I miss him. And you. When are you coming home?"

"I'm going to come visit next month. I told you that, re-member?"

"Will you be here for my birthday?"

"I'll do my best. If I'm not there, I'll send you something, I promise. And we can FaceTime. How was your day?"

"Good, except Robert took my cookie. I told him my brother would arrest him if he did it again."

"Um, that might be a little out of my jurisdiction."

His brother lived in a group home and went to a day program, where he worked part of the day in the cafeteria. "I don't even know what jury-whatever is," Patrick said.

"It means the FBI probably can't arrest someone for taking a cookie."

"But it was mine. I only took two and he ate one."

"Maybe you could pack three tomorrow and give him one."

"That's what Mom said." Patrick clearly was not a fan of that idea.

"See. Always listen to your mom."

"She wants to talk to you. Bye, Liam. I love you."

His brother's unfailing affection was like bright, blessed sunshine breaking through clouds on a stormy day.

"Hey, Mom," he said when his mother took the phone. "Is Patrick staying with you tonight?"

"No. I'm at his place. I felt like pizza today so I picked a few up and brought them over here for him and his roommates."

His mom was always doing things like that for her family. Whether it was baking a batch of his favorite cookies and mailing them to him in LA or taking his sister's little ones for the evening so Kat could enjoy a dinner out with her husband, Moira enjoyed life most when she was making someone else happy.

After her husband's death, Moira had finished her teaching degree so she could support herself and her three children. For more than twenty years, she had been a high school teacher at a small, exclusive private school outside Chicago—a school that had invested its employees' retirement accounts with Carter Rowland.

She was sixty-three years young and had been thinking about retiring in a few years to spend more time with her grandchildren, to travel, maybe to pursue a few of her own dreams.

Liam hated that Moira seemed to think that dream was out of reach to her now after losing her retirement savings.

"How are things? How's Los Angeles?"

He hadn't told his mother what he was doing. He had only told her he was working on a case. It hadn't been a lie, exactly. He just hadn't told her he was working off the books on this one, or how very personal it was.

"I'm actually in northern California right now on an investigation. I'll be here at least two or three weeks."

He couldn't imagine being able to meet his objective any quicker than that.

"An investigation. How exciting. Are you going undercover?"

"Kind of." Oh, he could lie to his boss about what he was doing during his vacation time but he couldn't bring himself to lie to his mother.

"Really? Should I be worried about you? You don't go out into the field very often. Are you undercover? Is it something dangerous?"

He pictured Meredith as he had just left her, with a smudge of dirt on her cheek and her hair coming out of a straggly ponytail.

He didn't consider her dangerous, but eating every day at the café with its delicious food might be hazardous to his waistline, at least.

"No. You know me. I'm an analyst. A money guy. We don't exactly live on the edge."

"Forgive me for saying this, but you should live a little more on the edge. I'm not saying I want you to do something foolish or dangerous. I worry about you enough as it is. But too much of the same thing can be suffocating."

She was not wrong. He worked long days, then returned home and spent most of his free time walking Jasper and thinking about work.

"That sounds like a seagull. Are you at least working near the ocean?"

He debated how much to answer, then decided there was no reason not to tell her a few details. If she had any idea what he was trying to do and that he was taking personal time to do it—or that it was all for her—Moira would insist he stop and return to Los Angeles.

He wasn't about to tell her the whole truth, unless he found the missing funds.

"I'm looking at the sunset right now. I'll send you a picture, if you want."

"Oh, yes. I'll live vicariously through you. I always wanted to go to Hawaii and sit on the beach for two or three weeks. I guess I never quite made it."

You might still have the chance.

He wanted to say the words but swallowed them down. If he could find the millions that Carter Rowland had squirreled away before he was murdered in prison, victims of his schemes might still be able to receive recompense for their lost investments. It was a long shot, he knew. The longest of shots. He knew it would probably end in disappointment but he had to try, for his mother and all the other victims.

He spoke with his mother for a few more moments, then they both said goodbye. He watched until the sun had slid down a little farther, then turned around.

"Come on, Jasper. Let's go back and pretend to work on a book."

He walked back to his cottage. Meredith was still working in her garden, he saw. She lifted a hand in greeting but turned quickly back to her work, and Liam resisted the impulse to go over again and talk to her.

Slow and steady. That was the only way he would be able to make this happen.

He only hoped he had the patience for it.

9

Tori

"I'm too tired to finish tonight. Why can't I just take the packet to school and work on it during lunch?"

"Because you won't. You've put it off all trimester and now we're down to the wire, Em. You've got to finish this, or you'll have to take summer school to make up the credits for those two failed classes."

Her daughter glared, throwing down her pen. "This is so dumb."

"Agreed." Tori fought for calm. "Do you think this is the way I want to spend my evening, after working since the break of dawn at the café?"

"That's not my fault," Em muttered.

A sharp retort hovered at the tip of her tongue, but she managed to swallow it. She let out a calming breath and tried for patience. "Help me out here. Neither one of us wants to be doing this right now. But would you rather fail two classes?"

"I'm only failing one class. I have a D in the other one."

"A D minus. Which might as well be an F, right?"

Em didn't answer, which gave Tori reason to suspect her daughter didn't really care either way.

"Try to make progress on the missing geometry assignments for another hour. Then you can stop for the night."

While her scowl deepened, at least Em didn't outright defy her. She picked up the pencil again and turned back to the packet of missing assignments.

Tori didn't want to be here, at the kitchen table working on her laptop. She would rather be on her bed reading a book or sprawled on the sofa watching a gardening or DIY show.

Good thing her love for her child and her desire to help said child succeed was strong enough to override those natural instincts.

Emilia had always been such a sweet kid. Growing up without a father could be tough on a girl, as Tori knew too well, but Em had been lucky enough to have a wide circle of people who loved her, including Javier's parents, who were supportive, devoted grandparents.

Until a year ago, she had had Frances as well. Tori's eyes burned as she thought of the grandmother who had really been the only mother she had ever known.

Em had taken Frances's death hard. Almost as hard as Tori had. It was only natural. Frances had been a daily presence in her child's life, the steady rock they had all relied on.

Had losing Frances played a part in the struggles she was having with school this year, this new malaise and misbehavior?

Tori had encouraged Em to go to grief counseling after Frances died but she had claimed she was okay, that she was handling her sadness in her own way. Maybe it was time they revisited that discussion. Or maybe it was time for Tori to make the unilateral decision that her daughter would benefit from talking with someone.

Right now, their focus had to be on the missing schoolwork, but she resolved to make a call to Em's pediatrician in the morning to obtain a recommendation and referral.

They worked in a silence broken only by the snoring of Emilia's tiny chihuahua-poodle cross, Shark.

After precisely one hour, Em slammed her textbook shut and slid her chair back.

"There. It's almost nine and I'm too tired to do any more."

She only had a few questions left, Tori saw. While she wanted to encourage her to finish the worksheet while she was on a roll, she decided not to push.

"Fine. You can have an hour of chill time, and then you need to put your phone in my room on the charger."

That was another point of contention between them. Em wanted her phone on her person at all times, but one of the conditions of her having a phone in the first place had been Tori's requirement that she relinquish it overnight so that she couldn't stay up texting her friends until all hours.

That had become one of the hardest rules to enforce. How many times had she heard that all of Em's friends were allowed to charge their phones in their rooms? Apparently, Tori was the meanest mother in town.

She tried to parent Em the way Frances had *her*. It wasn't easy.

As expected, Em's annoyed huff could have powered a couple of wind turbines. She said nothing, though, just tromped to her bedroom, where Tori figured she would go on social media and complain about the cruel dictatorship she lived under.

She powered down her laptop and took her teacup to the dishwasher. She was about to turn off the light when her phone buzzed with an incoming text.

She picked it up.

How did the homework battle go on your end?

Sam.

She was aware of a little glow of happiness bursting to life that she tried to quash as she answered him quickly.

I've still got all my limbs but barely.

He sent back the laughing emoji, which went a long way toward helping her feel a little less gloomy about the situation.

Have time to talk now about our predicament?

She leaned against her kitchen counter, as the glow flared into a bright flame of anticipation.

Oh, she had to stop this right now. Sam was her brother-in-law and she couldn't think about him any other way.

Sure, she texted back. *Do you want to give me a call?*

I could do that. Or you could walk outside. I'm on your porch.

She bit down on a swear word that would have gotten her in serious trouble if Frances had ever heard her say it. She had taken off her bra pre-homework session and was already in lounge pants and one of the faded, comfy T-shirts she slept in.

She almost answered that she couldn't come out, that he could call her, but she told herself she was ridiculous. Sam was family. She didn't need to dress up for him, especially since he wasn't at all interested in her romantically. Anyway, it was dark outside. What did it matter?

She pulled on a shapeless hoodie, shoved her feet into sneakers, quickly put Shark's harness and leash on him and pushed open her front porch.

She saw him in the light from her porch: tall, dark, handsome…and holding his cute terrier-mix rescue on a leash.

The two dogs greeted each other happily, tails wagging as they sniffed each other.

Was it wrong that she wanted to do the same thing to Sam?

"We could have done this over the phone," she said.

"I know. But Risa needed a walk and I can't seem to get

enough of the ocean, now that we're back in town. I didn't realize how much I'd missed it. Want to walk with us or hang out here on your porch?"

She couldn't remember the last time she had taken a moment to simply enjoy the moonlight on the waves, which was fairly pathetic since she lived on the beach.

"We can walk."

"Great."

The moon was only a thin crescent, giving space for a few bright stars to glitter above the waves. The beach was deserted, which wasn't uncommon after dark. Driftwood Beach, closer to downtown, often saw bonfires at night or sweethearts snuggling together and listening to the waves, but Starfish was smaller and a little farther from the population center.

"I'm glad you stopped," she said after a few moments of walking. "I need to apologize if I gave you the impression I hold anybody responsible for Em's mistakes but her. My daughter makes her own decisions. She always has."

"Who does she get that from? You or Javi?"

"Both, unfortunately. The poor kid got hit with a double whammy of stubbornness in her genes."

"You call it stubbornness. Others might call it determination," he said.

"True enough."

Javier had certainly been determined and stubborn. In the end, it had gotten him killed.

While he had supported their family by running a small bike shop around the corner from the café, he had loved his work on the local search and rescue team. When a call went out about a surfer in trouble on a beach without lifeguards, Javi had rushed to the scene. Without waiting for the proper equipment or even the rest of his team, he had gone out after the surfer. In the end, both of them had been taken by the sea.

She pushed away the memories. After seven years, she had

almost forgiven him for that one moment of poor decision-making, for wanting to be the hero to a stranger instead of remembering he was a husband and father first.

"Having Cristina here has been good for Em. That's what I should have said. She loves having her cousin close by."

Her gaze slid to Spindrift Cottage, where a small light glowed in what she knew was one of the bedrooms. She knew all too well how tight those family relationships could be. She and Meredith had been as close as sisters once. Maybe even closer.

"I think the two of them have been so focused on having fun together, they forgot the work side of things. We just need to help them readjust their priorities."

"Are you having any luck with that?" he asked as Risa sniffed at a clump of seagrass. "From what my mom said, Cristina worked all evening on homework and barely made a dent."

"Same," she admitted.

"I'm not sure the reality has set in. Maybe we should let them fail."

"I don't disagree. That would certainly get the point across, if they had to spend all summer making up the classes they failed."

Frances's philosophy had been to let her make her mistakes so she could learn from them. She felt another deep wave of gratitude for her grandmother, who had stepped in to raise her own troubled daughter's child and given Tori a loving, stable home.

If Frances had survived being a single parent of Tori, *she* could make it through Em's teenage years.

"Unfortunately, I found out from another mom that failed classes are now made up online. If they fail, we would both have to supervise their work closely through the summer, which would be miserable for all of us."

"Cristina's supposed to spend six weeks with her mom in Germany. I suppose I can pass the torch and make Joni deal with online classes, but that hardly seems fair."

"Being a single parent of an obstinate teenager isn't for the faint of heart. Running the show on your own is not easy, no matter how old the child."

"You would know. You've had loads more experience than I have."

Tori knew Sam had only had full custody of Cristina since fall, when his ex-wife's new husband, a military officer, had been re-assigned to Germany. Cristina hadn't wanted to go with them so their shared custody arrangement had become full-time for Sam.

"Cris must miss her mom a lot."

He picked up a small stone and skipped it across the waves. "They probably talk more now that we live thousands of miles apart than they ever did when they were in the same house. Cristina is always messaging Joni to ask about this outfit or that makeup choice."

"How is she doing? I tried to keep in touch with her after your divorce, but things have been a little different since she remarried."

She and her former sister-in-law had always been friendly. She liked the woman and had been sad when they split up.

"She seems happy. He's a good guy. They're expecting a baby in the fall."

She tried to gauge his expression in the moonlight, but Sam could be as inscrutable as the faces on Mount Rushmore when he chose. "How do you feel about that?"

He skipped another rock. "I'm not sure how I'm supposed to feel. I'm happy for Joni and Rob. I'm sure they'll be good parents together. And Cristina is excited about finally having the sibling she always wanted, even though they'll be so far apart in age."

He was quiet as the ocean murmured beside them and the dogs snuffled at something in the sand.

"All that said," he finally went on, "I guess you could say I'm conflicted."

"I imagine it's a tangle of different emotions. These situations are never as straightforward as they might seem on the surface."

"Exactly. I never wanted my marriage to break up. I felt like we both could have worked harder to make it work. For Cristina's sake, if nothing else. But it was over long before we finally signed the papers, and we've both built new lives without each other."

"Are you happy being back in Cape Sanctuary?"

"Cristina is. That's what matters. She needed her extended family around after her mom left for Europe."

"What about you?"

"It's definitely a slower pace. That's not a bad thing."

"You haven't been here during the worst of the tourist season yet, at least not since you grew up here. You might be singing a different tune by the end of the summer."

His teeth flashed in the darkness as he smiled, and her breathing hitched.

It touched her, knowing what he had given up for his daughter. Not many men would have been willing to shift their career path from a decorated detective in Los Angeles to becoming a small-town cop in a sleepy beachside town.

They reached the end of the beach where sand became impassable rock, and both turned around to head the other way.

This wasn't a bad way to end the day, she thought, enjoying the cool of the evening and the glimmering dance of the moonlight through the waves.

"So the girls," Sam finally said, turning the subject back to where they started. "We both have busy schedules. I was thinking it might be easier if we team up. Share the load a little."

"What do you mean?"

"We only have to get through the next few weeks, when the school term ends. What if we trade off? I could take a couple evenings a week to be the homework enforcer and you could take a few evenings?"

"How would that help?"

"The girls want to spend time together. We let them and

they'll think they're getting away with something, but if one of us is supervising the whole time, they won't be able to be distracted by their phones and social media."

"That's not a bad idea," she answered, considering the possibilities. Tori had a feeling Emilia would work harder when someone else was there to oversee her progress than she did for Tori. Maybe Cristina was the same way.

"So they go to your place two evenings a week and mine the other two, then work on their own the other nights. It's definitely worth a shot. If we find they're not working hard enough when they're together, we can change direction, but I'm certainly willing to try anything at this point."

"Great. Should we start tomorrow?"

"That works for me. Why don't I take the first shift? I've got something Friday and was trying to figure out how I could be the homework enforcer from afar."

"Hot date?" He looked down at her, and she could see the teasing glint in his eyes.

She gave a short laugh, even though his question made her face heat. "Hardly. We're hosting an after-hours birthday party that night."

"I didn't realize the Beach End offered private events."

"We don't usually. But Larry Wilson is turning seventy-five on Friday. He's one of our regulars, and his wife reached out asking if I would consider it."

"Ah. Understandable, then. As I recall from the year she taught me in fifth grade, Annette Wilson is someone who doesn't often take no for an answer."

She smiled, picturing the petite woman with her short steel-gray hair and bright red lipstick. "She definitely knows her own mind. I instinctively wanted to say no, but I took a vote with my cooks and they were all in favor of catering this one event. We don't plan to make it a habit, though."

"With all the prep that probably goes into something like

that, are you sure you have time tomorrow to crack the whip for our pair of miscreant girls?"

Right now, after wrestling with her daughter all evening, she didn't really want to do it all over again the next night, times two. But if Sam was willing to completely upend his life for his child, surely she could sacrifice an evening or two.

"It should be great. If you want to send Cristina over about six, I'll feed her and then glue them both to my kitchen table until we see some progress."

The wind had strengthened and now tugged tendrils of hair from her messy bun to flutter across her face. She tried to shove them behind her ears, but the breeze only grabbed them again.

"Why did you laugh when I asked if you had a hot date?" Sam said after a moment.

She thought about giving him some kind of trite answer, the kind she usually did when people asked about her love life.

Who has time to date?

When Em is a little older, I'll think about it.

The sincere curiosity on his features in the moonlight gave her pause. For reasons she couldn't explain, she didn't want to give him one of those trite answers.

"Dating is hard," she admitted. "Every time I decide to try again, I end up regretting it. I either ruin a friendship or hurt someone who wanted more than I could give."

"Maybe you haven't met the right person."

She tried again to tuck her hair back. "I did meet the right person. Javi."

His features twist with grief for the man they had both loved.

"He wouldn't want you to spend the rest of your life grieving," Sam said after a long moment. "Seven years is a long time to be alone."

He didn't have to tell her that. She was the one who had spent those years sleeping by herself, aching to be held and comforted and loved.

She had never set out to be a career widow.

A few years after Javi died, she had reentered the dating game, first by going out with guys her friends set her up with and then moving to online dating when none of those had turned into anything.

They hadn't all been bad experiences. She had dated a few guys she thought she could fall for, given a little effort. For one reason or another, none of those had worked out. She even had dated one man, an IT specialist who lived in Redding, for several months before they both mutually admitted they weren't quite right for each other.

That had been two years ago. And then everything happened with that damned Carter Rowland, Frances's health issues worsened, forcing her to step away from the café, and Tori had taken on more and more responsibilities, both with running the Beach End and caring for her grandmother. Since her grandmother's death, she had lost interest in even trying.

"Don't you think it's better to be alone than to be miserable with the wrong person?" she asked.

"Sure. I'm a walking testament to that. Joni and I weren't ever a good fit, no matter how hard we tried for Cristina's sake. But I also know you can't find the right person if you're not looking."

She sighed. "I know that. But right now, how about we focus on getting our daughters through eighth grade?"

His laugh slid down her spine like a caress. "Good plan."

They had almost reached the cottages, glowing against the darkness. She could see her temporary tenant sitting in his front room, remote control in hand. Next door, Meredith moved across the curtains she must have found somewhere.

Sandpiper Cottage was mostly dark except for a glow from the upstairs room she and Javi had created for Em from attic space.

Tori was thinking about the Adirondack chairs on the porch that needed a new coat of marine varnish this summer and not paying attention to where she was walking when she suddenly stepped on a small, uneven patch of beach.

She stumbled, trying to catch her balance so she didn't end up landing face-first in the sand, on top of her eight-pound little dog. Sam grabbed her instinctively, keeping her upright.

"Steady there," he said, his voice close to her ear, sending those little tremors down her spine again.

He smelled good. Some kind of clean, masculine soap with tones of sage and citrus and bergamot. She had to fight the urge to lean in to him, to rest her head against that broad chest and let all her troubles and fears float away on the ocean breeze.

No. This was Sam, her brother-in-law. Javier's brother. Her daughter's *uncle*, for heaven's sake. Wasn't her life complicated enough right now, with Em flunking out of eighth grade and Meredith back in town and insisting on working at the café?

She drew in a breath and slid away from him. "Thanks."

"No problem."

"It's late. I should…" She pointed to her house, feeling awkward and ungainly.

"Right. I need to go too. So we have a plan, right? Cristina will come here to work on homework, then Em will come to our house the day after that."

"Works for me. We'll get through this, Sam. They're good girls. They've just gone off track a little, but it's not too late to haul them back."

"Agreed. Night, Tori. Sweet dreams."

With another smile, he turned and walked in the direction of the house he had bought near his parents' place, a few blocks inland.

She rolled her eyes. Lately her dreams had been anything but sweet. And far too many of them involved Sam Ayala.

10

Meredith

She would like to say that her third day of work at the café was
an improvement on the first two.

Then again, she also would have liked to go back in time
and make completely different choices from around the age of
eighteen.

As her shift drew to a close, she pulled off her stained, sticky
apron, smeared with ketchup from an exploding bottle, orange juice from a glass that spilled and some other substance
she couldn't identify.

She either would have to figure out the mysteries of the ancient washing machine in the cottage or use some of her precious quarters to take her apron to a laundromat somewhere.

Denise angled her head toward the bag. "Want me to take
your apron home to wash?"

"I can't ask you to do that!" Meredith exclaimed, stunned
by the offer.

"It's no big deal. I wash Josef's and Aspen's all the time. Neither one of them has a washing machine. It's no problem to do
yours too."

After enduring three days of feeling clumsy and inadequate

and out of place, Meredith felt overwhelmed by the line cook's kindness.

"That would be...so kind. Thank you."

"Don't need to cry about it." The older woman looked dismayed. "It's just an apron."

It was so much more than an apron. Denise reminded her there were still good people out there, people who offered to help simply for the sake of making the world a little better for someone else.

"I'm sorry," she said, trying not to sniffle "You have just been so nice to me, even though I'm terrible at this and have no idea what I'm doing."

"You're trying hard. That's the important thing. Isn't that right, boss?"

Tori came into the kitchen at that moment, carrying the coffee dispenser. "Isn't what right?"

"We were just telling Meredith the important thing is, she's trying her best," Denise said.

"She'll get the hang of things," Ty added from the grill.

"Sure," Tori said, giving Meredith a sidelong look. "Today you only broke two glasses, spilled one cup of coffee on a customer and exploded a bottle of ketchup."

"See? That's an improvement!" Denise laughed, a warm, bright sound that made Meredith smile.

She was suddenly reminded painfully of Frances. Her grandmother had been the most kind, supportive woman she knew, always ready with an encouraging word and bright anecdote.

The two women had probably been great friends. But then, Frances had been friends with everyone.

A fierce longing to talk to her grandmother just one more time hit her hard. Oh, how she missed her.

She didn't have time to dwell on that, when Tori was looking her up and down, taking in the stained apron and her disheveled hair.

"You're doing fine," Tori said before heading back into the supply room.

Meredith stared after her cousin. It wasn't exactly a ringing endorsement but was far more than she expected from her.

The later shift was beginning to trickle in. After giving her apron to Denise to wash, along with her heartfelt thanks, Meredith walked into the supply room to grab her bag from the hook on the wall where employees kept their personal things.

Tori didn't say anything to her, though she knew her cousin was aware of her presence. She thought about slipping back out but figured she wouldn't have a better chance to talk to Tori away from the staff and customers.

"Do you have a minute?" she asked.

Tori looked up. "I'm in the middle of something."

"Okay."

She started to back out but Tori gave her an impatient look. "You're here. You might as well tell me what's on your mind."

"Thanks for what you said just now to Ty and Denise. I appreciate you not pointing to all my mistakes. I know I'm probably the worst employee the café has ever had."

"Close enough. I would fire you but the co-owner probably wouldn't allow it."

Right. She was the co-owner. Though she was not even close to pulling her weight, she wanted to try making a difference, if Tori would let her.

"In the middle of fumbling to figure out my job, I have had a chance to observe what's going on at the café. I, um, have a few suggestions."

Tori's eyes narrowed. "What kind of suggestions?" she asked, her voice dangerously calm.

Meredith instantly wished she hadn't said anything. "Not much," she said quickly. "Overall, the café appears to be well-run. The food is delicious and you have a steady clientele of regulars—mostly townspeople, it seems to me, with the occasional tourist who stumbles in."

"And?"

She should not have brought this up. Not yet. She had only been here three days. She should have given it at least a week before she started pointing out areas of improvement.

"And nothing," she said. "That's all. I have a few suggestions, just random thoughts, but they can wait."

She started to back out again, gripping her bag, but Tori shook her head.

"Nope. I won't let you get away with dropping that there and walking away. You started this. Have the guts to finish it."

This was a mistake. If she wanted to try healing the rift with her cousin, she couldn't start pointing out all the failings in the business Tori had effectively run by herself for several years.

But Tori was right. Meredith couldn't stop there. She had opened the door. She would only make things worse by not stepping through and saying what was on her mind, right?

"I've done a little internet research on how to improve a small business like ours and found a few things I thought we could implement."

"Internet research."

She gripped her bag more tightly. Not like she was planning to use it as a shield or anything, but experience had taught her something was better than nothing.

"Yes. I know it's not the same as practical experience, the years you've had running the café with Frances. You've done great and it appears to be a thriving operation. I just thought a few small tweaks might help."

"Such as?"

"For one thing, you don't have an A-board out front bringing customers in by letting them know the specials or dropping a funny line here and there to draw their attention. There's quite a bit of foot traffic in this part of town as people head for the beach. Why not tease them with something they could eat later? A good breakfast after beachcombing, a tasty lunch when they drop off their rental bike. That kind of thing."

Tori still didn't say anything. Was she annoyed with Meredith for suggesting the café wasn't perfect?

Stop talking now, she thought.

As usual, her mouth didn't want to cooperate with her brain. "Also, the interior is dingy and dated," she blurted out.

Now she didn't need to guess what Tori was thinking. Her cousin's gaze narrowed and her expression turned frosty.

"Dingy and dated." She echoed Meredith's words. "You think it's dingy and dated. I'll remind you this isn't the freaking Four Seasons. We're doing our best. I'm sorry if the décor doesn't meet your high expectations for a seaside eating establishment."

Meredith winced. This was not going well. She should have approached the conversation with much more tact. Tori was obviously touchy on the subject.

Better yet, she should have just kept her mouth shut.

"It's great. Really. Everyone obviously loves it. I was just thinking that one way to bring in more traffic might be through social media, which could only benefit if we made the place more…camera-ready."

"The Beach End is a café, not a nightclub, for crying out loud."

Yes. She was definitely losing ground here. "Let me start over. I love the Beach End as it is. I can see Frances in everything from the curtains to the silverware. I was just thinking that with a few small, relatively inexpensive changes we can freshen things up and make it even better."

"*We* were doing fine before you showed up to talk about how run-down and dated the place is. The only thing people should want to photograph here is the delicious food. That's what matters, not how cute we look when we pop up on somebody's news feed."

"You're absolutely right. The food is the star of the show." Meredith shifted. "But what could it hurt to brighten up the surroundings a little? We wouldn't be changing the main focus of the Beach End, the food, only trying to give the surroundings a refresh."

"I don't have time to redecorate right now. In case you didn't notice, I'm understaffed and overworked. I can't possibly jump into a redesign at the start of the busy season."

"I can do it." The words came out in a rush before she really had time to think them through.

"You?" Tori sounded doubtful.

"Yes. I could do everything." She might not know anything about food preparation or anything else that went into running a busy eating establishment, but she did understand color and design principles. This, at least, was something she could handle.

"I would love to. I would leave the exposed brick on the two walls with the windows but repaint everything else with a warmer off-white instead of the kind of dingy gray there now. I was also thinking it would be great to replace the dusty old framed prints that look like Frances bought them at a yard sale thirty years ago. We could display original artwork by local artists who maybe struggle to find gallery space in town."

She had learned to read people over the years, mainly as a protective mechanism. She could see that Tori instinctively wanted to say no, merely because she so passionately despised Meredith.

To her cousin's credit, she didn't. She actually seemed to be considering the merits of the idea. Meredith pushed on.

"I could do all the work after hours. You wouldn't have to be involved at all. I can even make arrangements with the artists. I'll get some names from some of the gallery owners, and you can have final say on everything I do. You'll love the difference, I promise. And if it draws in a little more business, that can only be a good thing for our bottom line, right?"

"Don't you have enough to do, trying to fix up the cottage?"

"I can manage both," Meredith said. She hoped.

After a long moment, Tori shrugged. "Whatever. As long as you're doing all the work and as long as you can do it so it doesn't interfere with our patrons, I guess you can give it a try."

Meredith let out a breath, as elated as if she had just single-handedly defeated a Roman battalion.

"You won't be sorry, I promise. I can start tomorrow night. I can at least start clearing the walls and washing things down."

"We have the birthday party here tomorrow night."

"Oh, right. I'll do it tonight, then, if you don't mind having bare walls for the event."

"Annette wanted to hang pictures and birthday posters around anyway. That would work, as long as you won't be too tired to come in tomorrow morning."

"I'll be here. I won't let you down."

More than you already have?

Tori didn't say the words, but Meredith could see the sentiment in her expression.

"I figured since the café closes early Sunday and is closed Monday, I could work through the weekend and have it all ready by Tuesday morning."

"Can you work that fast?"

"Yes. After Memorial Day we'll be busy so I should get it done while I can."

"You've really thought about this."

She needed something to think about while she cleared plates and washed off tables.

"You won't be sorry," she said again.

"I can't help you," Tori warned. "I'm in the middle of a crisis with Em and her homework and she needs my attention."

"I don't expect you to. You do enough. Let me do this part."

"I suppose you'll need a key fob so you can get in after hours."

It wasn't a huge gesture but Meredith still felt triumphant. "That would be helpful. Thanks."

"I'll see if I can find an extra. I keep them locked in the cash register."

She followed her out to the dining area and toward the old-fashioned register with its gleaming embossed metal and classic design.

After opening the register, she reached under the cash tray and pulled out a key fob.

"Don't lose it," she said, then handed it over to Meredith with clear reluctance.

"I won't. Thanks." Meredith slipped it into an inside pocket of her bag.

"Um. I hate to ask, but do you happen to have any painting supplies? Tape, a roller, paint tray and cutting brush?" If not, she would just have to dig into her budget for them and then repurpose for the work she was doing at the cottage.

"I've got a few things in storage. You can look through and see what you can use."

"Great." She might as well push for what she could get now. "Would it be possible for me to have an advance on my salary to cover paint and whatever other supplies you might not have? I shouldn't need much. Only a couple of cans."

Tori's long sigh stirred the air. "We can probably cover that out of my vast decorating budget."

Her dry tone made Meredith smile. "Thanks. I promise, you're going to love it."

"We'll see," Tori said. "If I don't, you'll have to paint it back in the original color."

"I will," she promised, savoring the rare and precious moment of peace between them.

11

Liam

Meredith Collins Rowland was going to paint a dingy, hole-in-the-wall café. And she wasn't planning to hire minions to do it; she intended to pick up the paintbrush herself.

Liam couldn't quite believe what he had overheard her talking about with her cousin. He wouldn't have expected the perfectly coiffed and manicured society wife who once owned a prestigious art gallery to even care about the interior design of the café.

But then, he hadn't expected to find her slinging trays and wiping down tables as part of the café staff either.

What was her endgame? Was she genuinely trying to settle into life here in Cape Sanctuary?

The woman was far more of an enigma than he was expecting.

He knew her routine after a few days and knew she would be leaving the café after her shift, so he had already settled his check. Now he quickly closed his laptop and shoved it into his battered leather bag, left money for a nice tip to cover monopolizing the table all morning and headed out right after her, timing his departure to coincide with hers.

"Hi. Looks like we're heading in the same direction. Mind if I join you?"

She turned, surprised. "Oh. Mr. Byrne. Hi."

"Liam. Please. It's a nice day to walk, isn't it?"

"It's lovely today. Cape Sanctuary is such a pretty little town."

She was not wrong. Flowers spilled out of baskets hanging from streetlights all along the business district of Cape Sanctuary, and the scent of them mixed with the salty tang of the sea and the rich sweet smell from a fudge shop they passed.

Though he had spent two hours drinking coffee and ordering the occasional small bite while he pretended to write, the chocolatey goodness still made his mouth water.

"How is the book coming?" she asked as they walked. She hadn't precisely told him he could walk with her...but she hadn't said he couldn't either.

"Not great," Liam admitted, grateful he didn't have to lie.

"Writer's block?"

"Something like that."

What would she say if he told her he wasn't a writer and wouldn't have the first idea how to start composing a book?

She gave him a sympathetic look. "I've heard that's tough. My friend who is a writer used to struggle with writer's block during the middle of every book. She told me she usually had to take a break and work on something else for a few hours while her subconscious figured out the problem."

"Maybe that's what I should do."

"Well, you've picked a good place for beautiful distractions. You could go mountain biking or sea kayaking. There are several outfitters who rent that kind of thing in Cape Sanctuary."

"Right. I've seen them around town."

"My friend liked to take long walks. She said something about being in motion helped her creativity. The area has some excellent hiking trails."

"Any you can recommend?"

"It's been so long since I spent any time here that I don't remember. But you could ask others at the café. I believe there's also a visitor information center near the city offices. They would probably have maps available."

"Good idea. Thanks."

A nice hike in the mountains east of town did sound appealing, but it wouldn't necessarily help him reach his goal of convincing her to trust him.

"Did I overhear you talking to your cousin about painting the café?"

She sighed. "What was I thinking? I mean, it's not like I'm an expert at decorating. I'm probably going to screw the whole thing up and make it look hideous, and then Tori will be even more furious with me."

This self-doubt was something else he wouldn't have expected from her.

"I'm sure it will look great."

She gave him a sidelong look. "Based on what?" she scoffed. "The beautiful job I've done so far on my cottage?"

"You haven't been in town long, right? You'll get there."

"I should be focusing on the cottage. At least there I might see some return on my investment of time and energy when I sell it. I should never have suggested a refresh for the café."

"Why did you?"

"I guess I just wanted to show Tori I have something to offer, since restaurant work is obviously not my strong suit."

He had no idea how to reconcile this woman who had insecurities and doubts with the one he expected to find here. Liam was beginning to think he should stop trying to figure her out and focus more on convincing her to trust him.

"Need a hand?" he asked. "I'm pretty good with a paintbrush."

She stopped walking to stare at him. "I can't afford to pay you anything."

"You wouldn't have to pay me," he assured her. "I don't need the money. But you were suggesting I take a break from my work to help the creative juices flow. This seems like a perfect outlet, with the bonus of helping you improve the appearance of what is becoming my favorite café."

"That is very kind of you," she said, still looking stunned. "But I can't be responsible for you not finishing your book, especially when you've come to Cape Sanctuary expressly for that purpose. As an avid reader, I would never want to discourage authors from putting their work out into the world."

"You said it yourself. I'm spinning my wheels and need a distraction. You can be my distraction."

For just an instant, something flickered in her gaze, something soft and warm and appealing. She gazed at him for a moment, then hitched in a breath and began walking again.

"I was talking about you enjoying the local scenery. I didn't mean for you to become my unpaid painter's helper."

He shrugged. "I'm not into sea kayaking or mountain biking. And who wants to go hiking alone? I might get attacked by a mountain lion or something."

He actually did love to go hiking alone and had spent a month backpacking the Appalachian Trail when he was in college. And he had tried both sea kayaking and mountain biking and enjoyed both. She didn't need to know any of that right now.

If he were indeed a struggling writer, he could imagine the gorgeous scenery of this quiet corner of northern California coast would be a constant source of both distraction and inspiration.

He wasn't, though. He was a federal agent on the trail of millions in missing funds. This woman held the key to finding it. If he needed to spend a weekend holding a paint roller in order to gain her trust, the effort would be entirely worth it.

"I would love to help you. This seems like exactly the distraction I need until I can figure out where I've gone wrong."

She appeared to mull his offer as they drew closer to the small row of cottages, looking like pastel macarons in the sunlight reflecting off the water.

"I suppose I could use the help," she said slowly, reluctantly. "I thought about asking Tori's daughter Emilia if she might give me a hand, but I seriously doubt Tori would let her anywhere near me. Plus Tori said she's having a homework crisis, so that's probably off the table."

Did she know that when she talked about her cousin, her mouth twisted down and her eyes took on an expression of deep sadness?

"You and your cousin don't exactly get along, do you?"

She stiffened and said nothing until they were almost to her cottage.

"She has good reason to hate me," she finally said, her voice soft. "I can't blame her."

"Why? What did you do?"

Her mouth tightened. "It's a long story."

He said nothing, letting the silence stretch out, a technique he had picked up from the limited fieldwork he had done before shifting focus to forensic accounting. She gripped the newel post on the porch railing.

She finally spoke, her voice low. "Once we were the best of friends until I ruined everything. I wasn't here when she needed me. That's what it comes down to. I wasn't here when her husband was killed, I wasn't here when our grandmother grew ill, I wasn't here after Frances died. I let her down, over and over again. And then my…" Her voice trailed off, and she drew into her shell like a baby sea turtle hiding from pecking gulls.

"Your what?" he prompted, certain she was going to say something, finally, about the bastard she married.

"Nothing. It doesn't matter. I let her down. That's all. Wounds that deep can take a long time to heal. Sometimes they never do."

The sorrow in her voice touched a chord deep inside. She

seemed genuinely sad about damaging her relationship with her cousin, though he wasn't sure what was real and true when it came to Meredith Rowland.

"Do you think painting her café will help you atone for hurting her?"

"First of all, it's *our* café. Our grandmother left it to both of us. Technically, I don't think I really need Tori's permission if I want to slap on a new coat of paint. Second, no. I can't make up for the choices I've made or for the actions of others I might have…brought into the family."

Carter had taken the life savings of Meredith's grandmother. Liam knew that much from the casefiles. He could imagine it would have been a natural thing for an older woman to trust the husband of her beloved granddaughter to manage her money. It wouldn't have been a great deal of money when compared with other accounts he had pilfered, a few hundred thousand dollars, but Carter had taken it anyway.

How soulless and immoral did a man have to be to steal the life savings of his own wife's grandmother?

And how could Meredith not have known what was happening?

He wanted to press her on the topic, to open the door somehow and persuade her to talk about her husband. Somehow, he sensed now wasn't the time.

"Yet you still want to try repairing your relationship."

She sighed. "Maybe a little. Or maybe I just want to prove to her that I can make a contribution. I have no idea how to run a café or order supplies or come up with new menu items. But I have a few ideas for driving more business to the café, and one of those is to freshen up the interior."

"When do we start?"

She gazed at him, the sadness giving way to an exasperated laugh.

"I'm going tonight to take pictures off the walls and scrub

them down, then I'm going to start painting on Sunday. If you want to come, I won't stop you. I would actually be grateful for the help."

"I'll be there. What time?"

"The café closes at 8:30. All the customers are usually gone by 9:00. It should only take us a few hours. Is that too late for you?"

"Not at all. I'm a night owl."

"Good. In that case, you can keep me awake." She gave him a tentative smile, her features soft and lovely despite the dark smudges beneath her eyes. "Thank you. I really appreciate it, Liam."

"No problem."

He left her at her cottage and walked next door to his own, doing his best to ignore his sudden misgivings.

He was doing the right thing. People like his mother—and her own grandmother—had been conned out of money they had scrimped their whole lives to save, that they had counted on for their later years.

Meredith held the key. He was convinced of it. She would be the one person who could make sure her husband's victims received as much compensation as possible and Liam intended to do everything within his power to make sure that happened.

12

Tori

She was definitely going to owe Sam for taking on the home-work monitor shift two nights in a row, Tori thought as she wiped down the table in one of the window booths.

Since Frances died, Tori tried to arrange her schedule so she rarely worked evenings. She liked to be home for Emilia after school, as it was sometimes the only chance they had to be together. Late that afternoon, though, both evening servers scheduled to work had called in sick and she couldn't reach anyone else to see if they might be available to come in. So here she was working a double shift.

She had texted Sam in a panic, and he had assured her he didn't mind and it would work out well for him, since he had a couple of late meetings the next week.

Maybe she would try to take him one of the pies she ordered from a bakery outside of town. Dutch apple was his favorite of the café's offerings, she remembered.

Would he think that was too much, that she might have ulterior motives for bringing food? The way to a man's heart was through his stomach, after all—or so Frances had always said.

She didn't want to find her way to Sam's heart. She *didn't* have ulterior motives. Sam was a police detective. He was probably smart enough to figure that out, right?

She grabbed the last pie from the shelf and put it in a box for him, then set it aside to take when she picked up Em from Sam's place.

"Order up," Jeremiah Kincaid, the evening grill maestro, called to her.

She picked it up, fighting a yawn, then carried the tray to a nearby booth, where one of her friends sat alone.

"You put in long hours, Tori," Deb McGowan said as Tori slid the plate of French dip sandwich and side salad to her. "Didn't I see you here this morning on my way to work?"

"What else can I do when I have a staffing emergency? You know all about that."

Deb owned a yarn shop around the corner, and they often complained to each other how hard it could be to hire dependable workers.

"The joys of running a small business, right? I think I spend more time at Another Yarn than I do at home. Sometimes I wonder why I even pay rent."

Tori smiled, even though the other woman's lament hit home with painful accuracy.

Deb was in her fifties and was also a widow, though she and her husband had never had children. The other woman frequently ordered a to-go breakfast sandwich and coffee on her way to work in the morning and often ate dinner here too.

Sometimes Tori suspected Deb frequented the café so often more out of a need for companionship than sustenance, though she wanted to think they provided both.

"How's business these days?" Tori asked as she wiped a nearby table.

"I've had a fairly slow shoulder season, but I expect things will pick up once the tourists come to town. I don't quite get it, but apparently people like to buy yarn when they're on vacation. Seems an odd souvenir, but what do I know? I'm not complaining."

"You know a lot. Which is why you have a thriving business. You're great at what you do and you've created a warm, welcoming store that carries exactly the kind of yarn crafters need."

"Thank you, Tori. That's a lovely thing to say." Deb looked touched and gratified by the words.

"It's true. I really admire all you've done. You're killing it."

"I'll never be rich but it keeps me busy and out of trouble," Deb said with a laugh. "For the most part, anyway."

They chatted for a few more moments, until Tori noticed a couple from one of the only other occupied tables was waiting at the register to pay. She excused herself and went to help them, struck again by how alone Deb seemed.

Was she destined to end up like her in five years or so, after Em left home? Pouring her heart into the café and spending her evenings eating another solitary meal?

She wouldn't pity Deb. The other woman had a full, rich life. She volunteered at the animal shelter, she served on the library board, she helped out during the town's annual Arts & Hearts on the Cape festival.

Tori could do far worse than to follow her example.

She worked for another half hour, until the last customers left and she had finished prepping for the next day.

"Do you mind closing up?" she asked Jeremiah, whom she considered not just an excellent grill cook but a trusted friend.

"Nope. Not at all. You've had a long day. Time you got off your feet."

"Thanks. You're an angel."

She headed to grab her bag just as she heard the front door chime.

Oh shoot. She hadn't locked up yet or turned the sign to closed. She hated turning people away, but at this point she couldn't deal with another customer, especially since she wasn't sure her tired legs would support her for five more moments.

She turned to greet the newcomer and was startled to find her tenant walking in. He had spent three hours or so taking up a table in the back. Wasn't that enough for him?

She set down her bag. "I'm sorry, Liam. The kitchen is closed but I can have Jeremiah make you a sandwich or something, if you're starving."

"No need," he assured her. "I'm here to help Meredith."

"Help her?" she asked, feeling stupid.

"Yes. Scrub the walls and prep for a new paint job."

She stared. "How did she drag you into this whole thing?"

"She didn't. I offered. You could even say I dragged myself into it, since she was reluctant to accept my help."

"Why?" she asked again.

He looked away, and she had the odd feeling he was hiding something. "My book isn't going well. I need the distraction."

"You must be truly hard up if you think scrubbing down layers of grease from these walls will be a party."

"I'm used to hard work. I don't mind."

Again, she sensed he wasn't telling her the whole truth. Working in a café since she was old enough to lift a coffeepot had given her interesting insights into people and the ways their minds work. Frances used to say working at a beachside café could be one big psychological experiment. She could usually guess the kind of tip people would leave based solely on how they talked to the server when they ordered.

It occurred to Tori suddenly that she knew next to nothing about Liam Byrne. He was living next door to her and her daughter. He could be a serial killer, for all she knew.

Then again, maybe she should stop listening to true crime podcasts.

"You said you're taking a sabbatical this summer to finish

your book. I'm not sure I ever asked what you do when you're not writing."

He met her gaze steadily. "Nothing very interesting, I'm afraid. I'm what most people call a numbers cruncher. That probably doesn't seem very strenuous. Not physically, though it can be mentally challenging. But when I said I was used to hard work, I was referring to my childhood."

"Let me guess. You had to slop the hogs and milk the cows at 5:00 a.m."

He laughed and Tori had to admit, he was cute in a sexy geek kind of way. "Not quite. I'm a city boy, born and bred. But I had a paper route from the age of about eleven and started my own lawn mowing business at thirteen."

"A business mogul."

"Something like that. What about you?"

"I grew up right here in Cape Sanctuary. I was raised by my grandmother, who owned this café. She died a year ago and I still miss her desperately."

To her horror, her voice broke a little on the last word as a rogue wave of grief and longing came out of nowhere to drag her against the rocks.

Oh, Lord. She must be tired. She usually tried to keep a much better lock on her emotions than this.

In effect, Frances was the only real parent she had ever known. Oh, her mother would pop in and out of her life but those visits were always harder than if she never came at all. Tori would be so excited for Caroline to show up, but it never turned out well. Her mother would make promises she wouldn't keep, about how she was working to get them an apartment so they could be together. Soon enough, she would have to leave again, searching for her next score. Tori would be devastated.

Inevitably, Frances would take her by the hand and the two of them would walk down to the ocean, where Tori would cry out her disappointment.

Finally Caroline stopped coming, around the time Tori was eight or nine, and Frances found out later she had overdosed by herself at a city park in Modesto.

She had grieved for her mother. Or the death of her dreams of what a mother should be, anyway.

"I'm sorry," he said, his voice low.

"Thanks," she said, never comfortable with sympathy. She hadn't known how to accept condolences with grace after Javi died, and Frances's death hadn't taught her that either.

Before she could come up with an answer beyond the banal, the back door opened and Meredith came into the dining area.

Tori felt those tears threaten again, curse it. She pushed them away. She would not cry for Meredith and their once tight relationship.

She focused instead on her cousin's appearance. This was a woman Tori hardly recognized. Meredith's elegant features wore no makeup and she wore, of all things, a baseball cap that said Find Your Sanctuary. She had to have picked it up at one of the cheap tourist shops in town.

She also wore a faded T-shirt and a pair of jeans with a gaping tear in the knee.

Meredith gave a tentative smile when she spotted them. "Oh. You're here already. I wasn't sure you would really come."

"I told you I would," Liam said.

"People don't always keep their commitments, unfortunately," Meredith said.

"You would know all about that, wouldn't you?" The words flowed out before Tori could stop them. She wanted to kick herself. She sounded bitter and hateful and *hurt*, which she hated. Worse, she had brought up their conflict in front of a stranger and dragged Liam into it.

She tried to patch over the crack she had made in the conversation. "So you're really going through with repainting."

After a pause, Meredith nodded. "Yes. We're only prepping

tonight. Taking things off the walls. Washing them. That kind of thing. I'll paint Sunday night after closing and do another coat Monday morning."

Meredith actually sounded excited about the project. Tori was overwhelmed, just thinking about how much work was involved.

"Knock yourself out, then. I've already worked a double shift. I need to go pick up Em from her cousin's house."

And hope she wasn't so tired that she let down her guard even further and made a complete fool of herself around Sam Ayala.

13

Meredith

Tori didn't slam the door behind her but she might as well have. Meredith couldn't help her wince.

She might have thought she would become accustomed to being despised. Why didn't it get any easier?

Because this was Tori. Her only family left, really. Her mother certainly didn't count.

"You guys good if I lock things up?" Jeremiah Kincaid, whom she had met earlier in the week, gave them an inquisitive look.

"Um. Sure," Meredith said, suddenly not at all certain of anything.

"Make sure that when you leave for the night, you turn off all the lights and pull the handle tight to make sure the doors stay locked. Sometimes they stick."

"Got it. Thanks."

He gave her a careful look. "You sure you'll be okay? I can stick around a bit if you need some help moving furniture around to wash behind or something."

"We'll be fine," Meredith assured him.

His phone dinged with a text and he looked at it, then looked slightly panicked. "That's my wife. She's pregnant with our second and has the weirdest cravings. She's asking me for tapenade. What the hell is tapenade?"

Finally. Something at the Beach End she actually knew. She smiled, even though she felt a familiar pang. "It's a Provençal topping made of olives, capers and anchovies. You should be able to find a jar at the grocery in the gourmet food section. It goes great with crostini or pita chips."

He rolled his eyes, which made her smile again.

"You'd better hurry. Wouldn't want to keep her waiting."

"Right. Guess I'm heading to the grocery store. Good night. Have fun."

He left out the back, tugging the door firmly behind him, and Meredith suddenly felt a wild flare of panic that she was going to be locked into the café with Liam Byrne.

She had a mental image of prison doors clanging shut and felt suddenly claustrophobia. She used to suffer terribly from it after being accidentally locked in a dark butler's pantry for several hours.

She thought she had gotten over it but since her life fell apart, all her childhood demons seemed to have crawled out from under the bed, completely intact.

"Everything okay?"

She nodded. Some sixth sense told her Liam Byrne wouldn't hurt her. The man seemed...kind. It had been a long time since she had met someone who treated her with open warmth.

Besides, if anything went south, she had pepper spray in her purse and an entire kitchen full of knives.

"Yes," she answered. "Though as I look around the café, I'm overwhelmed. I was thinking I only have to paint two walls so it wouldn't be bad but they're miles long."

"Not quite." He sounded amused.

"The last time I painted a room, I was in college. What if I screw it up?"

"You won't screw it up. *We* won't screw it up. You're not in this alone. We got this." He spoke in a low, steady voice and she wanted to sink into his gaze, to lose herself in his quiet assurance.

She inhaled a sharp breath, then released it more slowly. Calm seeped in to replace the beginnings of her panic attack.

Yes. She could do this. *They* could do this. For now, they were only washing the walls.

"I brought some cleaning supplies from home, things I bought to clean up my cottage."

She gestured to the bucket she had carried into the café.

"That will help."

"The first step I suppose is to remove the décor from the walls."

Some of her distaste must have come through in her voice because Liam laughed, a rich, warm sound that made her think of sliding into a tub at the end of a hard day.

"They're not so bad, as long as you don't mind pictures of guys holding fish."

"Those aren't the ones that bother me. It's the bland landscapes that look like they belong in a bad roadside motel."

"How many bad roadside motels have you stayed in?" he asked.

"Not many," she conceded. Precisely two, those she had stayed in on her drive out here from Chicago. But she had a good imagination.

They divvied up the walls and began pulling pictures off the walls, which were coated in a thick layer of dirt, grease and who knew what else.

"Looks like we're going to have some nail holes to fill before we paint," Liam commented after a few moments.

Meredith knew she probably shouldn't find the word *we* so reassuring. After enduring a long, difficult year where she felt more alone than she had ever imagined possible, hearing Liam lump the two of them together was comforting in a way she couldn't have explained.

She couldn't count on anyone but herself. That lesson had been drilled into her over the past year as friends had dropped away. Any minute now, Liam Byrne would probably grow bored and go back to his unfinished novel.

Still, he was here now. Even facing the magnitude of the project, he hadn't started making excuses to desert her the moment they started pulling off grimy pictures from the wall.

He pulled a small can and a foam brush out of a shopping bag on top of the table that Meredith had come to think of as his booth. "I thought we would, which is why I picked up some spackle at the hardware store."

She stared, as stunned as if he had just handed her a diamond tiara to wear while she was painting. "Oh!" she exclaimed. "Very smart. I should have thought of that. I'm so glad you did. Thank you."

"You're welcome." He smiled and their gazes held for a moment. He was the first to look away, and she thought for some reason he looked annoyed with himself.

"You said you brought cleaning supplies to wash down the walls?"

She nodded. "I'll go fill up a couple of buckets."

"I can help."

He followed her into the kitchen, where she headed for a small supply closet that held janitorial supplies. She picked up a few buckets and filled them with superheated water, then added the fume-free organic cleaning solution she had splurged on.

Liam took a bucket from her, along with a couple of sponges. "This shouldn't take us long. I'll work on the south wall, you do the west one."

She had to think a moment to figure out which way was west and then rolled her eyes at herself. The one running parallel with the Pacific was a good guess.

They both started on opposite sides of the room and worked in silence that should have felt awkward but somehow didn't.

"Why did you really offer to help me?" she asked, the final word coming out more like a grunt as she applied elbow grease to a particularly grimy section of wall.

He sent her a sidelong look. "I told you. I have writer's block. I'm looking for any distraction that will keep me from having to stare at the empty page."

"You'll never finish at this rate."

"I have to hope the muse is plugging along in my subconscious, and when she's ready, all the words will come spilling out."

"Is that the way it usually works?"

"So I've heard. I'm new to this, remember?" He sent her an inscrutable look. "To be honest, writer's block is only part of the reason."

"What's the rest?"

"I suppose I felt a little sorry for you. You seem…lost, somehow."

She was again stunned, this time that he could see her so clearly. She grew quiet, absorbing his words as she scrubbed. At her silence, he set down his sponge and gave her an apologetic look.

"Sorry. That didn't come out right. Sometimes I say things without thinking. My sister says I'm socially impaired."

She decided to focus on that instead of wondering how he could see her so clearly.

"You have a sister? Older or younger?"

"Younger," he said after a pause. "Four years."

"Does she live close to you?"

"No. I'm in Los Angeles. She's in Wilmette."

Dread clutched at her throat. "Wilmette, Illinois?"

He nodded. His back was to her, and she had to hope he didn't see how the information left her feeling vaguely ill. Wilmette was a suburb of Chicago. Even if Liam didn't appear to know who she was, his sister likely would.

"Katherine, Kat, is a pediatric nurse there. Her husband's an anesthesiologist. They've got a couple of adorable kids, a boy and a girl. I love them all dearly, especially my niece and nephew, mostly because their existence keeps my mother off my back about giving her grandchildren."

She told herself not to panic. Even if his sister had heard of her, why would she have reason to connect Meredith Collins with Meredith Rowland?

"Is she your only sibling?"

"I have an older brother," he said, suddenly guarded. "He lives in an apartment not far from my mom."

"Not your father?"

"He died when I was a kid."

"I'm sorry," she said softly. "That must have been tough."

He studied her for a long moment, as if she were a puzzle that didn't quite fit together. "It was," he finally said, returning to face his wall. "He was a New York City firefighter. He died on September 11."

She inhaled sharply. "Oh Liam. I'm so sorry."

She had only been in grade school but remembered the horror, the grief, all those lives changed forever.

"My mom moved us closer to her family and went to work as a teacher. She worked like hell to give us a comfortable life. We never had much, but we always knew we were loved."

"You're very lucky," she said. "Not everyone has that."

"I never forget it."

"What does your family think about your dreams of being a writer?"

He was quiet again, and she had the oddest feeling he was choosing his words carefully. "They're behind me, whatever I do. We're very close."

"How wonderful," she said softly. "My grandmother Frances was just like that. She supported me no matter what and always seemed to reach out when I was at my lowest point. The summers I spent here in Cape Sanctuary with her and Tori were magical."

Meredith ached knowing how she had repaid that steady, constant love by abandoning those who had always loved her.

Of all her mistakes, her weaknesses, that one tormented her most.

"What about siblings for you?"

She gave a ragged-sounding laugh. "My parents decided one child was all the inconvenience they could tolerate."

She hated sounding bitter so she quickly changed the subject. "Tori was as close to a sister as I had. She was raised by our grandmother. I don't know the whole story, but my aunt Caroline dropped her off with our grandmother when she was a toddler. She struggled with substance abuse. My aunt Caroline, I mean. Not Tori. Meth, from what I understand. Anyway, she died when Tori was about nine."

"That has to be tough on a kid," he said, his features twisted with sympathy.

Meredith immediately regretted saying anything. "I shouldn't have told you that. I'm sorry. It's not really a secret, but it's also not my story to share. It's Tori's."

"I won't say anything to your cousin," he assured her.

Somehow, though she had no real basis for it, she believed him.

With everything she had been through, it would be a long time before she completely trusted anyone again, if she ever could. But she was willing to believe Liam about this.

"So what's your story? What brings you back to Cape Sanctuary now?"

"I guess I just needed a change." She tried for a breezy tone but had a feeling she wasn't fooling him.

"A change from what?" he queried. "That sounds like a story."

"Not at all. My life has been pretty boring so far."

She almost choked on the patently ridiculous lie. Oh, she had stories. She just wasn't willing to share them, especially not with a man she had just met.

"What about school? Work? Marital status?"

Something told her he wasn't going to ease up. She could always tell him her past was none of his business, thank you very much, but that would probably only make him more curious.

She had to come up with something. A thirty-something woman didn't show up in a small beach café without any kind of past.

"I have a degree in art history. I've worked off and on at galleries or museums since I started college. My grandmother died a year ago and left me the cottage and a share of the café. Now seemed a good time to do something with both. So here I am. And I'm not currently married."

And that was all she planned to say about that.

"Do you have any idea how to putty the holes?" She deliberately changed the subject away from her least favorite topic. "I have no idea."

"I've done it a few times."

"Should we divide and conquer? When we're finished scrubbing walls, why don't I start taking out the nails and you can work behind me, filling in the holes."

He looked as if he wanted to press her about her past, but to her vast relief, he only nodded. "Sounds like a plan."

14

Liam

His prey turned out to be a tough nut to crack.

If he thought spending an evening with her while they scrubbed the dingy walls of a worn-out café would flip some magic switch, suddenly turn her into a babbling chatterbox, he was doomed to disappointment.

As they worked together for the next hour, she chose her words carefully and revealed very little about her background or personal life.

She certainly didn't tell him anything about the past tumultuous eighteen months, her husband's arrest and conviction for fraud and embezzlement or his subsequent death in prison.

And she absolutely positively did not offer any clues about where the missing money might be hidden.

She treated him with polite gratitude but kept herself concealed behind a spiny wall he couldn't breach.

Self-doubt began to creep in again. How could he convince her in only a few weeks to trust him with her secrets? As far as he could tell, this woman didn't trust *anyone*.

He had no idea where to start and was beginning to worry this whole thing was a colossal waste of time and resources.

She was a surprisingly hard worker, though. He had to give her that. Meredith had already put in a long day at work at the café and then had gone home and probably worked around her cottage. Now here she was at 10:00 p.m., humming under her breath as she pried out another nail.

"That looks so much better," she said after a moment, stepping away from the wall, hammer dangling from her fingers. "The original paint isn't as bad as I thought. It's just been covered with layer after layer of grime."

"Maybe you could clean the walls, hang new artwork in place of the old and call it good."

She looked momentarily tempted. "I could. But that would be the easy way out. I want to make the café pop, so it becomes more than just a local hangout. This should be the place where all the cool kids want to be."

But was that what the locals wanted? As far as Liam could tell after several days of occupying his booth in the corner, most of the Cape Sanctuary residents seemed perfectly happy with the café the way things were.

"You're going to start painting Sunday?"

"That's my plan. But, again, you really don't have to help me. You've been a huge help already."

"Are you kidding? I'm in this now. I want to see it through to the finished product." He smiled. "What color paint have you picked?"

"It's a nice neutral tan, a shade darker than what's here now. It should go a long way to making the exposed brick on the other walls pop."

"I wouldn't know anything about that. I have zero experience when it comes to designing spaces."

"I don't have much," she said with a rueful expression. "My... my late husband preferred to hire designers. I had a little input, but he had his own ideas about what he wanted."

Her statement shocked him on several levels. First, she had

been scrupulously careful not to reveal anything of her past. Telling him this much about herself seemed equivalent to letting him read a passage from her diary.

He also found her words disconcerting at best. Her husband hadn't let his wife, who had a degree in art history and owned a moderately successful gallery, decorate her own space. What the hell was that about?

He knew he had to tread carefully here. She didn't know he knew she had owned an art gallery.

"You're a widow? I'm very sorry for your loss."

"Don't be sorry. I'm not." She pried out a nail so hard, it clattered to the floor. "I'm not technically a widow as we divorced about six months before he died. I'm never quite sure whether to refer to him as my ex-husband or late husband or late ex-husband."

"Sounds complicated."

He held his breath, hoping she would reveal more.

"More than you can even imagine," she muttered.

As he was realizing she did as a defense mechanism when he probed too closely into something she didn't want to talk about, she turned the tables.

"What about you? Any wives in the picture? Late or ex or otherwise?"

"No. I'm one of those boring guys married to my job."

"I didn't realize anyone could be that passionate about accounting. Isn't that what you said you do?"

Liam gave an inward wince. He was really lousy at this undercover stuff. He had forgotten he had given her some vague story about working with numbers.

"That sounded like shade," he said, trying for a teasing smile. "What's wrong with accountants?"

"Nothing," she said quickly. "I have nothing against accountants. At least not most of them."

"That would imply you have something against some accountants."

She immediately backtracked. "Sorry. That was rude, wasn't it? I have nothing against accountants. Any of them. Even if it's not something I would personally enjoy as a career choice, you are certainly free to find meaning and purpose in it. I admire anyone who is passionate about what they do."

"I don't know if I would use the word *passionate*. But I'm good at what I do."

He loved digging into someone's financial background, poring over bank statements and credit card receipts to find hidden assets or embezzled funds.

It might not be as exciting or headline-grabbing as other areas of law enforcement, but what Liam and others who worked on white collar crime cases did was important.

Financial crimes were not victimless. He saw little difference between someone who broke into a house and stole someone's jewels and a criminal who preyed on someone's trust, then emptied their bank accounts.

If anything, the latter was worse, the crimes magnified because of the manipulation and deceit that were often involved.

"You've taken time off to write a book. Maybe that's where your passion is."

He certainly couldn't tell her that over the past few months, he had become pretty damn dedicated to finding out where her late ex-husband had squirreled away half a billion dollars.

"Right now, I'm passionate about finishing this job and going home to take a shower so I don't have to smell like pine cleaner all night."

To his utter astonishment, Meredith laughed. It was strangled, tentative, as if she didn't quite know where it was coming from, but it was definitely a laugh.

He hadn't heard the sound from her before and found he wanted to savor it. Progress. This had to be progress.

Should he stop here or press a little harder?

He knew the answer, though he didn't want to. "How long were you married?" he asked into the next silence, though he knew the answer down to the day.

"Eight years." She hesitated. "About seven years, three weeks and five days too long."

For reasons he didn't want to explore right now, her answer made something ache in his chest. "You must have been young when you married."

"Twenty-three. I met him the summer I finished at university, with starry-eyed dreams of one day working at the Louvre. He worked for my father at the time and was considered the company's golden boy."

"Was it love at first sight?" Liam tried for a light tone, even though he suddenly found the idea of the smooth, handsome Carter Rowland and this tousled-hair woman with a smear of dirt on her nose disquieting.

She yanked hard at another nail. "Something like that. On my side, anyway. But what did I know about love? I was young and stupid and had never had a real boyfriend."

"Really?"

That shocked him far more than it should have.

"Believe it or not, I was too focused on school. After graduation, I moved home for a few weeks while waiting to start a new job in Paris. Instead, I met my husband and ended up turning down the job."

"He really must have swept you off your feet."

"He was in his midthirties and needed a wife. Who better to help his inexorable climb to the top than the boss's daughter?"

She said the words in a light, mocking tone but he heard the underlying sadness, like a shadowy underpainting.

"He knew what he wanted and had no problem going after it. And I was young and stupid and pathetically eager to please my parents."

Her movements had lost their fluid grace. They were jerky, stiff. "Do you mind if we talk about something else? A lifetime of mistakes is my least favorite topic of conversation."

"We all have them," Liam said, his voice low.

She gave a short, mirthless laugh. "Other people make mistakes like running a red light and transposing numbers when they balance their checkbooks. Mine are a little bigger than that."

Despite her words, it was becoming increasingly difficult for him to see Meredith as Carter Rowland's partner in crime. The investigators on the case had cleared her of any involvement, but he had been certain they must have missed something. She had been married to the man. Had shared a house, meals, vacations. How could she not have known?

For the first time, he was beginning to wonder.

He had hoped this time together working to prep the café for painting might provide an excellent opportunity for him to gain her trust. He wasn't sure he was accomplishing that, but it *was* giving him a different perspective about Meredith, one he wasn't entirely certain he wanted.

15

Meredith

She stood back and surveyed the interior of the café, exhaustion weighing heavily on her shoulders. For the first time in months, her fatigue was strictly physical, not emotional.

"Thanks for helping me. It would have been a big job for one person."

Liam finished filling the last nail hole with spackle, then with a flourish scraped the knife over it.

"I enjoyed it," he answered, flashing a smile. She had the strangest impression he meant the words.

He angled his head to study the naked walls with the white patches of putty freckling the surface. "I'm afraid it won't be very pretty for your customers until we finish the job."

She made a face. "Is it worse, though, than all the hideous pictures that used to be hanging here?"

"What's your cousin going to say? Will she be happy about it?"

Some of that emotional fatigue came creeping back. "I don't think she'll be happy with anything I do, unless I decide to leave town."

He gave her a look of sympathy. "That must be tough. Is there any way to heal the rift between you?"

"In my experience, some wounds are too deep."

"I can't believe that. Tori seems like a reasonable woman. I'm sure she'll come around when she sees how hard you're working to make the café a success."

"You obviously don't know my cousin. I can't blame her. She's had to handle everything by herself for years, since her husband died. Her daughter, the café, my grandmother's care. I can't blame her for being angry with me."

"How did her husband die?" he asked as they gathered up cleaning supplies.

"It was a terrible tragedy. From what I understand, Javier was on the volunteer search and rescue team and saw a surfer in trouble at a beach outside of town. He called for help but then went out on his own to help the guy. They both died before others could get to them."

"Oh man. That's tough."

Whenever she was tempted to feel sorry for herself at the unexpected course her life had taken, she only had to remember that she did not have the monopoly on pain.

"In one terrible instant, Tori became a widow and a single mom. I can't imagine how tough that must have been, especially after my grandmother started struggling with her health. I should have been here to help her."

"You had your own life. I'm sure Tori understands."

She sighed as she finished stacking up the buckets she had brought and filling them with cleaning supplies. "When you care about someone, you find a way to help when they need it, even when it's hard. Maybe *especially* when it's hard."

He was quiet for a long moment. When he spoke, his voice was low, intense. "You can't go back and change decisions you made in the past, Meredith. The grime on those walls we cleaned accumulated year after year, not overnight. But a good scrubbing, some putty and a coat of paint can go a long way toward making things new again."

"I wish it were as easy to fix relationships as it will be to freshen up the café. I miss her. But if she doesn't want to repair things between us, there's only so much I can do."

He looked as if he wanted to say something else. Instead, he picked up the bucket of supplies. "I can help you carry this out to your car."

She turned off all the lights to the café, then followed him out into the cool night, where the half-moon gleamed on the waves. As Meredith pulled the door closed tightly to make sure it had locked, she breathed in the salty air, fighting the urge to lift her face to the breeze.

"Thank you again," she said as they walked to their vehicles, the only two in the lot. "Without your help, I would probably still be scrubbing walls in the morning when Denise shows up to start the grill."

"I enjoyed it," he repeated.

She had to laugh as she opened the trunk of her rattletrap sedan. "If you truly enjoyed scrubbing years of grease off the walls of a beach café, you have bigger problems than a manuscript that's not cooperating."

"Maybe I didn't enjoy scrubbing," he conceded, setting the bucket in the trunk. "But I enjoyed the company and the conversation."

His words gave her a little burst of pleasure, even as she tried to remind herself he wouldn't feel that way if he knew the truth about who she was.

"I probably gave you an ear full, didn't I?" she said ruefully. "Sorry about that. Unfortunately, you are about the only person in town I have to talk to. The only person in a while, actually."

She hadn't meant to add that last bit. She sounded pathetic, even though it was the sad, unvarnished truth.

She expected to see pity in the light from the moon and her open trunk. Instead, an odd expression flitted across his features, something that almost looked like guilt. It was there for only an instant, then gone.

"I'm glad I could lend a listening ear," he said with a warm smile. "Tell me all your secrets, Meredith. I'm here for it."

For an instant, she was tempted to tell him everything. The whole ugly truth seemed to well up in her throat like sludge coming up through a grate. All of it. Her mess of a marriage. Her blind acceptance of things she should have questioned from the beginning. The lies and betrayals and, ultimately, the shame of knowing others had been hurt because she had done nothing.

"You don't want to hear my secrets," she said, suddenly tired down to her bones.

"Try me," he murmured.

He was standing only a few feet away from her there by the open trunk of her car. She could feel his warmth, seductive and tempting.

What would he do if she stepped into his arms, rested her head on that strong chest and just let him hold her for a month or so?

Her gaze met his and something flashed there, something hot and hungry that sent butterflies twirling through her.

Impossible.

This gorgeous man with the ultra-blue eyes and the warm smile couldn't possibly want to kiss her.

Her breath seemed to catch, and for a long, suspended moment she could only gaze at him as the soft sea air eddied around them and a seagull cried out down the beach.

How long had it been since someone had held her, touched her? A year, certainly. Two?

She suddenly ached for the simple comfort of a physical connection.

She wasn't sure how long they gazed at each other there in the parking lot of the Beach End while a streetlight flickered on the corner and a dog barked somewhere in the distance. A minute? Two?

He was the first to look away.

"I, um, should probably go. Jasper will be wondering where I am."

His words seemed to jerk her back to reality. "Right. Yes. Of course. Good night."

She slid into the driver's seat and turned the key with trembling fingers, fiercely grateful when the engine sputtered to life at the first try.

Her mind whirled as she drove through the streets of Cape Sanctuary, all but deserted this late on a weekday evening.

Liam Byrne had wanted to kiss her. She had seen the light spark in his eyes like fireflies across a summer meadow.

He wanted to kiss her. Or at least the *her* he thought she was. Meredith Collins, part owner of the Beach End Café, not Meredith Rowland, the hapless wife of infamous swindler Carter Rowland.

The knowledge left her both giddy and terrified.

She pressed a finger to her lips, wondering what his mouth would taste like.

She quickly dropped her hand back to the steering wheel. She would never find out. If he knew the truth about her, Liam would never have looked at her like he wanted to kiss her.

He would not have helped her scrub the walls of the café or listened to her ramble on.

If he knew the truth, Liam would despise her. He would see her as the unindicted coconspirator along with her husband, as so many others did. The woman who enjoyed luxury and comfort, designer clothes and who had created a bougie art gallery with the money her husband stole from retirees and pensioners.

She had to tell Liam the truth. It was unfair to take advantage of him. He was offering friendship and help without having all the information.

As much as she might desperately need a friend, she couldn't take advantage of his good nature.

16

Tori

Tori missed the breakfast rush on Friday because she had to run to Redding to pick up a few things from the restaurant supply store there for the party later that night.

When she walked into the kitchen, everyone who worked the morning shift seemed to be watching her with sharp alertness, like a flock of magpies waiting for a crumb to drop at a picnic lunch.

The sidelong looks immediately set her on edge. What was up? Did she have something in her hair? She met Jenny Taylor's gaze with a smile, and the waitress immediately picked up a tray of glasses and quickly headed out into the dining room.

Tori frowned at the strange vibe.

"I told you all I would be in later, right?" she said to Denise. "I didn't leave you shorthanded for breakfast."

"You told us," Denise agreed.

So why was everyone looking at her like she was a hand grenade that had suddenly been tossed into their midst?

"How did the morning go?"

"Not too busy," Denise said. "We had a big group come in

about an hour ago. They just left. It's been slow since then. I think the rain has kept some people home."

The unpredictability was one of the things she loved about running the café. A stormy beach day could work both ways. Either it put people in the mood for breakfast out or they decided to stay home, snug and dry. One never knew.

She pulled on an apron and tied it, then scrubbed her hands.

"Have you been out front yet?" Denise asked.

"No. Why?"

"Just wondering."

She looked around the kitchen. Ty seemed inordinately focused on the grilled cheese sandwich he was flipping. Josef scraped off a plate into the garbage.

Suddenly wary, Tori pushed open the kitchen door and walked out into the café.

It looked…barren.

She had never been a huge fan of all the framed pictures her grandmother had hung around the café. Meredith had been right; they were outdated and tired. She should have made changes a long time ago and was embarrassed that she had become so used to the status quo and so focused on other things that she had let things slide here.

Still, the absence of the familiar seemed strange. When she was used to a space looking the exact same for more than a decade, any change was disconcerting.

The walls were faded around brighter spots where the prints had hung, and she could see patches of spackle covering what must have been nail holes.

Meredith stood behind the counter, a sanitizing cloth in her hand and an anxious look in her eyes.

"I know it doesn't look terrific now," she said. "It will when I'm finished painting, I promise."

Did Meredith think she would start yelling and throwing things around over some spackle on the walls?

Yes. Probably. She hadn't exactly given her any reason to think otherwise.

The rest of the staff certainly knew her better than that, except maybe Aspen, who hadn't been there much longer than Meredith.

"I'll have to take your word for it. I guess we have to paint now that you've patched the holes."

"I know. I'm sorry. I should have waited until tomorrow night, after the birthday party. I just didn't know how long it would take. Will it be too big of a mess for the private party?"

"It should be fine. I told you his family will be bringing banners and photographs to hang. I should have told you to keep the nails for them, though, in case they wanted to use them."

"We can spackle again, if they want to hang more nails. It's no problem."

"Don't worry about it. It's fine."

Meredith looked so relieved at her reaction, Tori immediately felt guilty, then told herself to cut it out. She wasn't here to make friends again with Meredith. That train had left the station a long time ago.

She headed back into the kitchen and didn't realize Meredith had followed her until her cousin spoke again. "Did you think of any local artists we could highlight after the walls are painted?"

Between her stress over Emilia and her schoolwork, these new and unwanted feelings she was having for Sam and her general unease about Meredith's return to Cape Sanctuary, she hadn't given it any thought.

"No. Sorry. I'll try to come up with some names over the next few days."

"Aspen is good artist."

Josef, usually so silent and watchful, spoke up unexpectedly.

He had been one of her best hires, after being recommended by a refugee center in the Bay Area. He worked hard, was courteous to everyone and seemed to bring out the best in all his coworkers.

She wasn't surprised he knew this about Aspen when Tori had no idea.

"I didn't know that!" Meredith exclaimed. "What medium?"

The young woman shrugged, turning her face away but not before Tori saw a new bruise on her cheek that made her stomach clench.

"Oil on canvas," she mumbled. "But I haven't painted anything in a long time. Art supplies are expensive. When it's a choice between my tips going for essentials like food or going for a tube of gesso, food wins every time."

Tori paid her workers much more than some of the local restaurants, as much as she could afford to attract quality help, but she knew it was still not enough.

"I would like to see some of your work," Meredith said, her features lighting up like Tori hadn't seen them since her cousin had come to Cape Sanctuary. "Do you have a portfolio? Or even photographs on your phone of some of your paintings?"

Something flashed in the young woman's eyes, something bright and hopeful, filled with possibilities. For an instant, Tori thought she was going to reach for her phone but then her hand jerked away and she picked up a tray containing the grilled cheese Ty had made along with a cheeseburger and fries.

"You've got better things to do than look at my crap art. It's trite and pedantic. Anyway, I'm not really a local. I'm only here for a few more weeks, then we're moving on. Josef, would you mind taking care of table four for me?"

She left the kitchen again, with Josef close behind her.

"Did you know Aspen was an artist?" Meredith asked.

Tori could feel color rising up her neck. "No. I don't know much about her. She's not a big talker."

Aspen had showed up about a month ago looking for work. She had experience and her references checked out. Tori knew she and her slimeball boyfriend were nomads, boondocking in the mountains east of Cape Sanctuary.

Though she seemed to wear the same two or three outfits to work, Aspen was always neat and clean, easygoing and friendly to the customers.

Apparently, the camping life was dangerous to her health, though. She was always coming in with a new bruise or scrape. Tori and Denise had both tried to give her info about shelters in the area, but she had shrugged them both off.

"I wonder who said her art was trite and pedantic." Meredith looked after the young woman, sympathy in her gaze.

"Probably the same bastard who gave her that bruise on her cheek," Tori muttered. "And the sprained wrist the week before that and the black eye the week before that."

"Oh." Meredith looked stricken, color draining from her her cheeks. "I... I didn't realize."

Maybe if you looked around at the rest of the world instead of focusing only on yourself, you might notice things like that.

Tori bit back the words. She was the last one to lecture anyone else about being more observant to the world around them, when she hadn't known her own server was an artist.

"Are you planning to come back tomorrow night after closing to finish prepping the walls?"

Meredith shook her head. "I thought we might need to but Liam and I were able to finish last night."

"So when are you planning to paint?"

"It's probably best if we stick to the original plan and start painting Sunday night, since the café closes early and doesn't open again until Tuesday morning. You're still planning to close Monday, right?"

"Yes. Frances always tried to close the café for one day the week before Memorial Day to give the whole staff at least one vacation day before the summer craziness starts. Monday is our slow day so that one makes the most sense."

"That will hopefully give the fumes time to dissipate a little before we reopen on Tuesday."

Tori quickly cycled through her weekend calendar, which mostly involved cracking the whip on Emilia over her homework.

"We're having dinner with the Ayalas Sunday evening to celebrate a couple of birthdays, but I might be able to come over after that."

Meredith looked at her as if she had just suggested they paint the café fluorescent green. "You don't have to. This was my harebrained idea."

"And it's my café."

"*Our* café," Meredith corrected.

For the first time in a week, Tori didn't have an overwhelming urge to snap back at her cousin.

"Right. Which means we both should be involved in any cosmetic improvements. I'll take Em home after dinner with the Ayalas. We're not eating until late, so it might be nine or nine thirty before I can make it back here."

Meredith looked as if she wanted to argue, but Ty asked a question about the menu for the evening's festivities and the moment was gone.

17

Meredith

Sunday evening, Meredith rode her bike through the rain-slicked streets during a break in the storm.

The lights of Cape Sanctuary sparkled through the evening, warm and cheerful against the darkness.

As she made her way down Main Street, she had to admire the lovely downtown, with its flower baskets and old-fashioned streetlights. Cape Sanctuary was charming but not pretentious. She loved that about it, the sense of warmth and welcome.

She had wondered whether she would feel the same pull to the place now that Frances was gone or if her grandmother had been the magnet drawing her back. Frances was inexorably linked to Cape Sanctuary in her mind, as much a part of the town as the honey-colored brick buildings and the ocean's constant song.

Meredith didn't expect that would ever change, but she found she could still love the town without her beloved grandmother.

This felt like home, or at least the home-shaped hole in her heart. Despite growing up in the Chicago area and then settling there with Carter, Meredith couldn't remember ever feeling the same sense of connection she felt here.

She loved the city buzz, the parks, the cultural offerings and restaurants, but there was something inherently peaceful about Cape Sanctuary.

Her father had held nothing but disdain for his hometown.

Any time he had to come visit his mother, Michael would be tense and strained until they headed away from the sea back toward the airport.

Meredith still wasn't sure why. Maybe he had bad memories of growing up here, especially with a sister who had taken a left turn into drugs and alcohol when she was still in high school. Or maybe he was embarrassed by Frances, with her ragged cut-off capris and her wild hair and her generous heart. His mother probably didn't fit the image he had cultivated for himself as a wealthy, sophisticated financier.

Cilla simply stopped coming to town after Meredith turned about nine.

I don't feel up to that long flight, Meredith could remember her mother saying at the dining table one day shortly before she had been scheduled to visit for the summer. *You can take her, darling. Or better yet, if your mother wants her to stay so badly, Frances should come to Chicago to collect her.*

That hadn't happened, of course. Frances had the café and Tori and a hundred other reasons why she couldn't leave Cape Sanctuary.

Michael had finally hired one of his employees to fly with her on her annual visits until he deemed Meredith old enough to fly by herself.

She had flown out a few times when she was in college, when she could squeeze out a few days between semesters. By then, her relationship with Tori had become strained and then nonexistent.

She knew Tori felt betrayed that Meredith had pulled out of the trip they had been planning, but this was more than that. She suspected Tori was beginning to resent the different paths their lives had taken.

By then, Meredith was at Smith College, pursuing her art

history degree, while Tori went to the local community college, got pregnant with Em and ended up marrying Javier before she was twenty.

Meredith was never sure if her cousin had stayed in Cape Sanctuary after Javier's tragic death because she loved it here or because she felt obligated to help Frances run the café. She hoped it was the former.

She pushed away the grim thoughts as she parked her bike in the empty parking lot of the café.

She locked it, then picked up the bag containing a few last-minute painting supplies.

When she unlocked the door, the silence in a place usually buzzing with life made her shiver a little.

She chided herself for the reaction. She wasn't afraid to be alone. It was better than being surrounded by people who despised her.

She flipped on the light and went to work preparing the space. She was covering the trim on the windows with tape when she heard a rap on the front door and saw Liam standing on the other side wearing jeans and a T-shirt that looked too nice to wear while painting.

Her pulse jumped and she frowned at herself for the silly reaction.

"Coming. One second," she called, though she knew he couldn't hear her through the door.

She hurried over to open the front door with its chiming bells. He came in smelling of rain and springtime and stood for a moment on the entry mat, shaking off excess moisture, then removing his jacket.

"Evening," he said with a smile.

"Hi." She cursed herself for the little tremble in her voice, blaming it on the fact she hadn't seen him since Thursday, when they cleaned the walls. He hadn't come into the restaurant Friday and she hadn't worked Saturday or that day.

The evening before, she had seen him on his back deck overlooking the water, chair tipped back and feet up the railing. He drank something from an amber bottle—beer, she assumed—as he watched the sunset.

She hadn't wanted to bother him. He had seemed lost in thought and maybe even a little lonely, though he had Jasper by his side.

Why would he be lonely? She was probably projecting her own emotions on him. More than likely, he was perfectly content with his life and only taking a moment to savor the beautiful surroundings.

"Are you sure you're ready for this?" he asked.

"Not even close," she admitted with a rueful smile.

"I'm sure it will turn out great. I'm here to help. Where do you need me?"

A wildly inappropriate thought popped into her head. Her cheeks suddenly felt hot, and she hoped he didn't see her blush and wonder what she was thinking.

"I'm still doing the prep work. I've started taping the windows and trim, then I need to lay down the drop cloths. Tori would kill me if I dripped paint on the booths."

"I can help tape, if you have more than one roll."

She had found a bundle of four rolls in Tori's paint supplies and hoped that would be enough. She hated to ask for more funds to pay for the project and wasn't sure her own tight budget would stretch any further.

He grabbed one of the rolls and headed toward the other wall.

"How's the book coming?" she asked as she finished one window and started working on the next one.

He made a face. "Not great but I'm making slow progress. How's the progress on the cottage renovation?"

"Your writing is probably going better than my renovation."

"I seriously doubt that," he said, his voice dry.

"The cottage is livable for now. That's what matters. I expect the renovation will be a long process. I can only do a few things at a time because of my time and money constraints," she said.

"What's the first priority?"

She made a face. "Everything. It's a disaster. I keep imagining what I would do if I had an unlimited budget. I don't, though, so I have to set realistic, attainable goals. Like cleaning the mold out from under the kitchen sink."

"Sounds like a good place to start."

"My grandmother used to complain about the constant battle she fought against mold and rust here on the coast. I finally get what she was talking about."

He gestured to the window she worked on. "Well, you're very good at taping. I would almost suspect this isn't the first café you've painted."

She had to smile. "I'm afraid you're way off there. This is the first and probably the last café I'll ever paint."

She moved to the last window on her wall, a window popping up like a noxious weed through a sidewalk crack. "I did repaint the guest half bath of our apartment one weekend on a whim. One wall was a hideous shade of brown, and I decided I couldn't stand it another moment so I ended up painting it a really lovely pale blue. My husband wasn't very happy about it."

He looked surprised. "Really? That seems odd. Most men don't care about that kind of thing."

She instantly regretted bringing up the subject. Her arm suddenly twinged, and she knew it was no coincidence.

"My husband did. Care, I mean. What's the point in paying a designer to come up with a cohesive theme for the house and shelling out a fortune to her if I'm only going to DIY something tacky?"

That had been the mildest thing he had said to her. *Stupid bitch. Talentless cow.*

"Wow. He sounds like a prince."

"Oh, you have no idea." Instead of facing him, she focused

on smoothing down the painter's tape to make sure the edges were secure.

"How long before you started to figure out he wasn't the man of your dreams?"

She gave a rough laugh that held no amusement. "Before the wedding," she admitted, something she hadn't told another soul on earth. "The day I was supposed to marry him, I pulled the covers over my head and cried, petrified I was making a terrible mistake. But it was too late by then. My father had spent fifty thousand dollars on flowers alone. All of my mother's friends were coming. It was the society event of the season."

Cilla had been over the moon. For the first time in Meredith's memory, her mother's focus had been laser-sharp on her. She had loved it, had thought maybe they were finally building the relationship she had always sought.

"I didn't know how to stop the train at that point. I thought it was too late," she said, to her vast shame. "Anyway, I thought I loved him. I convinced myself that he was sweet and attentive ninety-five percent of the time. Those times he wasn't had to be the anomalies."

"I'm guessing that didn't translate into a happy marriage."

How had they come to be talking about Carter? Her least favorite topic. She had brought it up, and she had the random thought that maybe some part of her was putting up the specter of her dead ex-husband as a barrier between her and this man who would despise her if he knew the truth about her identity.

She ripped tape off the roll with a particularly violent movement. "You would be correct."

He was quiet for a moment, his features troubled. "If you knew it was a mistake, why didn't you divorce him earlier?"

If you leave, I'll kill you. And nobody will ever find enough of you to bury. I know people who know people. Who would look for you, anyway? Your mother?

150

By the time he made those threats in a perfectly reasonable voice, she hadn't doubted him.

That had been three years into their marriage, when any pretext of love between them had been ground to ashes. After all the loss and pain of those years, she hadn't really cared what happened to her. She had been numb, hollowed out.

Death would have been a relief—or at least a release.

"I had...reasons."

They weren't good ones. She could see that now. Sometimes she looked back and wondered who that woman was, who walked through that vast, two-story penthouse apartment as insubstantial as a wraith, with no shape and certainly no spine.

Somehow she had managed to build a life. She had friends, she went to the opera and the theater, she volunteered with several organizations he had vetted and approved.

As long as she stayed out of his way, as long as she didn't contradict him, didn't question any of his actions, didn't say a word about any of his other women, they coexisted.

She had opened the gallery with the money her father left her, and had been quietly saving money, trying to separate their finances so she could finally step out from under the oppressive weight of their marriage.

If she had acted earlier, the truth about what Carter had been doing with his clients' assets might have come out in the divorce proceedings, and he could have been stopped sooner.

She expected the guilt would never ease, knowing that her own weakness and indecision had hurt others.

"I'm done here," she said abruptly, suddenly desperate to change the subject. "I'll go open the paint."

She hurried away from Liam and went to work opening the paint can and stirring briskly while he finished taping.

As she poured the paint into the two trays laid out on plastic sheeting and then old newspapers, she was suddenly struck by the enormity of the task.

She had no business believing for a moment that she knew what she was doing, that she could add some warmth and style to the café.

All those negative voices from the past seemed to rise up again in a chorus of dismissal and for a long moment, she could do nothing but stare at the liquid color.

"You okay?"

She looked up and met Liam's gaze. Some of her panic must have been apparent in her eyes.

He touched her arm, his gaze filled with calm and reassurance. "Steady on. You've got this."

"What if everyone hates it? People have been coming here for years and they like the comfort of the familiar. What if *Tori* hates it?"

"Then we'll start over until we find a shade she doesn't hate. Take a deep breath, Meredith. It's only a coat of primer."

She drew courage from his words. He was right. It was silly to panic about a simple coat of paint.

Maybe her panic wasn't about the paint but about the uncertainty of change. Everything in her world had shifted over the past year, and now here she was in Cape Sanctuary trying to scrape away the old mistakes and try anew.

This was her last refuge, the only thing standing between her and utter devastation.

What if she failed?

"Why don't I take the first swipe with the roller?" Liam said, his voice low and measured. "Once I do that, we're committed. We have no choice but to follow-through."

Why was this man helping her? It didn't make any logical sense. He was a stranger, simply passing through on his journey toward following his own dreams.

She had no idea but she was deeply grateful he was there, that he had offered to help her do this as a distraction from his own work that wasn't going well.

She took a deep breath and picked up a roller. "I'll do it. I think I need to do it."

He nodded and moved out of the way. She drew in a deep breath, coated the roller with paint, then moved to the wall. With another deep breath for strength, she rolled it on, watching the streaks of color overtake the tired, dingy old paint.

It was only primer, not the actual paint, but even those few rolls of paint managed to brighten up the space.

"There you go," Liam said. "It looks great."

"It won't be much different than what was there before, but at least it will be clean and fresh."

He picked up another roller. "Why don't I work on the opposite side of the wall again, and we can meet in the middle?"

She nodded, her spirits brightening with every sweep of the roller.

"You seem as if you've done this before," she said into the silence as they both worked in their respective corners.

"Paint a room?"

"That, yes. And also manage to talk down someone on the brink of a meltdown."

His mouth lifted into a small, surprised smile. "I'm definitely not an expert at painting. I helped my mother repaint rooms in our house over the years, and I painted the odd apartment. You probably shouldn't trust me with a roller."

"You're doing great," she assured him.

"As to the other thing, any alleged skill I might have in talking someone down," he began, then paused a moment as if trying to decide what to share with her.

"I told you I have a brother," he finally said. "Patrick. He's two years older than me. What I didn't tell you before is that he has been diagnosed with autism. In certain circumstances he can get overstimulated and end up having a meltdown. He doesn't have them as frequently as when he was younger, but it can still be a struggle for him. We all devised various coping mechanisms for helping him through them."

Maybe that was why Liam Byrne had a quiet air of calm and kindness about him that made her want to lean on his shoulder and spill every ugly detail about her life.

She didn't know what to say. "Has that been difficult?"

"Not really. Like I said, they don't happen that often now. Most of the time he's a great guy filled with curiosity about the world and a fascinating memory for details. He knows the batting average of every single Cubs player for the past twenty-five years, and he can easily spend an hour telling you every detail about a book he checked out of the library about boat motors or raising chickens. He has a girlfriend who goes to the same day program, and he lives in a group home with three other roommates. He has a good life."

"He sounds wonderful."

His features softened when he talked about his family. She wondered if he knew that about himself. She tried to ignore a pang of envy.

"He's pretty terrific. We all feel lucky to be part of his world."

She had to believe Patrick was also lucky to belong in a family that loved him and tried to help him live his best life.

"What does Patrick think about having a brother who will some day be a bestselling author?"

His mouth twisted, and he didn't answer for several long seconds. "He would say he's proud of me, no matter what I do," he finally said.

"Do you get the chance to visit often?"

"Not as much as I'd like. They like to come visit me. He loves Disneyland and is always looking for an excuse to fly out."

"Is it hard to be away from him and the rest of the family the rest of the time?"

"He still has my mom and my sister and her husband and kids. They all take care of him. His group home is only about a mile from my mom's house, and he often takes his roommates there for Sunday dinner. I usually have a video call with everyone to catch up, though it's so noisy and chaotic I usually can't hear what anybody's saying."

"It sounds wonderful." She had a feeling she wasn't very good at hiding the yearning that bloomed inside her at the picture he painted.

"No Sunday dinners for you, with a big, boisterous family?"

She shook her head, pushing down the pointless ache as she painted. "I'm an only child. My father died a few years ago and... my mother and I aren't close."

"I'm sorry. Is that a recent rift?"

He was very good at turning the questioning back to her, she noticed. Was he reluctant to talk about himself or simply interested in the lives of people around him?

"My mother was never especially warm and loving. I've come to accept over the years that Cilla is one of those women who probably shouldn't have given birth."

"That's tough."

She made a face. "I sound pathetic, don't I? Miserable marriage, no relationship with my mother. Let's add a distant, distracted father who was never there and I should probably be spending twelve hours a day in therapy."

"You don't seem a complete mess."

Ha. That showed how much he knew. "Frances and Tori gave me more than enough love to make up for it," she assured him. "I wish you could have known my grandmother. She was the most loving, generous person. You would have liked her."

"Sounds like it, from everything I've heard. It's good you had her, at least."

"The biggest mistake of my life was not returning to Cape Sanctuary earlier, as soon as she started to become ill. I had no idea she would go downhill so quickly. That's no excuse. I should have been here. I just…thought I had more time to sort things out."

"Time can definitely be an enemy," he agreed.

Yes. And shame. That had done more to keep her away from here than her husband ever did. She had been so ashamed at herself for her choices, for staying with him when she should never have gone through with the wedding and then for staying after the wedding once she knew for certain what a drastic mistake she had made.

"Did she like your late ex-husband?"

She shook her head. "No. Not from the very first. She wouldn't tell me why. I should have called off the wedding then. Frances was an amazing judge of character, probably because she interacted with so many people on a daily basis at the café. She used to say she didn't know much but she knew people. I should have listened to her. Instead, I buried my head in the sand and told myself things would get better."

"I'm guessing they never did. Do you want to talk about it? People tell me I'm a good listener."

Women people, probably. She could picture him going into bars and having women flock to him with their tales of woe and despair.

To her shock, Meredith found she wanted to be one of them, to tell him the whole sordid story. Every detail of the pain and loss she had endured and the cold shock of watching Carter's fragile house of cards not only tumble down but burn to the ground.

She hesitated, not sure how she could possibly condense the past miserable few years into a story that wouldn't take all night.

She also didn't really *want* to tell him. Once she did, he would no longer look at her with that warm compassion but with the same disdain she felt for herself.

"I told you my husband died shortly after we divorced."

"You did."

She drew in a shaky breath, then let it out in a rush along with the truth. "I didn't tell you he died in prison."

Oddly, he didn't look as shocked as she would have expected. Maybe all the other women who spilled the tea to him also were married to lying, cheating thieves.

"What did he do?"

"If I told you everything, it really would take all night. But the short version is that he was charged with more than a dozen different federal financial crimes and convicted on most of them."

The litany was painful. Insurance fraud, securities fraud, investment adviser fraud, theft from an employee benefit plan. Hundreds of counts he could have been charged with but prosecutors had settled on what they knew they could prove.

So many victims.

"Wow," he murmured. "That's a lot to deal with."

She gave a short laugh. "You could say that. It's been a little intense."

"Is that why you didn't come back to see your grandmother?"

"One of the reasons."

She was spared from having to go into all the gory details when the door unlocked with a click and Tori walked in, shaking off her umbrella.

"Sorry I'm later than I said. The party went long."

She never would have expected it, but she was actually relieved to see Tori. Even dealing with her cousin's antipathy was better than revealing the whole sordid truth about what the man she once thought she loved had turned into.

"You're not too late," Meredith assured her. "We're working on the first coat of primer."

"I can grab another roller for you," Liam said. He smiled at Tori, but Meredith had the odd impression he wasn't at all happy to see her.

18

Liam

As Tori Ayala came into the café with damp hair and skin sheened with moisture, Liam had to bite back a harsh oath.

He generally liked his landlady. But why did she have to come in now? He was close. Painfully close. Meredith had been on the brink of confiding in him, he was certain of it.

Meredith was beginning to trust him. She had told him about her mother and a few details about her marriage. It had to be only a matter of time before she trusted him enough to tell him the whole truth about her husband.

Time was not on his side, however. He had been in Cape Sanctuary a week, and he had nothing concrete to help him find the missing millions.

Not for the first time, he worried he was wasting his time with Meredith. She had been interviewed extensively by other investigators, who seemed convinced she had nothing to do with her husband's activities.

What made him think he miraculously would be able to uncover something new? Was it arrogance or blind faith?

Neither. His motives had more to do with desperation. He didn't know where else to turn.

Now, as both of them faced Meredith's cousin, he thought he might be further than ever from finding the missing funds.

Tori's gaze shifted from one to the other. Did she sense the tension in the room, the buried secrets Meredith had been on the brink of sharing?

"Am I interrupting something?"

Meredith's cheeks turned a soft pink. "No. Nothing important," she mumbled. "We've only started priming the walls. There's another roller for you."

Liam handed it over.

"I can do that," Tori said.

For the next few moments, the café was quiet except for the gurgle of pouring paint and the swipe of rollers against the wall.

"How was your party?" Meredith asked her cousin.

Liam thought for a moment the other woman wasn't going to answer, as if having a polite conversation with Meredith would betray all she held most dear.

"Fine," she finally answered. "We were celebrating Teresa's birthday last week as well as one of her grandchildren. The five-year-old daughter of Javier's sister Elena and her husband."

"Did Emilia stay at the party?"

"No. She's home. She's supposed to be finishing a couple of math worksheets on her own. We'll see whether that happens."

"Is she catching up with her homework, then?" Meredith asked.

Again, he thought Tori wasn't going to answer. She finally gave Meredith an inscrutable look. "Getting there. Sam and I are taking turns being the homework enforcer. This afternoon I spent three hours trying to keep two teenage girls on track. I have spent more enjoyable Sunday afternoons."

Meredith's mouth lifted into a hesitant smile. When Tori didn't return it, the smile slid away, he saw, and Meredith looked miserable.

159

The two women were so tense around each other. Was the relationship between the cousins irreparably broken?

If he could help repair it, maybe that might be one more way he could win Meredith's trust. His mind began to spin, as he wondered how he might bridge the chasm between them.

He dipped the roller into the paint and patted off the extra, shaking his head at himself. Helping her paint a café was one thing. Trying to insert himself into the tension between two women with a long history could only end in disaster.

Meredith seemed to believe she deserved her cousin's ire, but he couldn't tell if she truly believed that or was just being a martyr.

Why was he even contemplating trying to help her, more than he already had? She was still the woman who had been married to a criminal who had bilked thousands of people out of their life savings.

Plenty of people considered her as culpable as Carter Rowland.

Stick to the numbers, he told himself as he continued rolling primer on the wall while Meredith came behind him, cutting in color with a paintbrush.

He understood numbers. They were constant, comforting, endlessly fascinating.

Still, after moving to the other wall to help Tori, he gave the space an appraising look.

"The place already looks brighter, don't you think?" he asked Tori.

She sent him a sour look but didn't disagree.

"It's going to be great," Meredith assured her. "Especially after we start hanging artwork. I meant to ask you about that. Do you know a guy by the name of David Gallegos?"

"Sure. He lives a few blocks from here and his wife is good friends with my mother-in-law. Why?"

"I bumped into him on the beach this evening during a break

in the storm. He was flying a drone, capturing images of dark clouds in the sunset, and he was only too happy to talk to me about his work. I looked up his website before I came in, and he has some unique bird's-eye view shots of the sea stacks and the cliffs from his drone, as well as some overhead shots of Cape Sanctuary. I thought his work would look wonderful featured here."

Meredith seemed to be holding her breath, as if she feared her cousin would throw paint at her.

Tori only nodded. "Good idea. Dave is a great guy who does a lot for the community. He's served a couple of times on the city council and is the first one out with his chain saw to cut up fallen trees after a big storm."

Meredith looked shocked at Tori's receptiveness to the idea. She blinked a little as if she had been waiting to hear her cousin tell her what a dumb idea that was.

Who had left her feeling so inadequate, questioning her own instincts?

He had sensed it before in Meredith, as if she was always bracing herself to be dismissed or derided.

Or maybe that was simply a natural reaction to her cousin's obvious antipathy.

"Okay. Great. I'll start with him, then. I'll reach out tomorrow and ask if he's interested in sending us a few prints of his favorite shots that we could display."

"Sounds good. I did talk to my friend Stella, who runs the local art festival. She gave me a couple of names. You know more about art than I do so I'll let you reach out."

"I'll do that." Meredith's features were slightly rosy again, her eyes brighter than he'd seen them.

She was lovely. He had thought so before when he had seen pictures of her in the files, but those photographs had been cold, two-dimensional. They hadn't showed the softness of her skin, the angle of her cheekbone.

"I thought we could ask for a small commission from the artists. Maybe five percent from every sale that we could then give to help other local artists like Aspen, who might be struggling to buy supplies."

Liam had a feeling Tori wanted to find fault with the suggestion but couldn't.

"That's not a bad idea," she finally said.

Meredith blinked again, clearly both pleased and shocked by her cousin's approval. "Thanks."

"It's a great idea." Liam added his support, not that she needed it. "I didn't know Aspen was an artist. I suppose I should have guessed she's the creative sort from the tattoos and the piercings."

"I haven't seen her work but Josef has." Meredith moved the ladder so she could work on another part of the wall just below the ceiling. "He says it's really good."

"Sounds to me like she would be even better if she ever dropped that loser boyfriend of hers," Tori muttered. "I've never understood how some women stay with guys who treat them like garbage."

Liam couldn't help noticing that Meredith seemed to tense at that. Her expressive mouth tightened and she ducked her head, her gaze focused on the wall in front of her.

"Meredith tells me she spent lots of time during the summers here in town when she was a kid," he said, mainly to distract from whatever was suddenly bothering her. "What kind of things did you two do to stay out of trouble?"

Tori gave a rough laugh. "Who says we stayed out of trouble?"

Meredith lifted her gaze from the wall and the raw emotion in her eyes as she looked at her cousin left him feeling oddly off-balance.

"We didn't, did we?" she said after a moment. "We certainly made our poor grandmother want to pull her hair out a time or two."

"Do you remember that time we snuck out when we were

about thirteen or fourteen so we could toilet-paper that nasty Carly Little's house?"

"Was she the one telling everyone you made out with her boyfriend down at Sunshine Cove?"

"Yes. As if I'd go anywhere near Marcus Farley. He had bad breath and octopus hands. He's now her husband, by the way. And he still has octopus hands, from what I hear."

"Are you serious? Her name is Carly Farley?" Meredith asked, eyes wide.

"Yes. I find great satisfaction in that," Tori said. "But then, I'm a terrible person."

Meredith still seemed to be trying to digest the information and the memory. "Because she was omniscient, Frances somehow found out we were the ones who had toilet-papered Carly's house and she made us clean every bit of mess out of the trees. I remember we had to work about ten times as long to clean it up as we had spent throwing it into the trees in the first place."

"Isn't that always the way?" Liam said. "It seems to take so much longer to clean up any mess than it ever did to make it."

"Truth," Tori said. "I was always finding that with Em when she was little. Leave her alone in the kitchen for two minutes, and she could cover the floor with flour and sugar and drizzle maple syrup over the whole thing, just to ramp things up a notch. I would be hours cleaning up after her."

"My brother and I were the same way," Liam said. "He was older but I always seemed to be the ringleader, to my chagrin now. One time when I was about six, we wanted to play in the snow. Unfortunately it was July at the time, so we found some scissors and cut open two giant beanbags and scattered them all over the house. Our mother wasn't thrilled, but our father just laughed and grabbed his shop vac. In that particular case, cleaning up was more fun than making the mess."

Meredith watched him out of her serious eyes, a sympathy

there he didn't want to see. Was she remembering what he had told her about his father's death?

After a moment, she looked back at her cousin. "Do you remember the time we were about eight and I decided to cut my hair short like yours? Or more precisely I decided to have *you* cut my hair short like yours? Two weeks before I was supposed to be a flower girl at the wedding of one of my mother's friends."

Tori laughed out loud. "Oh wow. I had completely forgotten that until right this moment. Your mom was livid."

"I thought she wasn't going to let me come back. But she always did."

The two women shared what seemed to Liam to be a moment of peace. This had to be progress, right?

"How did Frances survive the two of us every summer?" Tori said ruefully.

"After everything we put her through, I still don't know why she welcomed me back, year after year."

"She loved you," Tori said simply, then her mouth hardened a little. "Even after all the years when you couldn't be bothered to come back and visit her, she loved you."

So much for the détente.

"I wanted to," Meredith said, her voice low. "Believe me, I wanted to."

The other woman didn't look convinced. "In my experience, when people want to do something badly enough, they find a way. No matter what."

Eyes filled with regret, Meredith looked down at the brush she was wrapping in plastic wrap in preparation for their next day of painting.

"You're right," she said, her voice tight, strained. "It seemed impossible at the time, under the circumstances I was in, but I should have figured out a way."

Liam sent her a curious look. What circumstances were so dire that she couldn't visit her own grandmother? Carter had been arrested nearly two years earlier. He was getting the impression it had been years before that since Meredith had visited the grandmother she claimed to love.

It was a puzzle but not the reason he was here, he reminded himself.

"What is Emilia going to do this summer while school is out?" Meredith asked, in an obvious bid to change the subject.

"Probably get into at least as much trouble as we did, if not more," Tori muttered.

"Uh-oh. That sounds like dark foreshadowing," Liam said. He had seen her daughter around the café a time or two and, more often, hanging out at Starfish Beach with another girl who looked enough like her to be a sister.

"What does she usually do during the summer?" Meredith asked. She sounded genuinely curious.

"Before Frances died, Em would hang out with her and they would keep an eye on each other or she would come with me to work. Sometimes she would spend the day with her grandparents on Javier's side and help them with little jobs around the house."

"That was nice," Liam said.

"Now that her cousin lives in town, I expect she'll want to spend every available moment with Cristina," she said. "She'll work here at the café a few days a week, and then she also babysits a few times during the week for a neighbor girl who's four so her mom can do shopping and go to the gym. She's trying to save up for a new computer."

"I understand she and Cristina want to buy cars when they turn sixteen."

Tori paused. "I hadn't heard that particular aspiration. We'll have to see about that."

"I don't know how you've done it all these years without Javier. Running the café, raising Em. It must be so hard on your own." Meredith spoke with an admiration that seemed to take her cousin by surprise.

"What choice did I have?" Tori said. "When you're a parent, you do what you have to do and push through the hard, one day at a time."

"That sounds like something Frances would say." Meredith looked amused.

The other woman shrugged. "Probably. I find myself channeling her all the time."

"She's a good person to emulate," Meredith said. "You could do far worse."

As they cleaned up the rest of the paint mess, Liam turned over the troubling conversation in his head.

Why hadn't she come back to Cape Sanctuary? Meredith clearly loved it here and seemed to have adored her grandmother. She couldn't have stayed away for financial reasons. With all the money her husband had pillaged, they could have bought their own private jet and flown it here dozens of times.

She hadn't even come home as Frances was dying. Why not?

He might have thought that behavior in keeping with the selfish, greedy bitch he had thought her before coming to Cape Sanctuary. But it didn't gibe at all with the warm, approachable, rather lonely woman he had met in this café.

Which was the real Meredith?

He still didn't know, but his life had seemed much less complicated when he thought of her as the cold, calculating, opportunistic wife of Carter Rowland instead of this paint-spattered, ponytailed, makeup-free woman he was beginning to find entirely too appealing.

19

Meredith

She had actually carried on a cordial conversation with her cousin.

Meredith almost couldn't believe it. She held her breath, not wanting anything to spoil the sheer wonder of the past half hour.

It hadn't been perfect. Tori still seemed to look at her with thinly veiled suspicion, but their conversation about Frances and the summers spent together with her seemed to have at least helped them achieve some sort of cease-fire.

She didn't want the moment to end. Too bad they were done priming for the night and had to let it dry before they could tackle the first coat of actual paint.

She wanted to hug Liam for nudging the conversation to the safer ground of their past, when the world had been right between them.

"Thank you both for helping tonight. Without you, I would have been here for hours," she told Liam and Tori after they finished stowing the paint supplies in the storeroom off the kitchen.

"My pleasure," Liam said.

Somehow she believed him.

"I can come back to help you paint in the morning," Tori offered. "I can be here about eight, after I get Em off to school."

"I'm free too. Just have to walk Jasper first."

Their willingness to help touched her deeply. "That would be great. Thank you. If we do the first coat early enough, we should be able to let it dry for a few hours and finish the final coat in the afternoon. We can open all the windows and let it air out all evening before the café reopens on Tuesday."

"Good plan," Tori said. "I'll see you in the morning, then."

She headed for the door. Before she walked through, she paused briefly, then turned around wearing a guarded smile. "This was a good idea. Something I should have thought to do a long time ago."

With that, she left, leaving Meredith almost breathless with joy.

One small act couldn't atone for all the harm she had caused Tori but it was a start, wasn't it?

"That went well, didn't it?" Liam said after she left. "Nobody brandished any kitchen knives anyway."

She had to laugh. "Not this time."

The two of them were alone in the kitchen, the café quiet and still around them. She was suddenly intensely aware of him, this gorgeous guy who had been so kind to her.

She remembered the night they had scrubbed the walls, when she had thought he meant to kiss her. Her toes curled in her sneakers. If he tried to kiss her right now, she didn't think she would be able to resist.

She wouldn't *want* to resist.

"Thanks again for all your help." She busied herself making sure all the lights were out and the doors and windows locked.

"It was really no problem. I enjoyed hearing you and your cousin reminisce. Sounds like you two were quite the pair."

"I had forgotten some of those things. It's funny but after I

168

stopped spending much time here, the memories faded. Some of the details, anyway. It was good to recapture some of them."

He took a step closer and her stomach jumped with nerves.

"Listen. I was thinking. Painting shouldn't take us all day tomorrow. You've got the day off. Seems to me you've done nothing since you came back to Cape Sanctuary except work."

She couldn't deny that. Her life had become an endless round of working at the café and then going back to the cottage to strip wallpaper and pull weeds.

"How would you feel about going on a short hike with me and Jasper after we paint the first coat tomorrow? I was thinking about checking out the headlands trail I've heard about, the one with the view down the coast. I would love some company."

She stared, her tired brain struggling to make sense of the invitation.

"You…want me to go hiking with you?"

"Sure."

"Why?" The question escaped before she could stop it.

He looked surprised. "Why not? I hear it's a beautiful view, and I thought you might enjoy taking a break on your day off and seeing some of the local scenery."

"Why me?"

"I like spending time with you. You're the closest thing I have to a friend here in Cape Sanctuary."

His words seemed to reach into a dark, empty place inside her. She wanted to wrap their warmth around her, let it comfort and soothe and heal.

How could she, when Liam still didn't know the whole truth about who she was?

"I don't…think that's a good idea."

Disappointment flashed on his expression. "Why not?"

I'm not who you think I am, some pathetic widow-slash-divorcée trying to build a new life for myself.

She opened her mouth to tell him everything she had been

about to reveal before Tori had interrupted them earlier. About Carter, about her own failings in her marriage, her cowardice and fear, the inaction that had subsequently hurt so many others.

She was still a coward. She didn't want to tell him. Liam was becoming a friend. He liked being with her, and she couldn't bring herself to destroy that yet.

"You're supposed to be writing," she said, instead of what she knew she should have revealed. "I shouldn't have even let you help me with the painting. You have work to do."

"Don't worry about that. I'm making progress. I can afford to take a day off. We can call it refilling the well."

"I don't want to be the reason you don't follow your dreams, Liam."

He looked as if he wanted to say something but then seemed to reconsider. "Let me worry about my dreams," he said. "I'm taking the hike tomorrow, with or without you. I would rather have your company and I expect Jasper would too, but you certainly don't have to go with us."

What would be the harm? a seductive little voice murmured. She was currently living in one of the most beautiful places in the world, and it seemed criminal somehow not to savor it while she had the chance.

"All right," she said, before she could change her mind. "I would enjoy that. Thank you for asking me."

"I... You're welcome." He faltered as if he had been gearing up to offer more arguments.

"We could even pack a lunch. I can do that. It's the least I can do to repay you for helping me paint."

She would be paid the following week and could probably squeeze enough from her budget to cover sandwiches, a couple carrot sticks and maybe a cookie or two.

"That would be great. We can hike, have lunch, and then come back and finish up the painting."

"Sounds good."

They both headed for the door. He waited while she locked up. The rain dribbled around them, soft and gentle. A cool wind blew off the water.

She breathed in the sea air, filling her lungs with the calm of the place.

"That's yours?" Liam said, gesturing to the rusty secondhand beach cruiser she had picked up at the thrift store for twenty-five dollars.

"Yes."

"How did you get the paint here?"

"I delivered it earlier, when the café was still open."

"It's raining again. Why don't you let me give you a ride, since we're going to the same place? You'll be soaked by the time you make it back to the cottage."

"A light rain will feel refreshing."

He frowned. "I can't just leave you. I'll worry about you all the way home."

"Good thing it's not far, then, isn't it? I'll be fine. Thanks again for your help. It was a lucky day for me when you decided to write your book here in Cape Sanctuary."

In the dim streetlights, she saw a strange expression in his eyes, something that looked oddly like guilt. It was there for a moment, then he seemed to blink it away.

"If you insist on being stubborn, I'll follow to make sure you don't have any problems on the way home."

She wanted to argue that she didn't need a babysitter, but she found it rather comforting to know he was watching out for her.

Grateful she had parked her bike under the café's roof over-hang, she climbed on and headed for Spindrift Cottage, her bike tires spraying water behind her.

They traveled in a strange procession, like she was a bicyclist in a painfully slow race and he was driving her own private support vehicle.

When they reached the neat row of houses, she saw hers was the only dark one of the three.

Tori's blazed with light, and she saw two dark shapes moving around. Tori and Emilia.

A soft glow emanated from Seafoam Cottage and she guessed Liam must have left a lamp on for his dog, which touched her more than it probably should.

As she might have expected, he didn't turn in to park at his house but followed her to her cottage, the farthest of the three from the café.

At her house, she climbed off her bike, doing her best not to let her teeth click together as the wind intensified here, closer to the shore, cutting through her windbreaker.

"Thank you for the escort but I'm home now. I made it without being attacked by pirates or falling into the sea."

"You can't be too careful," he said with a smile that left her feeling breathless again. "I'll see you in the morning, bright and early. We can carpool together so you don't have to ride your bike again. Why don't I pick you up at quarter after eight?"

She didn't see any point in arguing with him, especially as she expected he would only follow her back to the Beach End.

20

Tori

She was going to be late. Again.

Tori glared at the folder on the seat next to her, the one containing the history essay her daughter had worked hard on until midnight…and then promptly left sitting on the kitchen table when she left for school.

When did it become her responsibility to carry anything important Em left at home? Homework, packed lunches, permission slips. She sometimes felt like a cross between a fixer and a Sherpa, destined to always rush in to make things right when Em forgot something.

She wanted to let her daughter learn an important life lesson by having to face the consequences of her own absentmindedness in the mornings—probably because the girl was glued to her phone and her social media instead of focusing on anything she might need to do in preparation for the day ahead.

As tempting as that option might be, this didn't seem the right time to stand on principle. Em was one more missed assignment away from failing the eighth grade, and they were all working like hell to make sure that didn't happen.

So here she was driving to the middle school again when she was supposed to be helping to paint the café that morning.

Meredith would be wondering where she was.

Tori thought of her cousin, and how hard she had worked the night before to prime the walls of the café. This was important to Meredith, for reasons Tori didn't quite understand. She did know that short time while they had worked together, sharing one common goal and laughing about a few memories, had been a rare reprieve from her constant simmering anger.

What was she going to do about Meredith? She couldn't forgive her cousin for all the pain she had caused Frances. She didn't *want* to forgive her. Her grandmother had died longing for only one thing—to see her beloved granddaughter again. Even knowing all that Meredith's husband had done, ravaging her life savings, Frances had wanted to see her in person.

Her grandmother's focus on the one thing she couldn't have had filled Tori with anger...and, she admitted, plenty of jealousy.

All these years, she had been here, living next door to Frances. She had made countless meals for her grandmother, had helped her pay bills, had taken her grocery shopping and to the bank and then to chemotherapy appointments after her cancer diagnosis and subsequent cardiac issues.

Tori had been the one to sit with Frances all night when she had been too ill to get out of her recliner, had organized her dozen different medications, had provided steady, unwavering care.

Still, Frances had longed to see Meredith.

"She has had a rough time of things," Frances would say, making Tori want to scream.

Meredith had a rough time of things? The girl who had every advantage, who went to prestigious schools and wore expensive clothes and took trips to Europe on the regular?

Meredith knew both her parents. She hadn't been abandoned

by a mother who never even bothered to tell her who her father was.

Granted, *Meredith's* mother had been a narcissistic witch and her father had been an absent workaholic who ignored her. But something was better than nothing, wasn't it?

When she found out after Frances died that her grandmother had left Meredith Spindrift Cottage and half of the café, Tori had been stunned.

It had felt like the worst sort of betrayal, especially as she had no advance notice from Frances of her plans.

Underneath the anger had been a deep hurt that hadn't gone away, even a year after her grandmother's death.

She pulled into the parking lot of the school, doing her best not to brood.

Was she being unreasonable to carry her anger like a shield between her and Meredith? Frances had been willing to forgive. Tori wasn't at all sure she had it in her.

She found a parking space and gathered up the folder with Emilia's homework. As she headed toward the front door, her breathing quickened when she noticed a familiar figure coming from a nearby parked car.

Sam wore a rumpled dress shirt and loosened tie. He smiled when he spotted her, but that didn't conceal the deep exhaustion in his eyes.

"Tori. Hey. We seem to be making a habit of meeting at the school."

She held up the folder. "Em left her history report. I'm just trying to get it to her before the second hour starts."

He held up a textbook. "Mine is a math book. Cristina apparently forgot until she got to school that she was supposed to turn it in today. She gets ten points extra credit, which might just lift her from a D plus to a C minus."

"Every little bit helps. I guess. I can't figure out if I'm being a supportive parent or if I'm simply enabling bad behavior."

"Same."

He held the door open for her when they reached it. As she walked past, she smelled him, sandalwood and pine.

She shouldn't be noticing the way he smelled, curse it. Sam was her brother-in-law. Completely off-limits.

"You look tired."

He made a face. "Yeah. I was just headed home when Cris texted me."

"Did you work all night, after the birthday fun? You didn't say anything about being on the schedule."

"I was called out past one on an emergency."

"Uh-oh. When they call in the lead major crimes detective for the town, that can't be a good sign."

He nodded, the lines around his eyes more pronounced with his fatigue. "You're right. Unfortunately. Armed robbery at the convenience store on the south end of town. The clerk was stabbed."

"Oh no! Who was it?"

"Lisa Harrow. Do you know her?"

She felt cold, suddenly, as she always did when she heard bad news about a friend. "I run a café, Sam. I know most people in town. Lisa and her husband Rod come in for dinner a couple times a month with one of their grandchildren. Is she...okay?"

"She's pretty shaken up and lost a lot of blood, but the knife missed anything major. She had surgery this morning. Last report I had from the hospital was that they're probably keeping her another night for observation and she'll go home tomorrow."

"Did she know who it was?"

"Lisa's a great witness. She gave us a good description of the two who held up the store but said she didn't recognize either them or their vehicle. She got a partial plate number and the make and model. We're looking, but they were young so I'd lay odds it was a stolen vehicle and they were passing through. We've got a BOLO out for them, though, and might get lucky."

Sam dealt with horrible things on a daily basis, all with that calm courage. He had worked homicide cases in Los Angeles and probably thought coming to Cape Sanctuary would be a little more quiet.

"I'm sorry you didn't get any sleep."

He shrugged with a weary smile that made her want to loosen his tie, unbutton his shirt and hold him while he slept.

"I'll catch a few hours this morning. Unless Cris calls me to bring her something else."

They walked together into the office and handed the book and homework folder to the secretary.

"Which goes to which student again?" she asked, in the tone of someone who had already dealt with a long line of parents all morning.

They explained, thanked her and left the office as a few other parents were coming in behind them.

"What does Cristina do when you have to work overnight?" she asked.

"She generally stays with Mom and Dad. Last night I got called out so late, I left her sleeping with a note to let her know what was going on and to have her call me or her grandparents if she has any problems."

"You know she can always reach out to me too," Tori said. "I'm only a few blocks away, closer than your parents."

"Thanks. She's almost fourteen and is probably fine on her own, but the cop in me worries."

"Naturally."

"I was hoping I could let down my guard a little after she hit her teens."

Tori raised her eyebrows. "Seriously?"

"I know. What was I thinking? I have a whole new set of worries."

"Tell me about it. The difference is, I was a teenage girl. I know how much trouble we can get into."

177

She had ended up pregnant and married at nineteen. While she wouldn't trade anything about her life with Javier and Em, she sometimes wondered what might have happened if she had taken that trip through Europe with Meredith.

She could only hope her daughter would experience every opportunity life had to offer before she married her high school sweetheart and settled into small-town life.

"It's all so much harder than I expected having full custody and her mom out of the country."

"You're doing fine, Sam. Cristina is kind and funny and bright. She's the first one to help her *abuela* clean up the kitchen, and she loves playing with the little cousins. You and Joni have done a great job with her."

She rested a hand on his arm. He looked down and then, before she realized what was happening, he pulled her into his arms.

It started out as a kind of casual hug for comfort and reassurance, the sort of embrace she was used to from all the Ayalas.

The open, easy physical affection between his family had been one of the things that had first drawn her in when she started dating Javier. His mother and father were always hugging her, kissing her cheek, touching her arm to reinforce a point.

Frances had given Tori plenty of verbal affection and she had always known she was loved, but her grandmother hadn't been a big one for hugs or kisses.

Tori had adored the Ayalas for that.

This felt…different.

He held her for a long moment, his breathing even. She hoped he was finding peace in the embrace.

She certainly wasn't.

Her heart raced and heat seemed to soak her cheeks. The masculine scent of him swirled around her and she wanted, rather desperately, to rest her cheek against his chest and forget about her daughter and the café and everything else bringing her stress right now.

After several moments, he stepped away, features twisted into an inscrutable expression she couldn't read.

"Thanks for that," he said, his voice low. "I needed it. More than I would like to admit."

"All parents need encouragement," she answered when she could find her voice again. "Wouldn't it be great if we had our own personal cheerleading squad to stand and shake their pom-poms every time we have to make the hard parenting decisions?"

His mouth creased into a smile, brightening his tired features. He seemed lighter. She hoped he was.

"Who do you have on your personal cheer squad?"

"After Javi died, I leaned heavily on Frances for support. And your parents, of course, and Elena. They've always had my back."

Had she brought up Javier to remind him that anything more than the occasional hug was impossible between them? Or to remind herself?

He shook his head. "We all grieved Javi, but I can't imagine how tough it must have been for you, left alone with a young child."

After seven years, she was used to being alone, but she definitely remembered how lost and frightened she had been for months afterward.

"At the time, I didn't want to go on. But I had to focus on Em. I couldn't just curl up into a ball and wither away. She needed a mom, and not one who cried twenty-four hours a day, either. She was suffering too. She had adored Javier and struggled to understand why he was gone. So I had to put my grief away and focus on giving her everything I had left."

"If you gave her everything, what did you leave for yourself?"

Good question. She had focused so much on being a good mother, helping Frances and running the café, that hadn't left much room for self-care.

"I should probably work on that," she admitted. "Maybe once

179

summer comes, I'll take a long weekend down the coast at that new hotel and spa that opened a few years ago near Lost Canyon."

"If you need Em to stay with Cristina for a few nights, I'm sure the girls would love it."

She did her best to push down the sudden wish that she could go away for a long weekend with Sam.

"Thanks. If I haven't said it before, it's nice to have you home in Cape Sanctuary, if only to have one more adult Ayala on my cheer squad."

He smiled as he opened her car door. "Rah-rah-rah. Is that the only thing I'm good for?"

She shivered a little, not wanting to answer that even to herself. Something told her Sam would be good at any number of things.

This was getting ridiculous. She had to get a handle on this attraction to her brother-in-law or she was in for some really awkward family occasions.

"I should go. I'm supposed to be helping Meredith paint the café."

"How are things working out, having her back in town?"

She made a face. "Okay, I guess. Except she wants to change everything at the café. She has big interior design plans."

Something told her Meredith wouldn't be content at simply a new coat of paint and artwork on the walls.

Sam gave her an arch look. "She told you what to improve at the café and lived to tell the tale?"

"Am I really that cantankerous?"

"I wouldn't call it cantankerous. You're passionate about the café. You love it and it shows."

He yawned on the last word, and she shook her head ruefully.

"Go home before you fall over."

"A few hours. That's all I need, then I'll be ready to turn into the homework enforcer tonight. It's my turn, right?"

"Don't worry about it. I'll text Em and have her and Cristina go to my place straight from school so they don't bother you. I'm off today anyway, since the café is closed. It's no problem."

He shrugged. "I'm on it. Give me a few hours of sleep and I'll be ready to rock."

"I don't mind, really. You've had a rough night. You don't need to contend with two chattering girls."

"I'll be fine," he assured her. "But we could always combine forces to bring the full weight of our combined parental wrath against them. Maybe we're stronger together than we are apart."

"Good idea." She forced a smile despite the sudden longing his words sparked in her. "It's supposed to be a nice day, after what feels like weeks of rain. We could plan dinner on the patio after the girls finish their homework? The incentive of food always helps Emilia."

"Same with Cris. And me, for that matter."

"I was going to marinate some chicken breasts for dinner and then grill. I can easily toss a few more in the marinade for you and Cristina."

"Any time I don't have to cook is a win, as far as I'm concerned. And certainly as far as Cristina is concerned. She's not a huge fan of my cooking. I keep hoping she'll decide to try her own hand in the kitchen, but that hasn't happened yet."

"Why should she, when your mom and dad will always feed you?"

"True enough." His smile again split his weary features. "I'll bring some sides. At least salad and dessert."

Tori knew she shouldn't have this little buzz of anticipation crackling through her veins. It was only dinner, with her late husband's brother and his daughter.

"Sounds good. Get some sleep. You need it. I'll see you later."

"Something to look forward to," Sam said with a smile that left her feeling far more giddy than she should.

21

Meredith

She had been right. New paint was exactly what the café needed to feel bright and fresh again.

After finishing the first coat, Meredith set down her roller in the tray and looked around the restaurant with a deep sense of satisfaction.

Her neck and biceps ached a little, but she considered that a small price to pay in exchange for the deep sense of satisfaction she found looking at the walls.

"That should do it for the first coat," Liam said, taking a step back to admire their work.

"I'm done here too."

Tori, on the ladder, set her paintbrush in the small can of paint she was using to cut around the trim.

She said nothing for a long moment as she studied their work, while Meredith fought down her nerves, waiting to hear the verdict. She swallowed, realizing to her chagrin how much she wanted Tori to love it.

"The regulars won't recognize the place in the morning," Tori finally said.

Was that an insult or a compliment? Meredith couldn't tell.

"Sure they will," Liam answered. "Especially since you'll still have the same delicious food. I can't get enough. By the time I head back to my real life, I will have gained at least ten pounds."

From what Meredith had observed, that wasn't strictly true. Far from sampling the entire menu, Liam seemed to spend most days nursing one or two cups of coffee and maybe some avocado toast while he worked on his laptop.

Not that she was spying on him or anything.

"It looks good," Tori said. This time she met Meredith's gaze, eyes warm with approval. "It will look even better when we add some new art to the walls. I'll admit, I was skeptical when you first came up with this idea, but you were right. I'm really glad you started the ball rolling, Mere."

If she had been sitting, Meredith would have fallen out of her chair. Tori seemed genuinely pleased with the small refresh. Not only that, but she had called her Mere, the nickname she and Frances used to call her, decreeing Meredith was too much of a mouthful.

To her dismay, she felt the burn of tears and quickly blinked them away. She didn't want to be more of a dork than she already was so she simply smiled.

"Thanks. Isn't it amazing how a simple coat of paint can brighten up a space?"

Tori looked around. "When you see a place day in and day out for years, you don't always notice how run-down it's starting to look."

"Not run-down," Meredith corrected. "Just tired. All we did was give it a little more energy."

"It's nice," she answered, then looked at her watch. "What time do you think you'll be doing the second coat?"

"It needs to dry for at least a few hours. I thought maybe two or three this afternoon."

"We're going on a hike on the coast trail," Liam said. "Meredith has packed us a lunch. It should only take us a few hours."

"Are you?" Tori looked with interest between them, and Meredith could feel herself blush.

"I haven't been there in years. I hope I can still find the way," Meredith said.

"It's not hard. The trail starts right by the Skyline Campground. There's a parking lot with signs to the trailhead. Make sure you take plenty of water, especially since you're hitting it at midday."

"Would you like to go with us?" Meredith asked.

Tori looked briefly tempted but finally shook her head. "I can't. Sorry. I signed up to volunteer with Meals on Wheels today, since I had the day off."

"You volunteer with Meals on Wheels?" Liam look surprised. "After you feed people all week, you do it again on your day off?"

"It's a good program. Many of the seniors used to be our customers who can't get around as well as they used to. This is my one chance to help out."

Frances had lived by the philosophy to help others at every opportunity. She was always taking an extra pie to someone going through a tough time or passing some cash to someone else struggling to pay bills.

Tori had obviously taken that to heart, carrying on in Frances's footsteps.

Meredith needed to do better. Carter had encouraged her to volunteer with various organizations, but those were mostly made up of society matrons more interested in looking charitable than in actually living their mission statements.

Maybe Tori could suggest somewhere Meredith could volunteer while she was here in Cape Sanctuary.

"Have a good time," she said. "It's a beautiful day for a hike. Text me when you're on your way back here, and I'll try to meet up with you."

"Sounds good. Thanks."

All three of them worked together to clean up after themselves and then headed out of the café together.

"Do you want to ride together to the trailhead?" Liam asked when they reached the parking lot. "We don't need to take two cars, especially when we'll both be coming back here to paint this afternoon."

"I have to pick up the lunch I packed at my cottage."

"That's fine. I've got to grab Jasper anyway."

"Sure, then. We can ride together."

He held the door open as she slid into the passenger seat of his small SUV. It smelled like him. Leather and sage and Liam.

"I hope I don't slow you down today," she said as he started driving toward the cottages. "I'm not very athletic, I'm afraid. I don't want to hold you back, if you're looking to conquer mountains."

"I don't need to conquer any mountains today. I'm totally great with just an easy walk along the coast trail. It sounds perfect, actually, for such a beautiful day."

"It does sound nice, doesn't it? But I still don't like the idea of keeping you from working on your book all day."

He made a face at the mention of his work. "Don't worry about it. I need the break."

"Still struggling?"

"You could say I've hit a rough patch. I'm, uh, working through some plot things."

"If you need to talk about anything, you can bounce ideas off me. I don't know much about what it takes to write a book, but I've always been a voracious reader. I would love to brainstorm with you."

Her love of books had been forged right here, during those summer months she spent with Frances and Tori.

Did Tori read much anymore? She would have to ask.

"Cape Sanctuary has an excellent library. Or at least they used to. My grandmother would take me and Tori there at least once a week to check out books. She didn't have a television, which I thought was fairly barbaric. But spending summers here gave me a love of books that has lasted throughout my life."

"My mom has always been a big reader," he said with the same half smile he always wore when talking about his family. "Give her a stack of mysteries with some romances thrown in and she would say she's in heaven. She always said she wanted to spend her retirement years volunteering a few hours a day at our local library and with her nose in a book the rest of the time."

"That sounds absolutely dreamy. How close is she to retirement?"

He gazed out the windshield, but his hands seemed to tighten on the steering wheel. "She planned to retire next year, but it doesn't look like that's going to happen. She's had some…financial difficulties and thinks she needs to keep working to support her and my brother. She's an elementary school teacher, which can be a tough job when you're sixty-four and have bad knees."

He gave her a sidelong look, then shifted his gaze back to the road ahead of them. "And before you ask, yes. I have tried to help her but she won't hear of it. My mother might not have much, but she is overflowing with two things. Stubbornness and pride."

"I'm sorry. That must be frustrating for someone like you."

Again, he gave her a questioning look. "Someone like me?"

"You like to fix things. That's obvious by the way you stepped up to help me paint the café, even when you had far more important things to do."

"I didn't. Not really."

"Look at it this way. When you finish your book, publishers will probably be knocking down your door, big checks in hand. You can use the first advance to help your mom follow her retirement dreams."

"I'm doing my best in my own way to help her follow her dreams."

What did that mean? She wasn't entirely sure how to interpret the cryptic statement, but he pulled up in front of Spindrift Cottage before she had the chance to ask.

"Here we are. I just need to grab our lunch and change my clothes into something less paint-splattered and more comfortable for hiking. I need about ten minutes."

"Perfect. That will give me time to change my clothes too and to grab Jasper and his things."

"Should I meet you at your place?"

"Whoever is ready first can go to the other cottage. It's not like we're miles apart."

No. He was right next door and slept only a couple of flimsy walls away from her.

She climbed out. "Thanks again for helping me, Liam. It really means a lot to me."

He again had that odd, almost guilty expression. "It's really no big deal."

She didn't agree but didn't want to make him more uncomfortable with her gratitude.

After hurrying inside, she changed into a soft pair of yoga capris and a performance T-shirt and added a hoodie in case the weather turned. As she remembered it, the wind could blow on the headlands, winnowing its way through layers.

She grabbed the lunch of *jambon beurre* she had packed so carefully earlier that morning—a baguette slathered with butter and layered with thick slices of ham—as well as two apples and assorted raw vegetables. As she refilled her water bottle with ice, and water from the sink, she wondered if this whole thing was a mistake.

She didn't have a good feeling about this hike, almost as if she were teetering on the edge of the sea cliffs they would be walking on, with the ground crumbling beneath her feet.

She should be focused on rebuilding her life, and Liam should be focused on writing his book. Neither of them had time for distractions.

Maybe she should back out.

She didn't want to, though. The idea of spending time in nature seemed deeply appealing. And so did the prospect of a free afternoon with Liam.

She liked him, entirely too much.

She remembered his words of the night before.

I like spending time with you. You're the closest thing I have to a friend here in Cape Sanctuary.

She was deeply honored to know he considered her a friend.

He was hers, as well. Her only real friend in Cape Sanctuary right now.

Her coworkers at the café were all courteous to her, but her tangled relationship with Tori seemed to color all her interactions with everyone else. Given that her cousin had been there for years and Meredith for only a matter of days, they would all naturally come down on Tori's side of their unstated conflict.

Denise was kind to her, but it was the same friendly warmth she showed to all the other workers and customers of the café.

Meredith liked Aspen as well, though the girl had built so many walls, it was hard to read her.

Meredith suspected Josef had a thing for the young server. He was always quick to help her carry in platters of meals, forever watching her out of those dark, sad eyes that Meredith suspected had seen things she couldn't begin to imagine.

Aspen seemed unaware of Josef's admiration, though Meredith didn't know her well enough to question whether she knew and was only pretending she didn't.

Ty and the others who worked the morning shift with her all treated Meredith with politeness and courtesy, but they didn't share their private jokes, their observations, their pithy comments with her, as she knew they did with Tori.

Liam treated her with much more warmth than anyone else

in town. Was it any wonder she was drawn to spending more time with him?

A few times she thought she had seen him looking at her the way Josef looked at Aspen, but she told herself she was imagining things.

She should tell him the truth.

The thought seemed to lodge in her chest, hard and insistent, like a seed that had gone down the wrong way.

She had almost told him the day before, until Tori had come in and jerked her back to her senses.

Not yet.

She wasn't ready to reveal everything about her past to Liam. She knew it was selfish but when he found out about Carter and the whole terrible mess her husband had left behind, Liam would despise her. She wasn't ready yet to lose her only friend in town.

With a hurried glance at her watch, Meredith threw the lunch into the slouchy messenger-type bag she had picked up from a small boutique in New York City back when she was in college.

A backpack would be far more practical, but she didn't have one here in Cape Sanctuary—she wasn't sure she had ever *owned* a backpack. This one would have to do.

She hefted it over as a cross-body bag just as her doorbell rang.

For a moment, panic rushed through her, an instinctive urge to tell Liam she had changed her mind and wasn't up to a hike— or anything else—with him.

No. She wanted to be stronger than that. Coming to Cape Sanctuary was her chance to rebuild herself, to become someone her grandmother might have been proud to call her offspring.

She was tired of being afraid. She had let fear rule so much of her life. Fear of disappointing her parents, losing whatever crumbs of love they sent her way when she made choices that met their approval. Fear of not being the wife Carter demanded.

She had a long way to go, but she could start by not running away from those things that scared her.

Like Liam.

She drew in a deep breath and opened the door. He stood on the other side, looking lean and dark and gorgeous, even in thin khaki hiking pants and a plain blue T-shirt.

Before she could open her mouth to greet him, his friendly dog surged through, tongue lolling and paws clicking on the wooden floor.

The dog's enthusiastic greeting made her smile. "Hi, Jasper."

"He's a little excited, if you can't tell."

"Who can blame him?" Meredith said. "It's a beautiful day for a hike."

"Isn't it? Do you need more time?"

"No. I'm all ready." She held up the bag. "Do you have a water bottle?"

"Yes. I should have told you I'm taking a pack and there's plenty of room for your stuff in it. We can transfer whatever you want to take along once we're at the trailhead."

"That would be great. Thanks." She would be glad not to have to carry along her awkward bag.

On the drive to the trailhead on the edge of town, Liam asked more questions about her memories of Cape Sanctuary from her childhood. He seemed genuinely interested in the time she had spent here, though she couldn't help noticing he tended to deflect any question she asked in turn about his own childhood.

She wondered if the trauma of losing his father on September 11 had colored everything else.

When he reached the sign for the campground, which led up into the heavily wooded hillsides, he turned into the parking area.

Those taking the Skyline Trail had to park below the campground and then walk through it before reaching the actual trailhead.

They spent a few moments transferring her things to Liam's backpack and then headed up the trail.

As they were walking past an older-looking camp trailer, too run-down to be considered vintage, a man's voice raised in anger echoed through the campsite.

Stupid bitch.

Why can't you do anything right?

The words hit her like an avalanche tumbling down the mountainside, filled with sharp, jagged rocks.

A moment later, a door slammed and a young woman with purple hair raced out of the trailer and down the steps.

She stopped short when she saw Liam and Meredith walking past, her features cycling from pale and pinched to red and angry in seconds.

"Oh!" Aspen exclaimed, looking from Meredith to Liam. "What are you doing here? Are you spying on me?"

"No! Of course not!" Meredith replied quickly. "Why would we do that? We were only passing through the campground. We're heading to the Skyline Trail."

The server seemed nonplussed by the information, clearly still inclined to skepticism. "Oh. Well. Have a good hike, then."

She turned to go, but not before Meredith spied another angry bruise along her cheekbone.

She tensed, her stomach suddenly queasy. She knew exactly what could cause that kind of bruise. A hard, angry fist.

She stopped walking and Liam, walking with Jasper beside her, ordered the dog to stay.

"Are you okay?" She pitched her voice low so no one else in the campground could hear.

She had to ask, just as she knew exactly what the answer would be.

"Sure. I'm fine. Why wouldn't I be?"

Meredith knew she should drop the subject and continue walking. It couldn't be more obvious that Aspen wanted them to mind their own business and move along.

She couldn't seem to make her legs work.

191

Meredith knew what it was like to feel completely alone, as if no one else would ever believe what was happening in her world.

"Aspen," she said softly. "You don't have to stay. You know that, right? There are organizations that can help you get to a... to a more safe situation."

Aspen stared at her, eyes wide, then her shock turned to something else, something Meredith recognized only too well. Shame.

She glared at them both. "Mind your own business, Princess. What the hell do you know about my life?"

Nothing. And everything.

"You might be surprised," Meredith murmured.

Aspen didn't seem to hear her. She turned around and started walking in the other direction, as if she couldn't get away from them fast enough.

Meredith gazed after her, lost in a dark, murky, tangled web of memories.

She hated this feeling of impotence, knowing there was nothing she could do to help Aspen escape her situation. No matter what she said, how many website links or helplines or pamphlets she offered, Aspen had to take those first steps on her own.

She wouldn't have accepted anyone's help or advice either, she reminded herself. Even if anyone had suspected how things really were inside their carefully soundproofed penthouse apartment, Meredith would have denied and denied and denied.

Should she talk to Tori about it?

Or would that be a breach of Aspen's privacy?

What would Frances have done?

Her grandmother probably would have gone into that ramshackle trailer with a cast-iron frying pan and warned off the no-good boyfriend.

Meredith wasn't that brave. But she would talk to her cousin, she decided. That Aspen was in an abusive relationship would be no surprise to Tori. She had alluded to it before. But Meredith now had solid proof. Maybe both of them could talk to Aspen and try to make her see sense.

Tori was sensible and straightforward. She would know the right thing to say, and she had a much tighter relationship with Aspen than Meredith did.

She came back to the present to realize Liam was standing beside her, Jasper's leash in his hand and an odd expression on his face.

"Sorry about that," she muttered. "Let's go."

Without waiting for him to reply, she took off toward the trail, moving quickly though she knew she would never be fast enough to outrun her own demons.

22

Liam

Liam felt slightly ill as he watched Meredith stride toward the trailhead ahead of him.

That moment she had confronted the server seemed etched into his memory. She had been pale, her eyes haunted in her slim, elegant face.

A sick suspicion had taken root when he saw her face, one he almost couldn't believe.

He didn't want to think about it. But why else would she have responded as she had to Aspen's situation?

He had seen her expression of horror, and then her eyes seemed suddenly shadowed, dark with memories and pain.

He didn't think he could hate someone as much as he already hated Carter Rowland. He was wrong. The man was even more of a lowlife bastard than Liam imagined.

He wanted to make it all better. To hold her close and promise nobody would ever hurt her again.

Every single aspect of this investigation, all he thought and believed, had been turned upside down during the past week. Now he didn't know what to think, where to turn.

The trail was stunning here, going through old growth coastal pine and brush, with the ocean far below them, but Liam barely registered the breathtaking scenery or the heady mingled scents of dirt and pine sap and sea air.

His mind spun with questions. He didn't want to ask them. He wanted to be able to focus on their surroundings and pretend the world outside of this moment didn't exist, that her past was none of his business, like Aspen had shouted at her.

He couldn't.

He was coming to care for this woman with her curious mix of vulnerability and strength.

He caught up with her, and they walked in silence for another ten minutes before he could finally bring himself to open his mouth.

"When did your husband start hitting you?"

The words seemed to hover between them, greasy and ugly and raw.

Her footsteps faltered and she inhaled sharply, giving him a shocked look, then she picked up her pace on the dirt trail.

"I don't know what you're talking about," she lied. Badly.

She was that most fascinating of creatures, he thought. A woman both fragile and tough-skinned.

"Yes. You do. I'm not wrong. Your husband hit you, didn't he? When did he start?"

She walked another hundred feet before she finally stopped. Jasper caught up with her, tail wagging, and after a moment, she closed her eyes and dug her hands into his fur.

"Our wedding night," she finally said on an exhale.

Tension seemed to knife between his shoulder blades, hard and unrelenting. "Your wedding night," he repeated slowly.

They had reached a gap in the trees, and from here they could look down the coast for miles. She stopped, hand on an outstretched branch.

"We had a really beautiful day," she finally said. "My father paid to rent the ballroom at the Ritz-Carlton as well as three entire floors of rooms. I tried to tell myself I was the luckiest woman in the world. Marrying this handsome, successful man who adored me. What more could I want?"

She met his gaze and looked at once brittle and hard.

"We spent our wedding night there, in the Presidential Suite. It was like something out of a fairy tale, possibly the most beautiful room I had ever seen, with incomparable views of the city and Lake Michigan."

He could see her, fresh out of college, innocent and bright. His heart hurt, knowing what was ahead for that young, beautiful bride.

"He hit me before I could even get out of my wedding dress. Apparently, he didn't like the way I smiled at a couple of the groomsmen when they danced with me. He accused me of being a whore and said I needed to learn now that he wouldn't tolerate that kind of behavior from any woman of his."

His grip tightened on the leash to keep from pounding the nearest tree trunk. The worst part of the story, besides the obvious, was the matter-of-fact way she related what must have been a hideous shock.

"Why didn't you walk straight out of the hotel room and back to your parents?"

She gave a short, unamused laugh. "You obviously don't know my parents."

"Are you saying they would have tolerated someone hitting their child?"

"I don't know. I hope not, but I honestly couldn't tell you what they would have tolerated. I had always felt like a perpetual disappointment to them both, so I had no reason to expect anything to be different. The bottom line is, I didn't tell them. I should have walked out of the room, the hotel, the marriage in that moment but I didn't."

She was quiet, her gaze on something he couldn't see. "As soon as he hit me, he was so apologetic. He seemed more horrified than I was. Which was saying something. He said he'd had too much to drink, the events of the wedding had been taxing, he was stressed because his deceased parents weren't there and he missed them terribly. He knew exactly how to play on my emotions."

"You forgave him?"

"I was too shocked to do much else. He knew all the right things to say. My husband was a master manipulator."

Yeah, Liam thought. That was obvious by the many hundreds of people who had given him their life savings to invest.

"We fell into the classic pattern," she went on, features grim. "I turned myself inside out trying to make him happy, but of course nothing I did was ever enough. He would hit me and then apologize at length, blaming the alcohol or a deal going south or the person who scratched his Mercedes in the parking garage. Things would be better for a week or two but it never lasted long."

She absently picked a wildflower and began mangling the petals. Liam had a feeling she wasn't even aware of what she did.

He wanted to mangle much more than a wildflower. He wanted to rip a couple of saplings up by their roots and chuck them far out into the ocean.

"You didn't tell anyone?"

"What would I say? And who would believe me?"

"You really don't think your parents would have helped you?"

"They both adored him. Carter was the son my father always wanted. I knew they would take his side. My mother would tell me how much work it took to be the wife of a high-powered financier, how I needed to make sure his life was as smooth and trouble-free as possible, as she had done in her own marriage. My father would just pretend he didn't hear me."

He couldn't imagine a family dynamic like that, especially when his own family had always been nothing but supportive, no matter what he might be going through.

"Why didn't you leave?"

He knew it was an inane question as soon as he asked it.

He couldn't begin to understand what it was like to be in a situation that seemed hopeless.

She tossed the wildflower off the trail. The wind caught the petals, and they spiraled down toward the water below. The view here was spectacular, Liam had to admit, with the Pacific stretching out as far as the eye could see.

Being in the midst of nature's wonder made her story of one man's vicious ugliness even harder to hear.

"Why didn't I leave? I wish I had an easy answer to that," she finally said. "It seems so simple now. I had money of my own. Plenty of it. I could have moved out. I wanted to, desperately."

Her mouth tightened. "I tried once. After we had been married about a year, I had a miscarriage. I won't say it was because of the way my husband treated me, but I'm sure that didn't help. I was grieving and emotionally battered so I came here to visit Frances. I had no intention of going back to him."

"What happened?"

"He came after me. He was livid, more angry than I had ever seen him before. He told me if I pulled that kind of thing again, he would kill me and Frances both in our sleep, making it look like a tragic accident. Carbon monoxide poisoning. No one would ever know the difference."

Damn. For once, Liam wasn't a bit sorry the guy had been shivved in prison, even if it meant his secrets died with him.

Carter Rowland deserved that and so much more.

"So you chose to stay away from your grandmother."

Her mouth tightened. "I told myself I was protecting her, but I should have been strong enough to call his bluff. Like most abusers and bullies, my husband was a coward at heart. In hindsight, I don't believe he would have hurt Frances. She was tough as carbonite and would have stood up to him, and he would have hated that."

198

"Is that why you stayed with him? To protect her?"

"Maybe one of the more noble reasons. One thing I've learned is that fear and hope often go hand in hand. I was afraid of what he might do to me or someone I loved if I left for good. And I suppose some small part of me continued to hope, long after I should have, that things might get better."

"You were married to him for eight years. How did you manage without…"

"Ending up in the hospital?" she said when his voice trailed off.

"I was going to say without going after him yourself."

"Mostly by staying out of his way. I had two more miscarriages in the next two years. The third was actually considered a stillbirth because I was twenty-two weeks along."

She said the words in a matter-of-fact tone, but Liam could see the shadows in her eyes.

Good Lord. How much pain had she endured during her marriage? He couldn't wrap his head around it.

"Any love for him had died a long time earlier. But I loved those babies."

Her voice wobbled a little on the last word, and he fought the urge to pull her into his arms.

She shrugged. "After that, I didn't care about anything anymore. In a weird way, I think my own numbness gave me power. He knew I didn't care what he did to me, that he couldn't hurt me anymore. So he stopped trying."

"Just like that?"

"More or less," she answered simply. "When my father died, I opened an art gallery with the money I inherited and poured my energy into that as well as some charities I worked with. We lived separate lives, really."

She looked out at the ocean far below. "I should have left him the first time he hit me. I wish I had been strong enough to do that. Just as I wish I could convince Aspen to trust her own strength. She doesn't have to put up with a man who won't treat her with decency and respect, even if she thinks she loves him."

23

Meredith

What was she doing?

Was she really spilling every ugly detail of her life to Liam Byrne?

What was it about the man that invited such confidences? She never talked about this part of her life with anyone. Never. She hadn't even told her own grandmother, though sometimes she suspected Frances guessed the nightmare of her life with Carter.

That time she had come to Cape Sanctuary, after the miscarriage, Frances had taken one look at her, wrapped her arms around her and simply held her for a long time while Meredith had wept and wept.

When Carter had come to check on her, all full of love and charm on the surface, Frances had not been swayed by him.

She would never have invested her carefully tended savings with him. Meredith was certain of it. Frances believed her own son had charge of her funds. What Frances didn't know, what *Meredith* didn't know, was that her father had passed that task to Carter, who had raided Frances's funds for his own gain, as he had everyone else's.

No. Meredith hadn't told her grandmother the truth. With

Frances, as with everyone, she had become scrupulously care-ful about keeping her emotions under control.

Why had she told Liam the truth, then?

She didn't know the answer to that. She shouldn't have. Ev-erything would change now between them.

"I'm sorry. When you invited me to go on a hike, you had no idea you would end up forced to listen to the whole sordid story of my marriage."

His mouth tightened. "You have nothing to apologize for, Meredith. I get the feeling you don't talk about this with many people, do you?"

She shook her head, embarrassed all over again that she had chosen this man, this virtual stranger, to unburden herself to. "It's in the past. He can't hurt me or anyone else now. What's the point in dredging it all up again?"

"Your cousin doesn't know why you stayed away?"

"No. And I would prefer you don't tell her. She'll only see it as one more excuse, anyway. And she would be right."

He studied her, sunlight glinting off his hair. "Why did you choose to tell me?"

"I've been asking myself the same thing. I'm not sure I have a good answer. You asked me and seemed genuinely interested."

"I was. I am."

"And you're an easy man to talk to. I imagine people have told you that before."

"A few."

"I'm beginning to see how very much I needed someone to talk to. The past few years, I've mostly kept to myself. I haven't been able to trust many people."

"Because your louse of a husband was disgraced financier Carter Rowland?"

She stared at him, shock and dismay chasing through her. "How…how long have you known?"

He opened his mouth to answer, then appeared to change his

mind about something. "My family lives in the Chicago area," he said, obviously choosing his words carefully. "You could say I...followed the story. You're somewhat famous there."

"Infamous, you mean."

How much did he know?

A horrible, sneaking thought pushed its way in. Maybe that's why he had been so kind to her, why he had struck up a friendship with her, helped her with the painting, invited her along on this outing. He was a writer. Maybe he wanted to write a book about the whole sordid mess.

Had she just revealed everything dark and ugly in her marriage to a man who would betray her?

No. She couldn't believe it.

"You knew who I was and you're still here? You don't want to toss me over those cliffs into the water?"

She meant her words half in jest but he gave her a long, appraising look. "Why would I want to do that?"

"Most people in Chicago would. There, I'm a pariah. Mrs. Carter Rowland. Either a dupe or a coconspirator. If you followed the story, you know Carter raided pensions and retirement accounts for thousands of people in Chicago. This wasn't a situation of stealing only from the rich. He stole from those who didn't have much to begin with. Teachers, firefighters, service workers. Plenty of people think I hold as much blame as he does. I had to have known what he was doing, didn't I?"

His gaze seemed to see into every corner of her soul. "Did you?"

"I told you the sort of marriage we had. Do you think my husband would have confided in me about anything, especially the layers upon layers of fraud he was perpetuating on innocent people?"

He paused for a long moment, gazing out to sea. When he turned back to her, his expression was so full of compassion and understanding, tears rose up in her throat.

"I believe you," he murmured, though she had the odd impression he seemed as surprised by the words as she was.

She did her best to swallow down the emotion. Still, her voice came out shakier than she would have liked. "That makes one of you, then. The FBI and the Department of the Treasury certainly don't. They've been after me since Carter was arrested, convinced he and I were in cahoots and I've hidden our ill-gotten gains somewhere, waiting for the heat to die down."

"Have you? Do you know what he did with the missing millions?"

A mirthless laugh escaped her. "I wish. Then I could turn it over to the investigators and this whole thing would be done."

"Would you really turn it over? Half a billion dollars?"

"In a heartbeat, if I knew where it was."

He gave her a look of disbelief that made her bristle.

"I'm not a thief," she said fiercely. "But I'll be the first one to tell you I'm not innocent either. I *should* have known. Another wife might have had some sort of inkling about what her husband was up to. But I didn't want to know anything about Carter's business dealings or anything else. By that point in our marriage, the less I had to do with him, the better, as far as I was concerned."

"You don't have any idea what he might have done with the money?"

"My life would be so much easier if I did. Believe me, I have racked my brain trying to come up with the answer to that. Did I see something, hear something, unknowingly or not? Did he mention anything at all that could be used to find whatever overseas bank account he used? I don't know. As I said, I wish I did. Selfishly, I hate people thinking I would ever try to benefit from what Carter did. More than that, though, I hate thinking of the thousands of innocent people whose lives have been destroyed by a man I once thought had only destroyed my own."

He was looking at her with an expression on his features she couldn't read. "You're quite remarkable."

She could feel her face heat. "We both know I'm not. I don't need you to patronize me, Liam."

"Patronize you? Far from it. Other women might have crumpled after enduring what you've been through. You're finding your way to the other side, and you're still able to be compassionate for people you don't know as well as for those you do, like Aspen."

"It's not enough, though. I can never fix the harm that he caused to people."

"The harm that *he* caused. Not you. I think it's time you stopped blaming yourself."

"I should have known. If I had filed for divorce earlier, maybe some of what he had done would have trickled out."

"You can't know that. You're carrying too much weight on your own shoulders."

"Telling you has helped lift that a little, if only for a moment. Thank you."

"I'm glad."

He gazed at her for a long moment as the wind curled around them.

He was close enough to touch, she realized. And suddenly she wanted to touch him.

His gaze seemed to sharpen on her mouth. He seemed to be having an internal debate with himself. She didn't know if he won or lost when he took another step forward and brushed his mouth against hers with a stunning tenderness she found devastating.

He knew the worst of her, this man with the kind eyes and the sweet smile. Still, he kissed her as if she were a rare and precious gift he had stumbled upon in the mountains.

Her heart, which she thought had withered and died a long time ago, seemed to shiver awake as heat surged through her.

She was fiercely attracted to Liam. More than that, she *liked* him. He was funny, bright, compassionate.

She wrapped her arms around his waist and leaned into him as sensation after sensation rolled through her like afternoon clouds.

His kiss felt like a rebirth, cleansing and healing. She wanted to sink into his arms, to stay here on this oceanside trail while the sea air washed her clean from the ugliness and shame of the past two years.

They might have kissed all afternoon, except Jasper suddenly barked, the sound cutting through the birdsong and the ocean waves below.

She froze, stunned at the kiss and especially at herself for responding with heedless abandon.

He stared at her, his eyes slightly dazed. And then she saw reality hit him hard. His eyes widened, and his expression suddenly looked horrified.

Everything he had resurrected inside her seemed to shrivel again, becoming small and pitiable.

"Meredith. I—"

She forced a smile. "You don't have to say anything. Really. You don't. This was obviously a mistake."

She drew in a breath that shuddered slightly. So slightly she hoped he didn't notice. "Let's just eat our lunch and try to pretend that never happened."

He swore a vicious oath.

Right. She felt exactly the same way.

"I'm sorry, Meredith. We can eat lunch, but there's no way in hell I can pretend that didn't happen. I'm a numbers guy. My imagination doesn't stretch that far."

"And yet you're trying to write a book."

He looked briefly off-kilter by the reminder, as if he had completely forgotten. "Right. And struggling with every single word."

"Another reason we should eat our lunch quickly, then, and

head back. In fact, maybe we should forget lunch or eat in the car on the way back to the café. I've kept you long enough from your book."

He stared down at her for a long time, then he let out a breath. "You went to all the trouble to pack a lunch. And I'm suddenly starving. We can take ten minutes to eat."

"I think the waterfall isn't much farther. Do you want to press on and see if we can find it?"

"Sure. We've come this far. We can eat there."

He picked up his backpack, grabbed Jasper's leash and with one more searching look continued up the trail.

24

Liam

He had kissed Meredith Rowland.

They found the waterfall after only walking about ten minutes more. It was stunning, a stream that plummeted a hundred feet into the sea.

They ate her delicious packed lunch on a rock overlooking the falls. As Liam ate, five words seemed to echo through his head like a klaxon.

He had kissed Meredith Rowland.

And not simply a fleeting little peck. He had kissed her like he meant it.

He *had* meant it.

Liam wanted to smack his head against the closest boulder about twenty or thirty times.

What the hell had he been thinking? She was a source. That was it. He was trying to extract information from her about the missing funds her husband stole. He wasn't here to tangle tongues with the woman, no matter how tempting he might find her.

How had things come to this? He had completely lost any objectivity in this case. Meredith had become far more than a source to him. She was a woman who had endured pain and fear and loss, all with a quiet grace that astonished him.

He had kissed her because he wanted to kiss her. Because he was drawn to her, not because he saw her as some kind of damsel in distress, but because he saw her as a woman who had certainly been in a stressful situation where she had hit rock bottom and was doing her best to rescue herself.

He had kissed her because he was wildly attracted to her. She was lovely and courageous with a heart full of compassion for others who needed help, like Aspen.

He was in serious trouble.

If this kept up, he was going to find himself head over heels for her, the woman he had come here to investigate.

He could only be grateful he wasn't here in any official capacity or he would be so completely fired.

He still might be risking everything. When his special agent in charge found out he had tracked down Meredith here, had inserted himself in her life, had lied about who he was and what he was doing here, Liam very well might be fired.

The prospect didn't bother him as much as it probably should. He knew someone with his skills would always have a place in law enforcement. If not, he could always do private consulting.

What now? He had kissed her and couldn't take those moments back, even if he wanted to.

She said she had no idea where the stolen money may be. He believed her.

A week ago he had believed she was up to her eyeballs in her husband's crimes. Not now. She was an innocent victim. Perhaps even more of a victim than anyone else he was trying to help. Those who had lost money in Rowland's investment scheme had suffered a financial hit. Meredith had lost far more than money. She had lost her innocence, her self-respect and years of her life.

He had to tell her who he was and why he was there.

The realization hit him like a falling boulder. He didn't want to. It would hurt her, especially now that he had kissed her.

What a damn mess he had made of things.

"That was delicious," he said, folding up the paper she had used to wrap the sandwiches and tucking it into his backpack. "Maybe the best ham sandwich I've ever had."

"It's all about using fresh bread and excellent butter. I mean, it's not at all good for your arteries or your waistline. But maybe the hike in the fresh air will offset the carbs and the calories."

"We can only hope."

They headed back down the trail mostly in silence, both lost in thought.

With each step, his options seemed more complicated.

He could cut and run, leave town immediately without a backward glance.

He could tell her what he had done and enlist her help in looking for the missing funds.

Or he could just go on as before, pretending to be a writer while trying to probe in subtle ways to see if she might know more than she realized she did.

His conscience twinged. She didn't deserve to be manipulated and betrayed.

He should tell her the truth. That he wasn't really a writer, that he had no intention of penning the next bestseller about an art heist or anything else, that everything she knew about him was a lie.

He was no better than her husband. Lying and manipulating to get his way.

"Meredith. I have to tell you something," he finally said before he could change his mind.

She stopped on the trail at a spot surrounded by coastal pines, bent but not broken by the endless winds coming off the water.

"That sounds ominous," she said with a slight smile.

How did he start?

I am not and never will be a writer. I came here because, like everyone else, I believed you have been hiding millions that don't belong to you.

He opened his mouth, still not sure of the right words. Before he could say anything, Jasper barked at something down the trail. Liam looked in time to see a strange dog come bounding around the bend, a stick in its mouth.

The dog, a big German shepherd cross, froze almost comically when it spied them and then bounded over to greet Jasper, dropping the stick at the other dog's feet.

Liam braced himself, not sure if the dog would be friendly, but they started sniffing each other's butts and seemed to become immediate friends.

A moment later, two people came into view behind the dog.

He knew this guy, Liam realized. And so did Meredith. He worked in the kitchen of the Beach End.

"Ty. Oh. Hello!" she exclaimed. "What a surprise! I didn't expect to see you here."

The hipster-looking guy smiled at her. "Small world, I guess. Nice place to go on your day off. Have you met my girlfriend? This is Susanna."

"Hi, Susanna. I'm Meredith. I work with Ty at the café."

"Yes. He's told me about you."

The woman had dark, shining hair pulled back into a ponytail and a face that appeared guarded but friendly.

"Ty makes the very best nachos I've ever had," Meredith informed her. "People come from miles around for them."

"Yes. I really enjoy his nachos."

Somehow the woman managed to make the word sound vaguely sexual, though Liam couldn't tell if she meant it that way.

"And this is your dog? Hi there. You are a beauty."

"Well, it's Susanna's dog, anyway," Ty said.

"Do you mind if I pet him?" Meredith asked.

"Her." Susanna smiled. "Her name is Aggie. Go ahead."

"Hi there, Aggie."

Meredith petted the dog with enthusiasm. He might almost believe she didn't want to hear what he had started to tell her.

"Yes. Right. Well, enjoy your hike," she said, rising to her feet.

"See you tomorrow," Ty said. He gave Liam a bro nod, then the two of them continued up the trail with the dog leading the way.

"Ty is a good guy. He's kind to me, anyway, no matter how much I screw up."

"Kindness is an important trait in an employee."

"I agree. When I hired assistants at the gallery, I cared more about personality and customer service skills than I did about art knowledge. I mean, that was helpful, of course. A love of art, anyway. But what good was it to have someone with an art degree who treated every potential client as if they were fresh off the farm and didn't know their Manets from their Monets?"

She seemed to want to talk about anything but their kiss and her past, chattering for the remainder of their walk back to the trailhead about a few other hikes she had done in the area with Tori when they were teenagers.

As she talked, Liam debated how to broach the subject again and tell her he wasn't the man she thought he was.

Of those three options he had thought about earlier, not telling her at all held the most appeal.

It was also the one he knew he couldn't do. He had to let her know the truth about who he was and why he had come here.

But maybe not right now in these peaceful surroundings, where she was enjoying her first moment of relaxation since she had come to Cape Sanctuary.

25

Liam

Apparently, he was not cut out to be a secret agent, Liam thought after they dropped Jasper back at the cottage and headed for the café to finish the final coat of paint.

Oh, he was fine in data gathering and analysis, but when it came to deception and subterfuge, he sucked.

"This shouldn't take us long," Meredith said when they reached the Beach End.

She was right. The second coat went on much more easily than the first. With her cousin there, Liam didn't have a chance to talk even if he could have found the words.

"It looks really good," Tori said, this time with no reluctance in her voice. "This was a great idea. I'm glad you talked me into it."

Meredith glowed as they cleaned up the paint supplies and found room for them in the café's storage unit behind the restaurant.

As Liam drove Meredith back toward Starfish Beach and their respective cottages, he tried to figure out how to tell her the truth.

He supposed if he were good at this whole deep cover thing,

he wouldn't have this conscience scorching through him like a hot August wildfire. Either that or he would be able to ease his guilt by convincing himself the ends justified the means.

Unfortunately, he *did* have a conscience, one that was convinced Meredith Collins Rowland had not been involved in her husband's crimes and had no knowledge about where he might have hidden his ill-gotten gains.

He was going to hurt her.

The knowledge burned hotter than his conscience. He could see no way around it, other than not telling her anything and letting her go back to her life never knowing an FBI agent once tricked her into letting him into her life.

He didn't feel right about that either. What a damn mess.

How did he tell her? Possibilities rattled around in his brain, none of them particularly palatable.

Oh, by the way, I know we've kissed and you've told me all your secrets. I should probably mention that I work for the FBI and I'm here in an unofficial capacity—a personal vendetta, one might say—to earn your trust and find the money your bastard late husband stole from my mother and thousands of others. But thanks for the hike.

Yeah. He couldn't tell her that.

They reached the trio of cottages along Starfish Beach before he could come up with the right words.

She spoke as soon as he pulled up to her cottage. "Thank you so much again for your help painting and for inviting me along with you today. I'm sorry if I slowed you down on the trail."

"You didn't at all. It was perfect. And your picnic lunch was fantastic. You're very good at *jambon beurre*."

Color rose on her cheeks, and she gave him a soft, warm smile that only twisted the knife-edge of conscience that much deeper.

"There's not much to it. You just slather the butter on a baguette and add ham."

"Well, it was the most delicious thing I've had in a while. Not good for me, but completely delicious."

"Like all the best things in life, right?"

Their kiss would certainly fall into that category. Delicious, addictive and completely wrong.

She reached out and opened her door. "Oh," she said, turning back. "I totally forgot when we bumped into Ty on the trail but didn't you say there was something you wanted to tell me?"

Here it was. The perfect chance. He opened his mouth, still wrestling with the right words, when a woman stepped into view on her porch.

"Looks like you have company," he said.

Meredith looked up and her eyes widened with shock. "Aspen!" she exclaimed. She jumped from his SUV and up the steps to greet the other woman.

Aspen held up a large backpack. "Um. I was wondering if you know of somewhere I could crash for a few nights. That shelter you were talking about or a hostel or something. I have a little money."

"Yes. Of course."

"Leo packed up and left. He took most of my tip money."

"Oh Aspen."

Her purple hair danced as she shook her head. "It's fine. I'm glad he's gone. We weren't working out anyway. But now I have to figure out how to get back to Ohio. I just need to work for a few weeks and make enough for bus fare."

Meredith looked only too understanding. "You can stay here. It's not the most glamorous of cottages, but I have an extra bed and would be happy of the company."

"I can pay you," Aspen said again. She seemed determined to make it clear she wasn't looking for a handout.

"Don't worry about that. My spare room is empty. Oh, I'm so glad you're here. Let's get you inside and find some ice for that black eye."

Aspen looked overwhelmed at Meredith's compassion and care. "Thanks."

"I've got your bag," Liam said, reaching for the backpack at her feet.

He carried it into the small cottage. "Where do you want it?"

"The spare room is down the hall on the left. I guess you would know that, since it's in the same place at your cottage."

He carried it into the room, which was undecorated but clean, with only a twin bed and a single chair. He set the backpack on the chair, then returned to the living room.

"Can I use your bathroom?" Aspen was asking Meredith. "I walked down from the mountain a while ago and have needed to pee for about two hours."

"Oh. Yes. Of course. It's right across from the bedroom."

When she hurried away, Meredith turned back to Liam.

"I'm sorry. You were going to tell me something."

He did need to tell her the truth, but this didn't feel like the time, when she was distracted with her new houseguest.

"It's not important," he lied. What was one more? "Thanks again for the hike."

Her smile was radiant, more genuine than he had seen since she arrived at Cape Sanctuary. "Maybe we can do it again some time. But only if it doesn't take you away from working on your book. I'm off every day after two."

Liam forced a smile. He had no reason to stay in Cape Sanctuary, though he had paid for two more weeks at the cottage.

"Sounds like a plan," he said. He heard the water run in the bathroom and, suddenly struck by something, gave Meredith a serious look. "Listen. The most dangerous time for any woman in an abusive situation is when she tries to leave."

"I know," she said, her voice low to match his. Of course she would know. His heart ached, and he was filled with renewed fury toward Carter Rowland.

"Aspen said her boyfriend left her here but if he decides to come back, she should really go to the local shelter. Be careful, okay? I'm only next door. I can be here in an instant, day or night. And Jasper can be fierce when he needs to be, if you need a bodyguard."

"Thanks. I hope we don't need that, but thank you. I can't tell you what a comfort it is to know there are still good guys out there."

Yeah. He was a great guy, who had lied and manipulated her for days.

He forced a smile and left for his own cottage. His phone rang just as he let himself inside.

He looked at the caller ID and winced. His supervising agent, Danielle Trimbull, rarely called his personal number. Had she somehow found out where he was and what he had been trying to do?

He thought about ignoring the call. He was taking vacation time, after all. Because she called him so rarely, though, he knew it was probably important.

"Hi, Danielle."

"Liam. I'm glad I caught you. How's your time off been? Did you go to visit family?"

"No. I'm in northern California staying at a little town called Cape Sanctuary."

"Really? I've been there. I grew up not too far away in Ferndale."

"It's a lovely area."

"It is. I should go back for a visit. It seems like every time I have time off, I end up doing some project around the house. That's not why I called, though. I hate to do this to you but we have a problem. The prosecution in the Byte Right case has changed the order of witnesses. They feel like having you testify earlier in the trial than you were originally scheduled would be more effective for their case. They want you on the stand the day after tomorrow."

"The day after tomorrow? And they just decided this now?"

"They've been thinking about mixing up their strategy for a

few weeks but made the final decision this morning. I'm sorry to have you cut your vacation short. You still have two weeks, though. Your testimony will only take a few days and you could go right back to the beach. I'll make it up to you, I promise."

He didn't really have a choice. He had poured more than a year of his life into the case. He knew it better than anyone else and had to see it through.

"Yes. All right. I can drive down tomorrow."

He would come back after he testified to stay the rest of the time he had rented at the cottage, if only so he could tell Meredith the truth, he decided. That would give him at least a few days to figure out what to say.

He owed her that much.

26

Tori

Tori found herself ridiculously excited at the idea of spending the evening with Emilia, Sam and Cristina.

It was only homework, she reminded herself. The two girls were likely to be filled with attitude about it, at least judging by the past week.

The time for procrastination and messing around was long past. Em and Cristina had only a handful of days to finish their missing assignments if they wanted to pass their classes.

After going back to the café to finish painting with a strangely subdued Meredith and Liam, who both seemed in a hurry to be done with the project now, Tori stopped at the grocery store for a few things. Now she stood in the open kitchen/living area of the cottage, prepping a salad as she watched the shadows lengthen across the water.

She had already spent an inordinate amount of time getting ready for their guests, making sure all the cherry tomatoes were sliced exactly in half and the cucumbers weren't bitter or mushy.

She texted Emilia, up in her room, to come down and set the dining table out on the wide deck that faced the water, where they could listen to the waves while they ate.

"I wish we could just have Sam and Cristina over and didn't have to throw in homework too," Em said as she pulled plates down from the cabinet.

Tori managed to refrain from pointing out the girls were only reaping what they had sown by dropping the ball in their classes the last half of the term.

She already had argued that point ad nauseum, though. No sense rehashing.

"Wouldn't that be nice? We can plan on doing that over the summer. We'll have a big family barbecue for your birthday. We can invite your grandparents, too, or have it at their house where you all could swim."

Tori couldn't quite believe her daughter was turning fourteen soon. Where had the years gone?

She knew the answer to that. She had been busy trying to survive widowhood, helping Frances be as comfortable as possible during her last days, keeping the café going.

"Can I have a party just for my friends too?"

"That's a few months off, but I'm sure we can arrange something. If you wanted, we could even have it at the café after hours, like we did last week."

"That could be really fun. Could Ty make burgers for everybody?"

"We'll have to talk to him but that could probably be arranged."

"I was thinking just a bonfire on the beach, but dinner at the café might be cool. Good idea, Mom."

To her shock, Em gave her a completely spontaneous hug. Tori dropped her knife in an instant and hugged her back. In the rare moments her child wanted to hug her, she would always drop everything and open her arms.

Her daughter seemed taller even than the last time they had hugged. She was no longer a child but a full-fledged young woman.

Her throat felt tight, and she fought the urge to bury her face in Em's hair and beg time to stop moving so fast.

These affectionate moments had been few and far between this year. Tori knew she had to savor them where she could find them.

Most of the time, she was lucky not to earn an eye roll and a look that made her feel completely cringeworthy.

The quicksilver mood changes were one of the hardest things about parenting a teenage girl, Tori was finding. Had she been this quixotic? Poor Frances, if she had.

One moment, Em seemed like her usual, affectionate self, the next she didn't even want Tori breathing the same air.

She supposed she could endure those moody times for the payoff of moments like this, when Emilia still seemed to like having her around.

"Mom, why don't you go on more dates?"

She pulled away to stare at Em as she tried to process the completely unexpected question.

"And by more, of course I mean *any*," Em said with a teasing smile.

"I date. Sometimes."

"When was the last time you went out? When I was in fifth or sixth grade."

Tori went back to making the salad, avoiding her daughter's gaze in the hopes she could conceal from Emilia how uncomfortable she was with the topic.

"Why is everyone so interested in my love life? Or lack thereof?"

"Who else is interested?" Em asked.

Now she wished she hadn't said anything, especially considering whom they were expecting for dinner.

"Sam was asking me the same thing the other day."

Em looked intrigued. "What did you tell him?"

221

"The same thing I'll tell you. I have other priorities right now."

"Aren't you lonely? I mean, Dad's been gone for a long time."

She looked at her daughter and saw Javier in her smile, in her dimples, in the warm brown eyes.

"Sometimes it seems like Dad has been gone forever," Emilia said. "Other times, I swear I talked to him yesterday."

Her daughter grew quiet and, taking a chance and praying she wouldn't be rebuffed, Tori embraced her again.

"I miss him," Emilia said with a little sniffle, wrapping her arms around Tori's waist and resting her cheek against her shoulder.

"So do I," Tori answered, though she felt a little pang, knowing the sharp ache of loss was mostly gone now, after seven long years.

They stood together, both of them remembering the man who loved corny jokes and summer sunrises and dancing barefoot in the sand.

"Is that why you don't date?" Em asked after a moment. "Because you're still in love with Dad?"

Tori chose her words carefully. "Your dad was a wonderful man. Some part of my heart will always belong to him. Maybe deep inside I'm afraid I'll never find somebody as good as he was."

Em drew away with a sigh. "Sometimes I miss him so much it makes my stomach hurt. And other times, I can't remember what it was like having a dad at all."

Tori brushed a hand over her daughter's hair, her heart tangled with love for this lovely woman–child trying to figure out her way in the world.

"Your dad would have loved knowing the amazing young woman you're becoming. He loved being your dad. It was his greatest joy and his greatest honor."

The doorbell rang just then and Em made a face, wiping at her eyes.

"Oh great. Now my mascara is all runny."

"It's not. You look great."

"That's easy for you to say. You hardly wear makeup. I need to go fix it."

She hurried up the narrow staircase to her attic bedroom, leaving Tori to answer the door on her own.

After taking a quick look in the mirror by the entrance to make sure her own minimal mascara wasn't smeared, she opened the door.

"Where's Em?" her niece asked after Tori ushered them inside the cottage.

"In her room. Apparently, she needed a makeup repair before you spend the next two hours doing homework."

"I'd better check on her. Her mascara game is subpar."

Cristina hurried away, leaving Sam holding a box wrapped in the distinctive yellow ribbon from the local bakery.

"Is everything okay?" he asked, giving her a careful look. "You seem upset."

She shook her head. "I'm fine. Em and I are both fine. We were talking about Javier, and we both got a little teary. Hence the emergency mascara repair upstairs."

"Ah. Got it."

He looked at her with an odd expression, something glittery and bright that made her feel breathless.

"Oh. Sorry. Let me put that in the kitchen."

She reached across and grabbed the bakery box from him. Her fingers grazed his briefly and as skin brushed against skin, she shivered.

He followed her into the kitchen, leaning with his long legs stretched out and his arms behind him, holding on to the counter.

"All these years later, you can still get emotional when you talk about Javi. That's amazing. My brother was a lucky, lucky man. I wonder if he realized."

Their marriage hadn't been perfect. She had sometimes resented his long work hours and his volunteer efforts with the fire department, feeling like she and Em came a distant second to his commitment to public safety. She also knew she could be sharp, bordering on waspish, when she was upset about something. They had actually been talking about going to counseling when he was killed.

Instead of having couples counseling together, Tori had ended up seeing the same counselor, only for help with her grief and guilt.

"I don't get emotional all the time," she said now to Sam. "I was just telling Em how much her father would have enjoyed knowing the young woman she's becoming. I will always be sad that he never had the chance to know her beyond the little girl she was when he died. And that she doesn't have her dad. That's it. I'm not pining away for Javi, I promise."

"I still envy him."

To her shock, Sam reached a hand out and brushed at a tear right at the curve of her cheek.

At the feel of his strong fingers on her skin, she froze, all thought of her late husband vanishing in an instant.

All she could think about was Sam.

Everything inside her ached for him to do more than touch her face.

His gaze sharpened on hers, and she wondered fleetingly what he could see there in her expression.

Could he tell that she had started to have these wild, inappropriate thoughts about him? That she dreamed about him at night and awoke lonely and empty?

"Tori."

He said her name, only that. She swallowed and pressed her lips together. His gaze slid there and she caught her breath as he slowly, slowly lowered his mouth to hers.

At first, she couldn't believe what was happening. This was so much better than anything she had dreamed about him. This was flesh and blood, muscle and heat.

She kissed him back, unable to resist. He groaned low in his throat and deepened the kiss, and before she knew it, she felt the hard edge of her countertop at her back and his body trapping her there with delicious, seductive strength.

She was vaguely aware this was a mistake. The girls were upstairs and could come down at any moment. Beyond that, after a kiss like this, wild and unrestrained, they couldn't possibly cross back to their previous easy relationship.

All that hovered in her subconscious like some distant warning.

It was impossible to focus on anything else but the blood pulsing in her ears, the heat pooling inside her, the rising hunger for more.

She kissed him with all the weeks and months of repressed need, the secret awareness she had hardly even admitted to herself.

Still, that distant warning system was still at work when some small segment of her subconscious still on alert picked up the sound of footsteps coming down the stairs.

The girls.

She had to move. Now.

She jerked away, retreating to the opposite side of the kitchen just as Em and Cristina reached the bottom step and headed straight for them, talking and laughing about a boy in school who apparently had a crush on their friend Jenna.

Tori barely heard them over the pounding of her heart, the surge of blood through her veins.

Sweet heavens.

Sam had kissed her.

She couldn't seem to breathe around her shock. Sam had *kissed* her. And not in anything resembling a friendly, amiable brother-in-law sort of kiss.

This had been the real deal, full of heat and hunger and *want*.

The girls seemed to pick up that something was off in the kitchen, some subtle tension they must have sensed. Cristina's voice trailed off and she narrowed her gaze at them, which drew Em's attention as well.

"What's going on?" she asked.

"Nothing. Nothing at all," Tori assured her, though the lie seemed to scorch her tongue. "We were, um, just talking about… about your dad."

That part wasn't a lie. They *had* started out talking about Javier.

She knew as soon as she said it that she had made a mistake to bring up his brother again. A muscle jumped in Sam's jaw, but he said nothing.

That explanation seemed to suffice for the girls, however. After one more suspicious look between them, Em turned away.

"What time will dinner be ready? We were just thinking we should take a little walk along the beach for a bit to get out some of our energy so we can focus on our homework."

"I started the coals earlier. I only have to put the chicken on. It should be ready in about a half hour. Why don't you work on homework during that time while I'm finishing dinner? Sam can make sure you both focus. Then after dinner we can all take a quick walk before we get back to work."

There. That sounded at least somewhat coherent.

Still, neither girl looked thrilled at her words. She thought Em might argue, push the boundaries, but she only sighed.

"Come on, Crissy. The sooner we get done, the sooner we can get out of Homework Prison."

The girls grabbed backpacks and started to spread out at the dining table.

"What do you want me to do?" Sam asked.

For one wild moment, she wanted to tell him to kiss her again, then realized he was asking how he could help with dinner.

"You can grill if you want. I can do it, but I lack the equipment that seems to be required for the most effective grilling."

"What are you missing? I might have what you need."

Oh, she was 100 percent certain he did. That's what she was afraid of.

"I was thinking more about a Y chromosome and all its accompanying, um, baggage."

And now she was thinking about his Y chromosome and, um, baggage.

She flushed, horrified at herself. "Everything else is ready," she said quickly. "I only need to throw the chicken on the grill. I'll do that and you can be the homework police."

He studied her, and she truly hoped he didn't guess the direction of her thoughts. After a moment, he nodded and sat at the dining table, pulling out his phone.

She grabbed the marinating chicken from the refrigerator and carried it out to the deck, where the aroma of hot coals filled the air.

She threw the chicken on the grill and some of the marinade sizzled onto the coals, lemon and butter and spice.

Sam had kissed her.

Heat still pooled inside her, a deep ache to feel that exhilarating, sparkly desire again.

What was wrong with her? This was Sam! Javier's brother. Her daughter's uncle. She couldn't be this tangled up over him. She *couldn't*.

Her life was already too complicated, with Meredith and the café and Emilia's failing grades and wild behavior. Did she have to make everything so much worse by developing feelings for her brother-in-law, the one man she could never have?

Somehow, she wasn't sure how, she made it through prepping dinner and then carrying everything out to the deck, where the girls had set the table.

Despite the currents still zinging between her and Sam, dinner was actually a fun experience. The girls seemed happy, perhaps because they sensed their homework ordeal was nearly at an end.

"Delicious," Sam declared some time later, setting down his napkin. "Everything was so good. Thank you."

"Yeah. Thanks, Aunt Tori. You need to teach my dad how to do that marinade. I loved the lemony taste."

"I'll do that."

"Do we want dessert now? I brought cookies from the bakery we like in town."

"I'm stuffed," Em declared.

"Knowing the girls, they'll be hungry again in an hour. Maybe we should save dessert for a little later."

"Sounds good," Sam said.

"Can we take the dogs down to the end of the beach and back?" Cristina asked.

"You need to help clean up first," Sam said.

The girls hurried to clear the table and load the dishwasher, then grabbed the dogs' leashes.

"Fifteen minutes," Sam said, voice stern, after they had put the leashes on Shark and Risa. "That's about how much daylight we have left."

"If you can focus for a couple more hours, you'll both be done with all your missing work," Tori added.

"Fifteen minutes," Cristina agreed.

The girls hurried down the stairs and onto the path, the dogs leading the way.

She should have gone with them, Tori thought the instant Sam closed the door behind them.

She was afraid to be alone with him. Not because she worried he would hurt her but because she didn't trust herself around him, especially when her mind couldn't seem to stop reliving that kiss.

All through dinner, when she was listening to their conversation about a pool party one of the girls' friends was having the last day of school, she had been rehashing every second she had spent in his arms.

She wanted to lie but the words wouldn't come. She couldn't do it. Not to Sam. She gave a slight shake of her head, all she could manage.

"No, you haven't thought about us together?"

She met his gaze. "No. I can't tell you that. Because I would be lying."

Heat flared in his expression.

"What do you want to do about it?" he asked, his low voice sending ripples of awareness through her in concentric waves. She thought for a moment he would reach for her, but his hands remained at his sides and she realized he was giving her the choice.

"There is so much at stake here. We have to think about your family. Your parents. The girls."

"What about us? What about what we want?"

"We're parents. We can't only think about what we want."

She sighed, aching for him more than she could remember aching for anything in a very long time. "Say we gave in to these feelings and had a...a hot and steamy affair. Then what? How do we go back to Sunday dinners and pool parties and Christmas mornings with your family, with that kind of tangled history between us? It would be impossible. You might be able to handle it, but I know myself well enough to know I couldn't. I would start avoiding family gatherings, which would hurt Em *and* your parents. They wouldn't understand why I was suddenly declining all their invitations. And I certainly couldn't tell them it was because I'm all tangled up about their other son. Not the one I was married to but his brother!"

"What are you saying, then? That we simply go back to ignoring this heat sizzling between us?"

She didn't want to. Tori wanted so much to give in to that heat. To drag him to her bedroom and spend a week or two exploring all those hard muscles.

At what cost, though? She already cared about Sam. It would

only take a few more of those kisses, his teasing smiles, for her to fall completely.

The knowledge terrified her. She couldn't risk it. She wasn't willing to sacrifice her and Em's relationship with the rest of his family.

"Yes. That's the safest course."

"Life isn't always meant to be safe, Tori."

"You know, Javi used to say the same thing. And look how that turned out."

The sound of the girls coming in the door cut him off before he could answer. Sam gave her a frustrated look as she hurried into the living area to find Em and Cristina unhooking the dogs' leashes. They brought with them damp skin and smelled of the sea.

"Okay. Let's get this over with," Em said, taking off her jacket.

"Yeah. Let's kick this homework in the balls," Cristina said.

"Cris," Sam chided.

"I just mean we're going to work hard and get it done."

"I can't even tell you how happy I'll be when I finish the last of my missing assignments," Em said.

"Summer vacation can't come soon enough for me," Cristina said in agreement.

The girls sat at the dining room table, books spread out around them.

Tori grabbed her laptop and sat down at one end while Sam sat at the other with a book. It might have been a cozy, domestic scene if not for the tension that crackled in the air.

Every once in a while, she would look up from her laptop to find him watching her with a look that made her toes curl.

What had she done?

She should never have let him kiss her.

Even if they didn't have that hot, steamy affair she had talked about earlier, she worried everything would change between them now.

27

Meredith

Over the next week, Meredith felt as if her life was finally on a steady track, for the first time in nearly two years.

She was feeling more comfortable with the way things worked at the café and didn't feel like she was fumbling her way through the job. She now not only helped bus tables but sometimes delivered meals when an order came up while the server was busy with other customers.

She actually found herself enjoying the work. While she likely never would have chosen the job for her life's calling, she had come to appreciate many things about working at the Beach End Café.

Tori was a good boss. The café was well-run, the staff was happy and the food was consistently delicious.

Beyond delivering good, hearty meals, the staff treated the customers like family, even the tourists who would only eat there one or two times during a vacation.

She glanced over at the empty booth, the one where Liam usually sat.

That empty booth was the one blot in an otherwise improving situation. Liam hadn't been to the café since the day they finished painting it, more than a week ago. He seemed to have disappeared off the face of the earth. His vehicle was gone, and she hadn't seen him or Jasper on the beach in days.

She assumed he had left his rental early. Was it because of her? Because of what she told him about herself? What else could it be?

"It's time for your break, isn't it?" Tori asked after the morning rush had receded a little.

Meredith set down the glass she had been drying. "I'm fine. I don't need to take a break."

"Take one anyway. You've been running all morning. It's a lovely day. Go sit on a bench and breathe the sea air for a moment."

It sounded like an order. Meredith wanted to remind her cousin they were co-owners and Tori wasn't the boss of her, but that would be childish. Besides, she had agreed when she started working here that Tori *was* the boss, at least when it came to the café.

She had hoped her cousin was starting to forgive her, or at least was coming to tolerate her. She had seemed amiable enough when they were painting the café, even bordering on friendly. Since that day, though, Tori had become more distant than ever.

Something was bothering the other woman. For once, Meredith didn't think it was her. Over the past week, her cousin had treated everyone the same as she did Meredith, employees and customers alike.

She wanted to ask what was wrong but didn't know where to start. She was also wary about upsetting the fragile balance they seemed to have achieved. Tori wasn't exactly warm to her but she didn't snap at Meredith or treat her with obvious disdain, as she had when Meredith first came to town.

She looked outside the café, at the flowers dancing in the breeze in the window baskets and the waves sparkling in the sunlight. "I think I will go out for a few minutes," she said suddenly.

"No rush," Tori said, then turned to ask Ty something about an order.

On her way out the door, Meredith's gaze again went to the booth she had come to consider Liam's.

Had he left because of that kiss? She couldn't really blame him. She was a mess. Any smart man would run as fast as possible from her and her complicated past.

She walked outside the café and headed for her favorite spot, a gazebo along the coast walk between the café and the gift shop next door, with a bench overlooking the beach and the dramatic offshore sea stacks.

Meredith sat down on the bench and watched sandpipers run up and down the beach, scooping up unfortunate creatures brought in by the surf.

She was smiling as a couple of seagulls fought over something when she suddenly heard a single bark behind her. Her breath seemed to catch. That sounded like Jasper!

She told herself not to be ridiculous. There were hundreds of dogs in and around Cape Sanctuary. She couldn't recognize one canine bark out of all the others.

When the dog barked again, she couldn't stop herself from turning to find the source. A black lab with a braided green collar barreled toward her, tugging along the human at the other end of his leash.

Liam.

Happiness washed over her like those rolling waves over the sand.

She waved and gave what she hoped was a casual smile instead of the broad, bright, joyful one building inside her. She tried to tamp down her reaction. She had told him her life story, he had kissed her, and then he had disappeared. She had no reason to suddenly want to do cartwheels through the little gazebo.

He stepped into the wooden structure, led by Jasper. "Good

morning. I wasn't expecting to see you here. Aren't you working at the café today?"

"I am. We had a slow moment, and Tori told me to take a break."

"It's a beautiful today. So much warmer than it was when I left. I'm loving the quiet, especially since I've been driving in Los Angeles traffic all week and forgot how peaceful it is here."

"Oh. You went back to LA? Was it something to do with your book?"

He seemed to hesitate. "No. Work. I had an unavoidable obligation. Something I thought wasn't going to happen until later this month was rescheduled."

"Oh. I see." She paused. "I thought maybe you had left town early, trying to avoid me."

He frowned. "Why would I do that?"

She made a face. "Because you're smart? Because I'm a disaster? Because I'm Meredith Rowland, widow of one of the most hated men in the country and spilled my entire ugly life story all over you last week."

And then you kissed me and reminded me the world could still contain rare and precious moments of unalloyed beauty.

"No. That wasn't it at all. I just had a work thing. I thought I would only be gone a few days, but everything took much longer than expected."

He paused, then changed the subject.

"How's Aspen doing? I was hoping her ex stayed away."

"She's good. He texted her a few days after he left. He said he had made a mistake and wanted to come back to town to talk to her."

He looked wary. "What happened?"

Meredith gave a satisfied smile. "She told him where to go, said she was getting a restraining order against him and that if he contacted her again, she would call the cops and have him

236

arrested for stealing all her stuff and the trailer she paid the majority share for."

"Good for her! And she's still staying with you?"

"Yes. I told her she could stay as long as she needed a place."

Aspen had turned out to be an unexpectedly good roommate. She cleaned up after herself, she always made sure there was fresh coffee, she had even used random ingredients in Meredith's kitchen to create a couple of clever pasta dishes that were delicious and filling.

In lieu of rent, she offered to help with Meredith's efforts to spruce up the place. She was creative and artistic with her ideas, and Meredith enjoyed her company.

She liked Aspen, even if living with a nineteen-year-old made her feel ancient.

"How are *you* doing?" Liam asked, giving her a searching look.

Better now that I know you haven't left town because of me.

She couldn't tell him that, of course.

"I'm good. Things aren't perfect but they're…better."

"I'm so glad. You deserve to be happy."

His words sounded genuine. Still, she made a face. She didn't necessarily agree, but she didn't want to argue with him on such a lovely day.

"I'm sorry you didn't get the time you were planning to work on your book."

He shifted, looking uncomfortable, as he always did when she mentioned his manuscript.

"I hope you're able to take advantage of the rest of the time you have away from work. How much longer will you be here?"

"Some things at work have become more pressing while I've been gone, so I need to head back to LA earlier than planned. I'm leaving Saturday."

She felt as if the sunshine had dimmed, as if some of the color had leached from the flowers around them.

"I hate to sound narcissistic, but I truly hope I'm not the reason you're leaving early."

He sent her a swift look. "Why would you be?"

"I feel like everything is so...awkward now."

His features grew serious. "That is not your fault, Meredith. It's completely mine. I overstepped on our hike. I shouldn't have kissed you. I feel like I took advantage of someone going through a tough time. You shared something terrible and raw that had happened to you, and in response, I gave in to my... attraction for you and kissed you. It was wrong, and I've been kicking myself all week."

She gave a little laugh. "Would it make you feel any better if I tell you that kiss was one of the best things that have happened to me in a long time?"

"I still shouldn't have done it."

"I feel like I've been trapped under the ice of Lake Michigan for years. I learned how to swallow down all my emotions and put on a perfect show to my husband and the world. Being with you was the first time I felt like the ice was starting to crack. It was nice to remember I'm more than Carter Rowland's widow. And that I don't have to let the choices I made as a naive twenty-two-year-old impact the rest of my life."

He smiled. This time it reached his eyes, to the fine lines fanning out at the edges. "Exactly right."

He studied her, then seemed to come to a decision about something. "Listen, before I leave town, I wanted to have dinner at The Fishwife on Friday."

"Fancy."

"It's always on the list of best restaurants in northern California. I've heard really great things about it and would hate to leave town without trying it, but I really don't want to have dinner by myself. Would you come with me?"

He must have seen her instinctive hesitation because he was quick to clarify. "Not as my date. Just friends, though dinner would be my treat since you would be doing me a favor if you came with me."

She hadn't been to a really good restaurant in forever. One with pressed tablecloths and a professional waitstaff and gourmet dishes.

The food at the Beach End could hold up against any restaurant in town, but there was something to be said for a meal that didn't require ketchup.

"What time?"

"How does eight work?"

She mentally flipped through her calendar. "Can you make it eight thirty? Cape Sanctuary hosts a monthly gallery walk, where all the art galleries in town stay open late and offer refreshments and live music. I'm still looking for local artists to feature on the rotating display at the café. I thought it might be good to attend this month's event on Friday to make some contacts. I could do that first and then meet you at the restaurant at eight thirty."

"I would enjoy going to the gallery walk too. If you don't mind company, we could do that first and then walk to the restaurant. Everything is close."

"Sounds like a lovely evening. I'll look forward to it."

As it was only Tuesday, she wasn't certain how she would make it through the rest of the week with the anticipation already bubbling through her.

28

Liam

As he watched Meredith hurry back to the restaurant for the rest of her shift, Liam wanted to kick himself.

He was digging himself in deeper by the minute with her.

Why hadn't he come clean about who he was and his reasons for coming to Cape Sanctuary?

During the entire drive up the coast from Los Angeles, he had been telling himself that would be the first thing he did when he returned to town. He would go find Meredith Rowland, spill everything to her and prepare to face the consequences.

Instead, he had only perpetuated the lie and kicked the can down the road a few more nights.

He sighed, frustrated with himself. The hard truth was, he was afraid to tell her, loathe to cause more pain in the life of a woman who had already endured too much.

He grabbed Jasper's leash and continued down the path. It felt good to move. Necessary, even. After a week of court testimony and then driving for hours after the court adjourned the previous afternoon, he needed to work his muscles.

His testimony had taken far longer than anyone expected. The defense team for the accused had spent three additional days in cross-examination, going through his forensic audit in painstaking detail.

He had also taken time while in LA to let his boss know what he had done, about coming here on his own dime and on his own time in hopes of inserting himself into Meredith's life and gaining her trust.

As expected, Danielle had not been happy with him...at first. And then she had grown intrigued by the idea.

"Imagine what a huge coup that would be for the Bureau if we could do what the Treasury Department and the Federal Trade Commission haven't managed in nearly two years. Finding all those missing funds for innocent people hurt by Rowland."

Her eyes had turned sharp. "How long do you think you could keep things going? I would happily sign off for you to work remotely from the area for another few weeks."

"What's the point? Meredith doesn't know anything. I am a hundred percent certain of it," he had said.

"Maybe not consciously. But her subconscious might know more than she thinks. You're the best agent I have for lifestyle analysis. If anybody could pry those details out of her, it's you."

Lifestyle analysis when it came to fraud and white-collar crimes involved trying to quantify all the known sources of income and outlay. It involved studying a suspect's habits and expenditures. It was painstaking and laborious but could yield surprisingly accurate results.

"Surely all that has been done by those on the task force."

"Yes. But it sounds like you've been able to get closer to her than anyone has. You may have unique insights into her personality and might be able to suss out something she might or might not even be aware of. Did they take a second honeymoon to the Caymans? Are there any other dates in their relationship that might be significant in trying to locate where he might have stowed offshore account information?"

"She's an innocent woman, Dani, who has been raked over

the coals by the media, the investigative team and the public at large. By the time we were done with her, she had nothing left. Don't you think she's been through enough?"

Danielle had arched her eyebrow. "You didn't think so a few weeks ago when you decided to insinuate yourself into her life. What's changed now?"

I kissed her. I got to know her. I saw how kind she was with Josef, with Aspen, with the regulars at the café who came there for more than simply the good coffee.

"My gut now agrees with the task force."

Danielle had been disappointed, but she hadn't pressed him.

He hadn't told her he was returning to Cape Sanctuary for a few more days so he could tell Meredith the truth about his identity. Danielle probably would have tried to talk him out of that too, urging him to leave the door open a crack in case an opportunity arose in the future to push his way through it.

No. He had to tell her, though he knew that when he finally told her his real identity, she would hate him.

A week ago that might not have bothered him. Now it did. He didn't want to be one more person who had betrayed her. Her mother, her friends in Chicago—they had all abandoned her when she most needed someone to stand by her side.

He had started this with his egotistical idea that he could succeed where other investigators had failed. In doing so, he had set Meredith up for more hurt. The easy thing would be to leave without telling her the truth. But *easy* wasn't the same thing as *right*. More than likely, she would find out eventually and would feel doubly betrayed that he hadn't told her.

So he would take her to the art gallery walk, to dinner at a lovely restaurant…and then he would have to tell her the truth, no matter how hard.

29

Tori

"I can't believe the girls pulled it off after all. They worked so hard! I knew they could do it. You must be absolutely thrilled."

Tori stretched her feet out in the booth at the Beach End, listening to her mother-in-law gush over the phone.

"I'm beyond thrilled. It kind of feels like our own little miracle."

Teresa laughed. "They're good girls. They just got a little off track."

"I hope so."

"You and Sam were smart to team up so you didn't have to fight the homework battle alone. The two of you make a good team."

She fought down a little shiver at the words. They really didn't. What would Teresa say if Tori confessed that she and Sam had kissed the other night…and that she couldn't seem to get the memory of that kiss out of her head?

She had not seen much of Sam the past week, once the girls finished their homework and turned in their assignments. Today was the last actual day of class, with the rest of the week taken up by honors assemblies, field trips and yearbook day.

"They passed all their classes, then?"

"Yep. Somehow they both managed to push every grade up to either a C plus or a B minus."

"I hope they learned a lesson," Teresa said. "Don't put things off. You never know what's going to happen tomorrow. If you want something, you have to work for it and don't let anything stand in your way."

"Absolutely right."

"I think this calls for a party. Why don't you come over tonight? Papi can make pizzas in his oven."

Her father-in-law, without a drop of Italian blood in his veins, was obsessed with making homemade pizza in the backyard pizza oven the family had gifted him the year before. He was retired now from working as an engineer and loved to tinker with recipes. While pizza was his latest craze, Tori loved all the dishes he made from his native Oaxaca. She especially adored his tamales with mole and his enfrijoladas with chorizo.

"Sure. Pizza sounds good. We don't have anything planned tonight."

"Good. Good. Sam and Cristina were already coming for dinner. I'll call Elena and Jason and see if they want to bring their kids over. It's supposed to be a warm night. They can swim if they want. We'll have a party, especially since we missed Sunday dinner this week."

She steeled herself, not sure she was ready to have a family party with Sam.

"Sounds good. What can I take?"

"Just yourself and Emilia," Teresa said, fondness clear in her voice. "We'll handle everything else. It will be our way of celebrating the end of school for the kids and to honor Emilia and Cristina for remembering they can do hard things."

That was one of Teresa's favorite sayings from her own mother, whose Danish ancestors had traveled across the country by wagon in the 1850s, hoping to make a new start in California.

"What time do you want us there?"

"Let's do seven. That should give Papi time to make the dough and proof it."

"Sounds good."

She was about to hang up when Teresa stopped her. "You know, this is a celebration for families. Why don't you invite your cousin?"

Tori looked across the café, where Meredith was cleaning up after a particularly messy party of moms with their toddlers, probably enjoying the last gasp of the school year before their other children were out for summer vacation.

Things had been better with Meredith, but Tori wasn't sure they were better enough for her to invite her cousin to tag along to an Ayala family gathering when she wasn't at all connected to Javier's family.

"I don't think so."

"She's your family. All you have left now, isn't she?"

"No. I have you. Aren't I lucky?"

Teresa chuckled. "*We* are the lucky ones. The smartest thing our Javi ever did was marry you."

And the dumbest thing Tori had ever done was to kiss their other son and risk ruining the most important relationships in her life.

What was she going to do about Sam?

"Thanks. That's a lovely thing to say."

"If you change your mind, she's more than welcome. We always have plenty of food. I saw her in the grocery store last week, and she seemed so sad and alone. I introduced myself and she lit up like I was some kind of celebrity or something. Think about it, okay?"

Their conversation drifted to Em and Cristina's plans for the summer, which mostly involved hanging out with friends.

"They can come here any time they want to swim."

"I'm sure that will definitely factor into their plans," she said.

RaeAnne Thayne

After they hung up a few moments later, Tori looked across the café, where Meredith was smiling at the group of regulars in the corner, old men who came in for coffee and lunch and to flirt with all the restaurant staff.

What would be the harm in asking her along to the family party? She would probably say no anyway.

Her chance came a short time later, when she went into the kitchen and found Meredith there, working at the sink and chatting with Denise.

"Did I see you sitting outside with our hunky writer earlier?" Denise was asking. "I hope you told him we've been missing his pretty face. Where's he been keeping himself?"

Meredith looked down at the dishes she was rinsing in the sink. Tori saw with interest that her cheeks had turned rosy. "Apparently, he had to go back down to LA for a work emergency," she answered.

"I wondered why I hadn't seen him around," Tori said. "I hope he doesn't want me to discount his rent."

"I doubt he does."

"I'm curious about what kind of work emergency an accountant might have."

Meredith frowned, as if she hadn't thought about that. "He didn't say. He just said he was needed back in the city and that he drove a lot in LA traffic."

"That's enough to make anybody need a vacation," Denise said. "My sister lives down there, and every single time I leave, I feel like I've gripped the steering wheel so hard I must have left finger impressions in it."

Tori smiled. She hated even driving around in Redding or Eureka. She couldn't imagine how bad Los Angeles traffic must be.

Aspen came in and handed an order to Denise, who turned back to the grill. Meredith rinsed off the last plate and rose to go back out to the dining area, but Tori held a hand up to stop her.

246

"Listen. Em and her cousin somehow snatched victory out of defeat and passed all their classes. The Ayalas are throwing an impromptu party tonight to celebrate, and Teresa asked me if you might want to come. I told her I would ask."

Meredith looked stunned at the invitation. "How nice of her. I talked to her in the grocery store the other day, and she was so kind to me."

"That's Teresa. She's pretty terrific."

"You really lucked out in the in-laws department, didn't you?"

Yes. Except Sam. She could have done without having a brother-in-law who pushed all her buttons.

"Anyway, my father-in-law is making pizza. We gave him an outdoor pizza oven for Christmas, and it's kind of become his passion. I imagine the kids will swim and the adults will mostly sit around eating pizza and drinking beer. It won't be anything big, and you're under no obligation. She asked me to invite you. Now I've done it."

She felt stupid and wished she had never started this, especially when Meredith narrowed her gaze and studied her. She suddenly remembered that her cousin once knew her better than anybody else on earth.

"Would you rather I not go?"

"If you want to go, it's fine with me," Tori answered. Somewhat to her surprise, she realized she was speaking the truth. Her relationship with Meredith was so tangled with hurt and regret, but maybe things were beginning to unwind and unsnarl to the core of the love they once had for each other.

"I'm sure Emilia would enjoy the chance to spend a little more time with you. She was saying the other day that she's hardly had a chance to even speak with you."

Meredith seemed to be considering. "Sure. That sounds fun," she finally said. "Thanks for the invitation. Wow. That's two social events in one hour to add to my calendar."

"You're a party animal. What's the other one?"

Meredith's color seemed to rise again. "Liam asked me to have dinner at The Fishwife with him on his last night in town, Friday. He wants to try it before he leaves but doesn't want to go alone so asked me if I would accompany him. Not a date," she added quickly. "Just as friends."

"You're buying that?" Tori didn't. She had seen them together the weekend they had painted the café and had definitely picked up a vibe between them. Besides the fact that Meredith grew flustered every time she talked about him, Liam couldn't keep his eyes off her.

As if to prove the point, her cousin colored. "Yes. I believe him."

She looked away. "Even if he wanted more, which he doesn't, you know it's impossible. Not with my baggage."

Tori didn't miss the thread of sadness in Meredith's voice. She had a wild impulse to hug her cousin in sympathy, one she quickly pushed down. They weren't quite at the hugging stage.

"If you want to come for dinner, we're eating around seven. I can text you their address."

"Thank you. That's very kind of your mother-in-law. Are you sure it's okay? I wouldn't want to make anyone uncomfortable by crashing what sounds like a family party."

"As Teresa was quick to inform me, you're my family. All that I have left, not counting Aunt Cilla. Which I don't."

Meredith didn't appear offended at the dig against her own mother.

"That makes two of us," she said with a rueful laugh. "Thanks. I'll think about it and let you know by the end of my shift."

"Sounds good."

After Tori returned to her booth and her paperwork, she decided she might actually appreciate having her cousin along as an additional buffer between her and Sam. Anything to distract her away from wanting the one thing she couldn't have.

30

Tori

Any hope she might have entertained that Meredith would provide an additional buffer to help her avoid Sam was dashed as soon as she pulled up to the Ayalas' house with Meredith and Em and spotted Sam and Cristina arriving at the same time.

The girls squealed as if they hadn't seen each other in months and were soon talking a mile a minute.

Sam, looking tall and gorgeous in jeans and a T-shirt the color of new leaves, smiled a greeting to both of them. And all Tori could think about was that mouth pressed against hers, his arms pulling her tight to that chest and his hands exploring her skin.

She felt hot, suddenly, though the evening was mild.

Teresa bustled over while Tori was still trying to rein in her rabid imagination.

"Here you all are at once. I'm so glad."

She pecked everyone on the cheek, even Meredith.

"Thank you for inviting me tonight," Meredith said, looking bemused and a little shy.

"Of course. Of course. You're more than welcome. We're thrilled to have you."

Elena moved forward, the spitting image of her mother minus about twenty-five years.

"Hi. I'm Elena. You can call me El. Most people do, except my mother."

"Hi, El. I'm Meredith."

Elena, who ran a computer store along with her husband, gave her a bright smile. "I know who you are. Tell me how you're enjoying Cape Sanctuary."

She tucked her arm through Meredith's and led her toward the covered patio. Meredith sent Tori another bemused look but went with her.

"We're going to go swim before dinner, okay?" Em announced, then she and Cristina rushed off without waiting for an answer, leaving Tori alone with Sam—exactly what she had been hoping to avoid.

She folded her hands together to keep from reaching for him.

"I'm not sure if *Congratulations* are really in order. What do you think?" Sam asked, gesturing toward a gold banner hanging along the soffit of the covered patio.

"Well, they did pass eighth grade and are moving on to ninth. A few weeks ago we weren't sure that would happen, or that they would manage to somehow squeak through with passing grades in everything."

"Can you believe we pulled it off?" Sam shook his head.

"I feel like I just went through the eighth grade all over again in the matter of a couple of weeks."

He looked out at the girls, splashing each other and their younger cousins. "How are we going to keep them on track next school year?"

She made a face. "We have two months where we don't have to worry about that. How about we just enjoy the accomplishment tonight?"

"Good idea."

He smiled, teeth gleaming in the sunset, and Tori felt like someone had just kicked her in the chest.

Oh. Oh no.

She wasn't simply attracted to Sam. She was falling for him. Maybe she was already there.

"It was nice of you to invite your cousin along."

"That was all your mother. She doesn't like the idea of anyone being alone."

He gave her a long look. "So what makes you think she would be happier if you spent the remainder of your life as a widow, dedicated to preserving the memory of Javier?"

"I never said that," she said, her voice low. "I have no doubt your parents would both be fine if I moved on. I'm not sure, though, that they would be fine if I moved on with *you*."

A muscle flexed in his jaw, and he looked like he wanted to argue, then apparently thought better of it.

"What's the story with this end-of-year party the girls want to go to Friday night? What do we know about this girl, Sierra?"

She relaxed a little. Talking about teenage parties was much easier than digging into her own past.

"What do you want to know? Em has had classes with Sierra since kindergarten, and they played on the same soccer team for years. Her mom and I were room mothers together when the girls were in fourth grade. She's a good friend. The mom, I mean. Celeste teaches at the high school, and she and Jeff, Sierra's dad, are fairly involved parents."

"So you think it's okay if they go? Is it going to be coed?"

"Em says she's not sure. I'm going to guess yes or she would be much more transparent with her answer."

"Yeah. Cristina's been pretty evasive when I've asked her the same thing."

"I'm a hundred percent positive Celeste and Jeff will keep a close eye on things. It won't be some kind of drunken free-for-all. They're thirteen and fourteen years old."

"I don't know. I was pretty wild at that age."

She had seen pictures of him in family albums, a skater boy with long hair and a troublemaker smile.

"And look how you turned out," she said. He still had that troublemaker smile but now he was a tough police detective.

"So you're letting Em go?"

Tori shrugged. "The girls have worked hard, at least the past two weeks. I thought letting her go would reinforce the rewards of good decision-making."

"Excellent point. Anything to avoid having to go through this last-minute homework blitz again."

They heard laughter from El and Meredith, who had been joined now by El's husband, Jason. Sam looked over with interest.

"How are you really doing, having your cousin here? I know you haven't been thrilled about her coming back to town."

Tori relaxed a little more. They could do this, as long as they avoided talking about the heat swirling between. "She plans to stay in town for several months. We work at the same place and live two houses apart. I think I have to at least try to get along. I'm not sure I'm able to stay in a perpetual state of war."

"That sounds wise."

"I'm not saying I'll ever forgive her for all she's done over the years, but I can at least try to get along. Maybe with time we could be, if not friends, at least polite acquaintances."

"Sounds like progress to me."

She smiled and met his gaze and caught her breath, suddenly shaky at the blazing heat in his expression.

"Don't do that," she hissed.

"What?"

"Look at me like that."

He blinked. "How was I looking at you?"

Like you want to toss me over your shoulder and carry me home with you.

"You're giving me all your hot cop mojo. Cut it out."

He gave a strangled-sounding laugh. "I wasn't aware I had hot cop mojo."

She snorted, not believing that for a second. She couldn't be the first woman who had pointed that out to him.

"I knew this wouldn't work," she muttered. "I knew we wouldn't be able to act normal with each other after we...after we kissed."

"I, for one, can't get that kiss out of my head."

His voice, pitched low, made her shiver. She couldn't believe nobody in his family seemed to notice the heat they were generating. It was probably rolling off them like the steam from the pizza oven.

"The first two pizzas will be ready in five minutes," Pablo announced. "Since the kids are playing in the pool, this one is for the grown-ups."

"I guess that's us," Sam said.

"I should go see if your mom needs help bringing anything out."

She hurried toward the kitchen, determined she would spend the rest of the evening trying her best to avoid him.

The food, as always, was delicious. She had two pieces of pizza and had to restrain herself from going back for a third.

Meredith seemed to have lost her initial awkwardness as she alternated between helping Pablo shape pizza dough, working with Teresa to keep the salad bowls full and chatting easily with Sam, Jason and Elena.

Tori didn't have the chance to talk to her cousin until after dinner, when they were both helping clear away the food and carrying it back inside to the kitchen.

"You seem to be enjoying yourself," she said.

"They're all lovely," Meredith said. "Everyone has been so kind and welcoming."

"They're a pretty terrific family."

Meredith nodded, then gave Tori a careful look. "Is something going on between you and Javier's brother?" Meredith asked.

She nearly dropped the empty plate that once held garlic breadsticks. "Why would you say that?" she snapped.

"Oh, no reason. When you were talking to him before dinner, I thought you looked like you wanted to either throw him into the pool or drag him into a dark corner somewhere."

Or both. Was it possible to pick both options?

"Nothing's going on," she lied. As soon as the words were out, Tori reconsidered them. Why not tell Meredith the truth? She could use a little perspective, and Meredith was the one person not emotionally tied to Sam and this family.

She looked around to be sure none of the family was in earshot. "Okay, the truth is, we've spent a lot of time together the past few weeks doing homework with the girls, and last week Sam kissed me. Not a brotherly kiss, either."

"Is that the reason you've seemed distracted all week at the café?"

She released a breath. "Maybe. Probably. It's such a mess. He's put me in a horrible position."

"Why?" Meredith look genuinely confused.

"It's obvious, isn't it?"

"Not to me. Sorry. Is he a terrible kisser? I mean, he's great looking but from what I used to hear from my girlfriends and gallery assistants, sometimes the hot guys are the worst kissers. They have no game whatsoever because they've never had to work at it."

"That is not the problem," Tori assured her. "Sam is not a terrible kisser. At all."

This felt so much like when they were younger, when they used to talk endlessly about boys and friends and school, even when they were separated, through text messages and emails and IMs.

"Then what's the problem?" Meredith said with a baffled frown. "Javier has been gone a long time. He wouldn't want you to pine for him the rest of your life."

"I am not pining for him! Why does everyone think that? I loved my husband deeply. I still grieve that he's not here, especially that he never had the chance to get to see Emilia grow up. That doesn't mean I want to lock myself in my room and pull my hair out in despair."

"Help me understand, then."

Why was everyone determined to be obtuse about this? "I was married to his brother! We're practically family. It's just wrong."

"But you're not family. Not really."

"The Ayalas are my family. Em's family. I love them dearly. But what happens if I…if I date Sam and things go wrong between us? There's more at stake here than only a broken heart. I can't risk it."

"I know where you're coming from," Meredith said, surprising her. "It seems to me, though, that you're only looking at the worst-case scenario, that if you have an affair with Sam it will eventually burn itself out. But what if it doesn't?"

She couldn't even think about that as a possibility.

"You care about Sam, don't you?" Meredith went on.

She considered lying but knew there was no point. Meredith would see right through the lie. "Yes," she murmured.

She couldn't bring herself to say the words, to admit to Meredith and to herself that she was very much afraid her feelings ran much deeper than she wanted to acknowledge.

Meredith seemed to pick up the gist anyway. "We both know I'm the last person to give advice about love or marriage. My track record is certainly nothing to brag about."

"True enough. Yet something tells me you're going to give me advice anyway."

"Yes, I am," Meredith said, ignoring her barb. "Sam strikes me as a good man. He loves his daughter, he's close to his family, he's respected in the community. He's the kind of man any woman would be lucky to have in her life. I know a little about fear, and I can tell you it would be a shame if you let your fears about something that might not happen rule your decision-making and keep you from finding happiness together. That's all."

She walked away before Tori could reply, leaving her remembering exactly why she had never liked debating with her cousin.

She made too much blasted sense.

31

Liam

"You don't need to give me that sad-eyed look. I'll only be gone a few hours, I promise. And then tomorrow we'll go back to LA, where you can play with all your friends at your doggie day care again."

Jasper wasn't swayed by the promise. He kept his face turned away, clearly annoyed that Liam had changed out of jeans into dress khakis and a button-down shirt.

Maybe Jasper was mad because the dog wasn't excited about going back to the hectic pace of LA. Liam certainly wasn't looking forward to it. He liked it here in Cape Sanctuary. He liked the people, the scenery, the pace of life.

He liked all of it.

Cape Sanctuary felt like home.

It wasn't, though. Not even close. He was here under false pretenses. The nice people of Cape Sanctuary would not take kindly to finding out he had duped them.

He planned to come clean to Meredith that night.

Any enjoyment or anticipation he might be feeling about spending the evening with her was tempered by the hard truth that he would hurt her before the evening was out.

All day he had been debating whether he should tell her before they went to dinner.

He had talked himself out of it.

She had clearly been looking forward to the gallery walk, connecting with artists whose work she wanted to feature on the walls of the café. He didn't want to ruin that for her.

He wasn't being a coward by keeping the truth from her a little longer, he told himself. He would tell her, just not yet.

Feeling as if he were carrying the heavy weight of the truth under his shirt, he walked next door to her cottage and knocked on the door.

Spindrift Cottage already looked much nicer than it had when he first arrived in town a few short weeks ago. Potted plants in colorful containers brightened the porch, and the rickety old furniture had received a new coat of white paint that sparkled in the sunlight.

When no one answered at first, he considered knocking again. Just as he lifted his hand, the door opened and Aspen stood on the other side.

She seemed like a different person from the frightened, belligerent young woman they had encountered at the campground. She still had purple hair and tattoos, but her bruises had faded and she seemed lighter somehow, as if she had set down her own burden along the way.

She seemed surprised to see him there. "Oh. Hi. It's you."

"Sorry to disappoint you."

"You didn't. It's fine. A friend is picking me up, and I thought he might be the one at the door. Meredith is almost ready."

"Okay."

"You can come in."

The inside of the cottage was clean, though clearly in the middle of renovation, with the walls bare except one that was half-stripped of wallpaper.

He had an impression of light and color, with bright pillows on the chairs and a blanket thrown over the sofa.

"How are you?" he asked carefully. "No problems with the ex?"

"No. He's gone and he won't be coming back. I told him I would press charges if he did, and he knows I meant it."

"Good for you."

She fiddled with a tassel on one of the pillows. "I feel stupid I was ever in that situation in the first place. I always told myself the first time a guy hit me, I would be gone. It's not as easy as I thought it would be, when we were living the nomad life, moving from town to town and leaving before I had a chance to make friends who might care enough to help me."

He was grateful that Meredith had stepped up to help Aspen. He only wished she had been able to find someone to offer help when *she* had needed it.

Meredith hadn't been living on the fringes of society, like Aspen had, living out of a run-down camp trailer and always on the move. But he suspected she had felt every bit as trapped by her situation.

"I'm glad to see you doing so well," he said, filled with compassion for both women. "Are you off to do something fun tonight?"

When Aspen smiled, her whole face seemed luminous. "My friend Josef and I are going to the gallery walk."

"That's what we're doing too. Maybe we'll see you there."

"Maybe. If Josef ever gets here."

As if on cue, the doorbell rang and Aspen jumped up to open the door for the quiet man who worked at the café. He wore a white shirt and black slacks and gave her a small smile that told Liam he clearly adored Aspen.

At that moment, Meredith walked into the living room. She looked so lovely, she took his breath away.

Her hair was curled, the first time he had seen her wear any hairstyle other than a ponytail since he had been in Cape Sanctuary. She wore a pretty, flowered dress and a sweater the same apricot of the blossoms.

She looked soft and beautiful, and he didn't want to look away.

"Sorry I'm late. I couldn't decide what to wear." She gave a little laugh. "And that's probably the first time that's happened to me in about eighteen months."

Somehow he knew the reason it hadn't happened in so long wasn't because she couldn't choose her clothing but because she hadn't cared what she wore.

He should be flattered, but he only felt the low thrum of unease.

He hated knowing he would hurt her before the night was over. Again, he was tempted to wait for Aspen and Josef to leave and then tell her everything now. It seemed so wrong to withhold information she needed to know.

Not yet. A few more hours.

He forced a smile. "I don't know what the other options were, but you made an excellent choice. You look lovely."

She gave a little laugh. "I didn't tell you that because I was fishing for compliments. I just don't have many nice clothes to choose from. I sold or donated nearly everything when I left Chicago and only kept a few favorites."

"What you're wearing looks perfect," he said.

"You are…very beautiful," Josef said in his accented English. "The two most beautiful women in all of the town. We are lucky men, yes?"

Liam smiled. "Yes. Very lucky."

Aspen only rolled her eyes. "We should probably go. I told Denise we would meet her and her husband at Horizon Art and start there."

She tucked her arm through Josef's, who looked as if all his dreams had just come true.

"Enjoy your evening," Meredith said. "I'm sure we'll bump into you at some point."

"I don't know. There are twenty-seven galleries in town, and they're all part of tonight's gallery walk," Aspen said. "The odds of our paths intersecting aren't all that high."

"We'll look for you, though. Have a good time."

Aspen pulled a fringed shawl over her sundress and the two walked out of the cottage, leaving Liam alone with Meredith.

He wanted to kiss her again.

He ached to pull her into his arms and mess up that expertly applied makeup.

Memories of the kiss they had shared on the trail kept him up at night.

It would be easier to tell himself that guilt at his deception was tangling up his thoughts.

He knew it was more than that.

He was drawn to this woman, as he hadn't been to another in a long time.

As much as he longed to taste her again, touch her again, he couldn't do it. Not with the lies between them.

His lies.

He couldn't kiss her again until she knew the truth about him. Yes, he knew the trouble with that logic. As soon as he told her the truth, she would be furious and want nothing more to do with him.

Any further kisses—or anything else—would be completely off the table.

"Twenty-seven galleries," he said. "I had no idea Cape Sanctuary hosted that kind of a thriving art scene."

She smiled, reaching down to a side table and picking up an elegant clutch only large enough for a cell phone. "Don't worry. We don't have to hit them all. I was thinking maybe five or six. I can't imagine we'll have time to see more than that before your dinner reservations."

"That's a relief. Five or six is a little more manageable."

"Do you mind if we walk? Everything is close, and I think that would be easier than trying to find a parking space at each of the galleries."

"I guess that's why they call it a gallery walk."

She smiled and led the way out of the cottage into the pleasant evening that smelled of flowers, salt spray and regret for all the things he couldn't have.

32

Meredith

Years from now, when she was old and withered and gray, Meredith expected she would remember every detail about the lovely June evening she spent with Liam Byrne.

They ended up making it through six galleries, all fairly close to the restaurant. She loved every single art show they were able to see, from nature photography to graceful sculptures to modern abstracts.

They were all different, yet exciting and fresh. She felt invigorated by the art, the walking and the company.

Now she and Liam sat on the stone patio of the elegant restaurant overlooking the ocean. On this night, only a few weeks away from the longest day of the year, the sun was still setting, sliding into the ocean in a burst of color. They had gorgeous front row seats to nature's own nightly art showing.

The food was delicious, fresh and flavorful. They had each opted for chef's choice sampler menu, a selection of small unique plates, each more flavorful than the one before.

They had tried a salad of shrimp, avocado and mangos, squid ink risotto, phyllo-wrapped halibut with lemon scallion sauce.

She loved every bite, especially sharing them with a man she suddenly realized could easily capture her heart if she let him.

She was the worst kind of hypocrite. She had told her cousin that she should take a chance with Sam Ayala, despite all the obstacles standing in their way.

That was great advice for Tori, but Meredith knew she couldn't take it for herself. She had already let Liam into her mind and heart too far. The man knew things about her that no one else did. If she lowered her defenses completely and let herself truly care for him, as she knew she could, he would leave her devastated.

Anyway, Sam and Tori were a different situation. They at least lived in the same zip code while Liam was leaving town in less than twelve hours.

She likely would never see him again after tonight. The knowledge lent a particular edge of poignancy to the evening.

Liam smiled at her now across the table, the sunset turning his features amber.

"Wow. That was delicious. The hype was spot-on. Too bad I only discovered this place on my last day in town."

"I guess you'll have to come back," she said, trying for a casual tone.

He smiled again. "I'm sure I will. There's something about Cape Sanctuary. I can't put my finger on it. The town seems to welcome you in and make you feel like you're exactly where you need to be."

"Maybe when your book is published, you can come back to town for a signing. I'm sure the local bookstore would love to have you, especially when you let them know you wrote a good portion of the book here. Make sure you mention the Beach End in your author note. It would be fabulous publicity for the café."

He set down his napkin, his jaw suddenly set. "About that," he began.

Before he could finish the thought, a woman whom Meredith had noticed at a nearby table suddenly rose from her seat and headed for them.

She was stylishly dressed, lean to the point of gauntness. When she spoke, she had a Midwestern accent that immediately put Meredith on alert.

"I've been looking at you for a half hour trying to place how I know you. I finally figured it out. You're Meredith Rowland, aren't you?"

Meredith drew in a sharp breath at the unexpected vitriol in the woman's tone, so much worse because she hadn't been expecting it here at the quiet, peaceful stone patio of a northern California restaurant overlooking the ocean.

"Yes," she said, her voice low.

The woman's face turned a blotchy red and her hands curled into fists. "I can't believe you have the nerve to show up here, in a decent restaurant. You're probably dining on the money you and your husband pillaged from people's retirement accounts, aren't you? How dare you."

Meredith felt as if she were shrinking into her chair, disappearing more with every harsh word.

"My sister and her husband lost everything to you and that scum. I'm glad someone killed him in prison. I only wish you had been there right beside him. You're a miserable, pathetic excuse for a human being. You should be ashamed of yourself. And so should anybody willing to be seen in public with you."

"I'm sorry you feel that way," she finally said when the woman started to wind down. What else could she say?

The woman gave her one more hate-filled look, then stomped away, dragging her sheepish-looking companion with her.

Meredith carefully pulled the napkin from her lap and set it on the table as if were radioactive waste.

When she reached for her water glass, she realized her hand was shaking.

"I'm so sorry," she whispered to Liam. "What a horrible ending to what had been a lovely evening."

He narrowed his gaze. "You can't think that was your fault."

She wanted to press a hand to her stomach, to the ache there, but she knew nothing would make it go away.

"He hurt so many people. The ripple effects will go on for years. When people are angry and hurt, they want someone to pay for the harm they have suffered. Unfortunately, the man responsible is dead. I'm the next best thing."

"You shouldn't be. You were not involved in your husband's crimes. It isn't fair that you're being blamed, when you're a victim too."

He looked as if he wanted to go after the woman to set her straight. While Meredith was touched by his concern, that was the last thing she wanted.

"Please. Can we go now?"

After a moment, he nodded reluctantly.

She was still shaky and upset but did her best not to let it show as he took care of the check.

"Are you up for walking home or do you want me to call a ride service?" he asked as they walked outside the restaurant.

Their cottages were about three blocks away from the restaurant. Maybe a walk through the cooling evening would help her calm down.

"I'm fine to walk."

As they made their way past the charming, whimsical stone cottages of this part of town, Meredith could feel some of the tension seep out of her shoulders.

She and Liam walked mostly in silence, though one or the other would point out something they passed, like a mailbox that matched its corresponding house exactly, down to the cables and the trim. Or the house across the street with a wild country garden that exploded with color, even at night, snapdragons and wisteria and climbing roses.

When they were nearly to the cottages on Starfish Beach, he stopped at a small overlook along the road, a grassy area with a bench overlooking the ocean. To her surprise, Liam led her over to it and then sat beside her.

"I need to tell you something, Meredith. Something I should have told you before but the circumstances never felt quite right."

She suddenly felt more anxious than she had when that woman had confronted her in the restaurant. "Okay," she said slowly.

Something told her she did not want to hear what he had to say. That it would change everything between them.

"I haven't told you before now because I know it's going to hurt you. That's the last thing I want to do."

The sun had gone down completely now, though a tiny slice of light still rode the horizon. She could see Liam's silhouette but couldn't make out definition in his features.

"Now you're scaring me. Just tell me."

He let out a long, drawn-out sigh. "I've been lying to you, Meredith."

Everything inside her wanted to jump up from the bench, to run the rest of the way to the cottage, rush inside and lock the door against whatever news he had to impart.

She remained frozen, forcing herself to breathe past the growing dread.

"About…what?"

"I told you I work with numbers. That's completely true." He paused. "I didn't tell you that I work with numbers as an analyst for the FBI, specializing in forensic accounting."

She stared at him, fighting again the urge to press a hand to her stomach and the sudden roiling pain there.

"The… FBI." To her, that meant long hours of questioning, depositions, search warrants that peered into every nook and cranny of her life.

He nodded. "I work out of the Los Angeles office. Last week when I had to leave town, I was called to testify in a case I've been working for more than a year, a money laundering case against an attorney for one of the Mexican cartels. I wasn't supposed to testify until next week, but the schedule was rearranged."

She couldn't seem to make sense of things, as if someone had taken a shelf full of jigsaw puzzles, dumped them on the floor and expected her to put the pieces back in the correct boxes.

"But...you're still writing a book, aren't you?"

He again sighed, a sound of regret an apology.

"There is no book," he said slowly. "I lied to you about that too. I used that as an excuse to explain why I was here."

"And why were you here?"

She knew, though. Even before he said the words, she knew.

"I came to Cape Sanctuary because you were here. I came hoping to get information that might lead to the missing funds Carter stole."

A hot wave of betrayal and hurt and shock washed over her then, slick and greasy. She covered her mouth to keep from retching.

"You...you've been lying this whole time. Everything. Everything is a lie."

His shoulders were taut. "Yes. I'm sorry."

"I was told I was no longer being investigated." Her voice came out small, thready.

"Officially, no. The case against you is closed. The task force leading the formal investigation has concluded you were not involved in Rowland's scheme."

She tried to pick up a few more pieces. "So why are you here?"

"I'm not part of the official investigation. My visit here has been completely unsanctioned."

"Why?" she asked again. The corrosive betrayal seemed to eat away at everything that had been bright and good in her world this week, casting dark, sinister shadows instead.

He had come here alone, without FBI resources, to investigate her.

"It's a long story. I told you my mother was a teacher. I didn't tell you she works for a small private school outside Chicago that was ill-advised enough to invest their employees' entire 401(k) plans and retirement pension accounts with Carter Rowland. My mom lost everything."

Meredith closed her eyes. He had spoken in such glowing terms about his mother, a September 11 widow who had rebuilt her life to take care of her children, who lovingly cared for a son with special needs. Who had delayed the retirement she had been planning and now continued to work despite her own health challenges.

Because of Carter, Meredith realized. Because her lying, cheating, greedy bastard of a husband thought he was entitled to steal from Liam's mother and so many others.

This would never end. No matter how far she fled from Chicago, how hard she worked to rebuild herself, the ripple effects of what Carter had done would go on the rest of her life.

"I'm...sorry," she said.

He made an impatient noise. "You need to stop apologizing for what he did. It's not your fault. I'll admit, for a time I wasn't sure. I thought you had to be involved, that you had completely snowballed the task force. That's the reason I came here, a desperate effort to somehow insert myself into your life and persuade you to tell me everything you might know that might lead to the missing funds."

"You were working undercover, all this time."

"Not officially. Again, this was not an agency-sanctioned op. They wouldn't let me near the investigation because of my family connection. That was the reason I first came to Cape Sanctuary. I was desperate, for my mom's sake. Not only hers. Patrick too. She put my father's life insurance proceeds into a trust for him that was also managed by Rowland."

Patrick, his sweet brother who remembered obscure Chicago Cubs statistics and had a girlfriend and read esoteric library books.

She felt like she was going to be sick again.

"You should have told me from the beginning. I could have saved you a lot of time and bother. I can't help you. As I've told the other investigators, if I had any idea where Carter hid the money, I would tell you."

"I understand that now. I didn't when I first came to town, before I met you and spent time with you."

She had sudden flashes of memory, of him coming daily to the restaurant, ordering coffee and pretending to work on his laptop. Of him helping her paint the café and being so kind to her, walking her home and teasing her and bringing her slowly back to life.

Of him kissing her with an aching tenderness that made her want to cry all over again.

She had told him everything. This man knew more about her life than anyone else on earth, the true ugliness behind the closed doors of her marriage.

About her miscarriages, her stillbirth. Everything.

She had shared her deepest secrets and the entire time, he had pretended to care.

She had been falling in love with him.

Good Lord, she had atrocious taste in men. The first man she ever loved had been an abuser and a con man.

The second, this man she had let herself begin to care for over the past few weeks, was only feigning interest in her in hopes she could lead him to the ransacked funds stolen by her ex.

She would find it all hysterical, if it weren't so painfully tragic.

"You're telling me you went rogue from the Federal Bureau of Investigation and decided to launch your own undercover op? Do you really expect me to believe nobody there knew what you were doing?"

"They do now. When I went back to LA last week, I confessed

everything to the special agent in charge of my division." He paused. "She wanted me to continue with what I was doing. To dig harder, push you more. I refused. I told her I believe completely that you have no knowledge of your husband's activities."

"Am I supposed to give you a medal for that?"

She rose from the bench, unable to be close to him another second.

He followed her as she walked toward Spindrift Cottage, desperate for the refuge she had started to create there.

"I'm sorry, Meredith," Liam said, following at her heels. "I wish I had been honest with you from the very beginning about who I was and why I was here. I especially should have told you the truth after we went hiking, when you told me about your life with Carter."

It would never be over, she thought again. No matter how hard she tried to reinvent herself, to become someone new and better, she would forever be trapped by the decision she had made when she was twenty-two years old, to fall in love with the wrong man.

Tears threatened and she willed them away. Not yet. Once she reached Spindrift Cottage, she could give in to the hurt and humiliation and betrayal tangling through her.

She dug her nails into her palms. "I suppose I should thank you for finally telling me the truth, right before you leave town," she said when she finally reached the bottom step to her porch, what felt like twenty years later. "I'm sure your conscience feels better now. But that wasn't for me, was it? That was all for you. I would have been much better off if you had merrily driven away tomorrow and gone back to your life in LA without telling me that one more person I… I cared about has lied to me."

She didn't wait for him to answer. She simply hurried up the stairs, let herself into her cottage and locked the door behind her.

After making sure the curtains were closed, she sank onto the couch, buried her face in her hands and wept.

33

Tori

Why did she suddenly feel like the whole world was partying except for her?

Tori sighed as she waged her constant battle against sand in the cottage and finished sweeping off her porch.

When Cape Sanctuary hosted its monthly gallery walk, she usually tried to make the rounds with Em or with a friend, if only for the free drinks and appetizers and the chance to dress up and socialize outside of the people she talked to on the regular at the café.

She had completely forgotten there was a walk that night. By the time Meredith and Aspen had reminded her of the event earlier at the café and she reached out to a few of her friends, it was too late. They all had other plans.

Em and Cristina had gone to the big bash at their friend Sierra's house, and Sam was working. Not that she had asked but Cristina had offered the info when Tori had dropped the girls off at the party.

She could have gone to the gallery walk by herself. It probably would have been easy enough for her to bump into a friend or two and ask to tag along with them. Or she could always have attended alone. She was a strong, independent woman. She had no problem going to social occasions by herself.

Instead, she decided to stay home and catch up on laundry and housework while listening to a couple of her favorite podcasts. The exciting life of a single mom.

Friday nights made her wish she still had a significant other, if only to take advantage of the ready-made date night opportunities like the Cape Sanctuary Gallery Walk.

Okay, there were other times she longed to have someone in her life. She missed the little things about being married. Having someone to share all the highs and lows of life with. A shoulder rub when she was working at her laptop. Cuddling up on the sofa and watching a movie together.

"If I need to cuddle someone, I guess I always have you," she said to Shark. Em's weird-looking chi-poo rose from his spot on the rug by the front door, did a funky little dance around in a circle, and then settled back down.

She had just finished sweeping the porch and was shaking the sand off the broom into the grass—for it to all be trailed back in again—when Shark lifted his head, gazing intently down the road toward town.

If she hadn't already been out on her porch with her broom in hand, she never would have seen Meredith walking back to Spindrift Cottage with the sexy writer.

Tori picked up Shark and eased back into the dark corner, into her favorite chair. She wasn't spying, she told herself. She simply didn't want Meredith and Liam to see what a solitary loser she was on a Friday night when everyone else seemed to be out having fun.

They were arguing, she realized as they walked past. No voices were raised, but she could tell by the tones and the tension that rolled off them in waves.

Meredith walked a few steps ahead, and she could hear snatches of their conversation on the sea breeze.

I'm sorry.

Should have told you.

Lied to me.

A moment later, she heard Meredith's door shut. She didn't slam it, but the finality still echoed through the night.

She waited for Liam to go next door to his own cottage. In the glow from his porchlight, she saw him walk up the steps and unlock the door. He didn't go inside, though. He finally sank onto the rocking chair there, the one that had been Frances's favorite, and raked a hand through his hair.

This was odd. What could they be fighting about? Tori was wildly curious. She wanted to traipse over there and ask him but also didn't want to be the nosy landlord.

After a moment, he rose and turned to go inside the cottage, looking suddenly weary.

Tori always hated when people had tiffs in the café, mainly because she couldn't know the whole story or who she should root for just by eavesdropping on snippets of conversation.

What did it matter why Liam and Meredith were fighting? Liam was leaving the next day. She couldn't extend his stay even if she wanted to now since the cottage had booked rapidly once he told her he was leaving. It was booked every day until Labor Day.

She still wasn't thrilled about renting out Frances's cottage. It seemed odd somehow to see someone else staying at her grandmother's house, sitting in her rocking chair. Whenever she thought how strange it was, she reminded herself she was saving every penny from the vacation rentals for Em's education.

In her arms, Shark seemed restless. She set him down and he pranced to the edge of the porch, then looked back at her expectantly.

She sighed. "I just took you for a walk an hour ago. Do you seriously need another one?"

The dog continued to stare at her. Amazing how with one

look he could so clearly communicate *You know what to do, human. Grab my leash and the bags and let's do this.*

"Fine. I could use another walk anyway," she muttered. A moment later, she attached his harness and leash and grabbed the poop bags, then headed down toward the grassy spot where Shark liked to do his business.

Fortunately, he was quick and a few moments later she headed back to the cottage. On impulse she decided to walk a few extra steps and go past Spindrift Cottage.

She wasn't being nosy, she told herself. Just concerned.

And, okay, a little nosy.

The windows and blinds were closed, but she thought she heard the sound of someone crying inside.

None of your business, Tori told herself.

But she had a sudden random memory of her first heartbreak when she was fifteen, when her first boyfriend Luke Donahue had dumped her for a ditzy cheerleader with big teeth and bigger boobs.

Meredith had stayed on the phone with her for six hours straight that night, consoling her, commiserating, making her laugh when she was certain her life was over.

She should check it out. Make sure Meredith was okay. It was the decent thing to do, what Frances would have wanted.

After waffling a moment more, she drew in her courage and marched up the steps. This was a mercy mission. That's all.

She knocked softly. "Meredith? Is everything okay? It's Tori."

Silence greeted her for several moments. She was debating whether to knock again or leave Meredith to her misery when the door finally opened and her cousin's pale face peered through. The dim glow from the porch light didn't hide her splotchy skin or red eyes.

"Uh-oh. Is it that bad?"

Meredith let out a tiny mewl, like a kitten whose tail had been stepped on, then looked ashamed that she had made the sound.

Tori sighed. She had to do something. Driven by habit ingrained from the years when they were as close as sisters, she closed the door behind her and stepped forward, opening her arms.

Meredith looked at her for a shocked moment, as if she didn't quite know how to react. And then she sagged against Tori, shaking with sobs.

Not the way she would have chosen to spend her Friday night, she thought as she held her weeping cousin. Next time she would definitely make plans in advance.

Still, she had to hope she was offering a little bit of comfort.

"What did he do?" she finally said.

"It's not only... Liam." Meredith choked out the words. "There was a...a lady at the restaurant. She was so angry at me. If Liam hadn't been there, I think she would have sp-spit in my food."

"Why? What did you do?"

Meredith seemed to compose herself a little. She worked to get her tears under control and wiped at her nose with a paper towel.

"I married Carter Rowland," she said, her voice small. "Family members of the lady at the restaurant invested with him and lost their life savings."

Tori had no answer to offer. What could she say?

"I thought I would be safe here. This was always my haven. My literal sanctuary. But it doesn't matter where I go, what I do. My past will always be around my neck. I could move to Zanzibar, change my name and sell homemade jewelry on the beach and people would still find me and blame me for what my b-bastard ex-husband did."

Tori blinked. She rarely heard Meredith swear. All told, that was a pretty mild pejorative for Carter Rowland. Tori could give her a few better names.

"Was selling jewelry on the beach in Zanzibar ever an option?"

"Doubtful," Meredith admitted with a small, watery laugh. "I couldn't have afforded the cost of a plane ticket."

"Explain something to me. You had money before you married Carter. Your dad was loaded, and you must have inherited some when he died. Why are you so broke?"

Meredith was quiet. To Tori's relief, she seemed to be regaining her composure, inch by inch. "I ended up selling everything after Carter was arrested. I put it all back into the victims' compensation fund."

Tori stared at her cousin's lowered head. In that moment, she knew. Frances had been right to defend Meredith. She should have trusted her grandmother, who was always an excellent judge of character.

"You didn't know anything about what Carter was doing, did you?"

Meredith met her gaze briefly, then looked away. "It doesn't matter whether I knew or not. But no. I didn't have any idea. He didn't tell me anything. If I had known, I would have tried to stop it somehow. I was beyond caring what he did to me."

What had he done to her?

The implications seemed to hit her all at once and she frowned, remembering something else Frances once had said to her.

Meredith is dealing with things you can't possibly understand. She needs our support and our love, not our condemnation.

She could remember being so angry at her grandmother for the blind spot she always had toward Meredith. Now Tori felt a little light-headed as she tried to reassess everything she thought she knew.

They had so much to unpack between them, but something told her this wasn't the time for them to dig into the ancient past, when Meredith was dealing with something else that had only happened hours ago.

"What did Liam do to upset you so much?"

Meredith gripped the paper towel.

"He's not a writer. He lied to me. To everyone."

She thought of Liam coming day after day to the café, working away at his laptop. "Why is he here, then?"

Meredith sniffled a little. "He works for the FBI. He's an analyst in forensic accounting. Apparently, he started his own rogue operation, going undercover in hopes of persuading me to reveal all my secrets and tell him where Carter hid the missing funds."

Wow. Double wow. Talk about betrayals. No wonder Meredith was so upset.

"I'm sorry. That stinks."

"I told him...so much about my life. Everything. Things I haven't told anyone else. I can't believe I could be so foolish. I trusted him. And these days, I don't trust anyone. I thought I was starting to care about him."

Meredith started to cry again, softly this time. She sank down into a chair and to Tori's surprise, Shark, the little beast, trotted over to her and jumped into her lap.

After a startled moment, Meredith cuddled the dog to her chest, sniffled a few times and then seemed to calm.

"What can I do? Do you want me to march over there right now and tell him to get the hell out of Frances's cottage?"

Meredith gave a watery laugh. "He's leaving first thing in the morning anyway. I don't think there's anything either of us can do. It's over. Now I need to figure out how to move on."

"You could always save up for a plane ticket to your backup plan. I hear Zanzibar is gorgeous."

As she had hoped, Meredith smiled slightly. "I think I'll stay right here, thanks. Cape Sanctuary is exactly what I need right now."

Tori's phone rang before she could answer. Nobody called her these days. Em could text all day and all night, but she hated talking on the phone.

She looked down and was startled to see Sam's number on the caller ID.

She stared at it for a long moment, then with an odd sense of foreboding, she picked it up.

In the background, she thought she heard sirens and people yelling.

"Hey, Tori. It's Sam," he said, unnecessarily. "Is somebody there with you?"

She frowned. "Yes. Meredith. Why?"

He paused for about two seconds, long enough for fear to spurt through her. "Good. I don't want you to panic. I'm glad someone's there. I wanted you to know as soon as possible. The girls have been in an accident."

She rose without really being aware of it, the blood rushing from her face. "Where? What kind of accident?"

"A car accident. Up on the Cliff Road."

"That's impossible. They weren't going anywhere. I dropped them off at Sierra's party. I'm picking them up in an hour."

"They left the party and met up with some older boys, apparently. One had a license, even though he's only sixteen and wasn't supposed to be transporting anybody else. He was speeding around a bend and lost control and the car rolled."

She couldn't think, couldn't move. This couldn't be real. People died on the Cliff Road. Every year, someone took a turn too fast and rolled into the water.

Not Em. Not Em. Not Em.

The ocean had already taken Javi from her. It couldn't take their daughter too.

"Don't panic, Tori. I know it sounds bad, but right now everyone is okay. I've talked to everyone in the car and they're okay. Panicked but okay. They've got some minor injuries. Broken bones and so forth. Right now, we're focused on getting them out safely. It's a little complicated but we're working on it."

"This can't be happening. There has to be a mistake. Are you sure it's them?"

"There's no mistake, Tor. I have to go. Now I need you to

be calm and meet us at the hospital. Have Meredith drive you. We'll get them out safely, I swear it."

He disconnected the call, leaving her bereft and terrified. She inhaled sharply, panic beating through her with barb-tipped wings.

"What is it?" Meredith asked, features concerned.

"I've got to go to the hospital. There's been an accident. I have to…"

The panic gripped tighter and she felt frozen, until she felt Meredith's arms around her, offering comfort to her now in an abrupt reversal.

"I'll drive you to the hospital. Let's take Shark back to your house and grab what you need there. You probably want a phone charger and your purse. Do you have insurance info?"

She didn't know how to answer.

Not Em. Not Em. Not Em.

To her vast relief, Meredith took charge, and Tori, not knowing what else to do, followed her out the door.

34

Meredith

Nothing like a potentially life-threatening emergency to put her problems into perspective.

As Meredith helped Tori gather things she might need while at the hospital, her own confrontation with Liam seemed miles away. It was still there, still raw, but right now she had more important things to worry about.

She would have time later to give in to her vast sense of betrayal. For now, she had to focus on helping Tori and Emilia.

The regional hospital in Cape Sanctuary was a modern facility with gleaming windows and pale brick.

Meredith pulled up to the emergency room parking. Before her rattletrap sedan came to a complete stop, Tori jumped out and raced for the entrance.

Meredith finished parking and followed her in as quickly as she could manage, arriving in time to hear Tori speaking impatiently to a woman behind the reception desk.

"I know she's not a patient yet. She will be. She's on her way in. My brother-in-law is a police officer and he's at the scene. He called and told me to meet the ambulance here."

"Oh, was she involved in that rollover up on Cliff Road?" the young woman asked.

Tori nodded, looking vaguely queasy. "That's the one."

"It's been all over the news for the past ten minutes or so. Apparently, somebody is broadcasting live from the scene and the rescue has gone viral."

She pointed to a television in the waiting area. Meredith looked up and saw a horrendous scene. Flashing lights, emergency vehicles and a mangled car teetering on the edge of a guardrail, ready to plunge over the side at any moment.

A little crawler across the bottom read Live from Cape Sanctuary, and she heard something about a dramatic rescue in progress.

"Turn it off," Meredith commanded sharply. She wasn't great at being assertive, but in this case, someone had to be. "Right now. Turn it off!"

"No," Tori said, following her gaze, eyes huge. "That's my baby in there!"

"You can't watch this, Tori. Let's wait somewhere else."

"I have to. I have to. That's my baby."

Her cousin moved closer to the screen, eyes wide. On the screen, all the emergency workers seemed to be standing in a half-circle, watching a figure lying on his back as he worked his way under the teetering body of the vehicle with the end of a towrope. The other end was already hooked to a huge fire truck that had a winch attached.

"He lied. Sam lied!" Tori exclaimed, hands covering her mouth. "He said they were safe. They're not safe. They could plunge over the cliff at any minute."

Meredith couldn't look away. "No. They're safe. Look closer. They're not going to plunge over the cliff. That guy is putting a towrope on the car. They're going to tow it off the railing."

"What if the girls fall out? What if the towrope slips?"

"They won't. It won't."

Tori reached out blindly, and Meredith gripped her trembling fingers. Both of them watched, barely breathing, as the rescuer attached the end of the tow to something on the underside of the vehicle.

Watching this scene play out on live television was excruciating. Soon, a small crowd had gathered around the TV in the emergency room waiting area, watching as the rescuer slid back along the gravel, spider crawling away until he was clear of the vehicle.

Slowly, painstakingly slowly, the fire truck began pulling the car away from the edge. They all gasped in unison when the winch seemed to stall and the car lurched back again toward certain disaster, but after a few seconds, the vehicle again began moving toward safety.

Whoever was holding the camera zoomed in to show frightened and bleeding faces peering out of the vehicle before they panned away again.

When the car was finally several feet away from the edge and rescuers swarmed in to get the teens out of the car, the entire emergency room erupted into cheers.

Tori stared, her expression somewhere beyond shocked, bordering on sheer panic.

"Sit down, Tori," Meredith urged her cousin, who seemed to be swaying on her feet. "You need to sit down or you're going to fall over. What help will you be to Emilia if you're in the ER yourself with a concussion from passing out and hitting your head on the way down?"

Tori looked at her with a numb expression but finally sank into one of the waiting room chairs, her gaze still fixed to the screen.

"There you are, folks." A perky blond anchor spoke up as the broadcast cut away from the dramatic scene. "You saw it live first here on Channel 6. Looks like a happy ending for four teenagers in Cape Sanctuary who literally ended the school year with a cliff-hanger they won't soon forget."

Meredith rolled her eyes at the avaricious inanity of some news stations. As she knew only too well, some at the station were probably sorry the car hadn't gone over the edge into the water far below.

Sure, several teenagers might die, but think of the ratings.

They had been watching the live feed for no more than four or five minutes, but it felt like an eternity. She could only imagine how much worse it must be for Tori, whose daughter's life was at stake.

Tori was still clutching her hand so tightly Meredith might have worried about the circulation if she wasn't so determined not to let go.

She would rather be teetering on the edge of that guardrail herself than to let her cousin down when Tori needed her.

"I wish you hadn't watched that," Meredith said after a moment.

"I had to. That's my baby. If you had a child yourself, you would understand."

Meredith felt a familiar ache in her chest, one she had almost grown used to over the years. She had lost three children. One, after she had felt her move around inside her and had come to love with all her heart.

If she had carried her first pregnancy to term, her son would have been the age of the boy she could see across the waiting room, playing on a tablet.

She pushed away her grief as the waiting room numbers suddenly swelled with an influx of people.

The woman they had first met behind the reception desk hurried toward them, a clipboard in hand. "Mrs. Ayala? They're bringing in the ambulance now with your daughter. She was the first one to be extricated from the vehicle and transported. She should be here in five minutes or so. The others aren't far behind."

"Thank you."

"As soon as the ambulance arrives, I'll come and take you back to her."

"Thank you."

After the woman walked away again, Tori looked over at Meredith. "You don't have to stay. I can catch a ride with someone or call a taxi."

"I'm here," she said firmly. "I'm not going anywhere."

Tori nodded, gratitude meshing with the fear on her expression. She gripped Meredith's hand more tightly in hers.

"I'm glad you're here," she said.

Her voice rang with so much sincerity, Meredith had to believe her.

"So am I," she answered. "This is exactly where I need to be."

They sat in silence for another few moments, in the strange time warp of hospitals, until the receptionist approached again. "The ambulance is almost here. Follow me and I'll take you back to the trauma room."

Meredith and Tori rose together. The woman gave Meredith a curious look. "I'm sorry. Only immediate family is allowed."

"Meredith is family," Tori said firmly, still gripping her hand.

Meredith followed her, feeling as if they weren't only crossing the emergency room waiting area, they were bridging the deep chasm that had been between them for years.

35

Tori

There was no hell more acute for a mother than seeing her child in pain and not being able to do anything to make it better.

Twenty minutes after the ambulance arrived, Tori sat beside a pale, frightened Em in the treatment room gurney, clutching her hand and murmuring soft reassurances that were mostly meaningless.

Meredith was sitting in the corner, where she had retreated as soon as Em had been wheeled in, with doctors and nurses bustling around her. Tori supposed she could have tried to send her home again, but Meredith's presence was calming, in a way Tori couldn't have explained.

Em whimpered and shifted on the hospital bed to find a better position. The girl was a mess. She was covered in blood, her features bruised and swollen. She had two black eyes, a broken nose, shattered wrist and a likely concussion.

Still, she was alert and conscious. The first thing she had done when she spotted Tori was burst into tears, though Tori could tell they weren't tears of pain. These were tears of guilt and regret. She was familiar with them, because she had cried plenty of her own over the years.

"I'm so sorry, Mom. I'm so sorry I lied and we went with Hunter and Nick when we told you we would only be at Sierra's house. I'm so sorry. When I thought we were going to die, all I could think was how mad you were going to be that I lied to you and left the party and I lied to Sierra's parents too and said you were picking us up."

Tori wanted to say she hoped Em learned her lesson and that maybe having to have reconstructive surgery on her nose and wear a cast on her wrist all summer would be enough of a reminder. The words hovered right there, but she swallowed them down, knowing now wasn't the time to twist that particular knife.

"You didn't die. You're here and you're okay."

She was so very grateful, only too aware what a close call the teens had survived.

She remembered the precise moment when she had realized the identity of the rescuer crawling through gravel and dirt, risking his own life to attach the towrope to the vehicle.

Sam.

She had known in that moment that the girls would be okay. He would make sure of it.

He was there, somewhere nearby. She hadn't seen him, though she had heard his voice in a nearby room. The treatment rooms in the ER were small and fairly close together. She couldn't hear words, but she could definitely pick up the timbre of his voice.

She wanted to go to him and wrap her arms around him to thank him for helping to save their girls. Right now, though, she needed to be here for her child.

Em looked over at the corner. "When we first got here, I thought maybe I was hallucinating from the drugs they gave me in the ambulance. But that is Cousin Meredith, right? Why is she here?"

Meredith smiled in that calming way Tori was coming to deeply appreciate.

"She gave me a ride to the hospital after Sam called to let me know what was happening to you."

Sam hadn't told her the full truth. She would have to have a word with him about that. He hadn't told her the girls were still at grave risk, that they weren't yet safely on solid ground.

"Hi, Emilia," Meredith said. "I'm so glad you're okay."

"Hi." Em looked between the two of them out of her swollen eyes. "Are you guys talking again?"

Tori thought of Meredith's revelations earlier in the evening, what felt like a million years ago. Her cousin needed her. They were family. More than that, they were friends. The embers of the bond they had once shared were still burning; they only needed to be fanned into a full-fledged flame.

"Yes. I guess we are. We still have a ways to go, but things are…better."

Em smiled. "I'm glad."

She closed her eyes and seemed to drift off again as a nurse came in to monitor her condition.

"Is she okay?" Tori asked in a low voice. Em had never been one for napping. During her difficult toddler years, Tori or Javi used to have to drive her around every afternoon so she would drift off.

"She's sleeping. That's not unusual, with the medication going into her IV. We're waiting for the orthopedic surgeon and the plastic surgeon to consult about who gets first dibs. Either way, she's going to be our guest at least overnight. Somebody will be operating tomorrow."

Em had rarely even been sick with a cold. She was now facing multiple surgeries and reconstructive surgery on her nose. Cristina was in a similar state.

"Thank you."

"Can I get you anything?" Meredith asked after the nurse left again. "Coffee? A soda? A snack from the cafeteria? You might be in for a long night."

Tori shook her head. "I'm okay for now. I don't think I could eat anything. But thanks."

"Okay. Let me know if you change your mind."

"You really don't have to stay all night, especially after the rough evening you had. You look like you're ready to fall asleep too."

"I don't feel right about leaving you without a ride."

"I'll be fine. The Ayalas will be descending on the hospital soon, I'm sure. Someone can drop me off at the cottage if I need something."

"Okay. I'll get out of the way. But call me if you need me, okay?"

"I will," she said, and meant it.

"Can I take care of Shark for you? Will he do okay at my cottage?"

She hadn't even given Em's dog a second thought. "That would be great. Thanks for thinking of it. There's a key under the pink flowerpot on the back patio."

"Got it."

Meredith reached out and hugged her. It was awkward, framed by the years of discord between them. But that only made it that much more sweet.

After Meredith left, Tori felt restless, on edge. Em was sleeping soundly, so she left to use the restroom out in the hall.

As she was returning, the door to the room next to them opened and a nurse exited. Behind the woman, Tori could see Sam sitting beside Cristina's bed. He looked completely exhausted, hair messy and a smear of blood on the sleeve of his blue shirt.

On impulse, she turned into that room first. Em was still sleeping. If she awoke and needed something, she could push the nurse call button. This would only take a minute, Tori thought.

Cristina was sleeping as well, she saw. She looked small and fragile against the white pillows.

The instant Sam spotted her, his eyes lit up. He rose, arms open and she sank into them, trying not to cry at the vast relief bubbling up in her. It felt so good to hold him, to lean on each other for support.

"How is she?" Tori murmured against his chest. "I was just coming to check."

"Sore. Sleeping. She's got a broken foot and collarbone and a bunch of cuts and scrapes. They're setting the foot tonight, and she'll have to wear a brace for the collarbone. She'll be okay, though. How's Em?"

"Broken nose and wrist. She's going to need a couple of surgeries. What about the boys who were in the car? Do you know anything about how they're doing?"

His muscles seemed to tense. "Better than they should be. One has a concussion, the other a couple of broken ribs. The driver is in big trouble with the law and worse with me. What were two sixteen-year-old football players doing with a couple of thirteen-year-old girls? They all could have been killed."

"They weren't, though. You saved them. I saw the footage. That was you hooking up the cable, wasn't it? Even though you could have been crushed if the car had moved in the wrong direction."

He made a face. "Damn cameras. You can't get away from them these days."

"You risked your life. I can never thank you enough."

"It was a team effort. I just happened to be the guy who volunteered to crawl under the car."

"I have never been so scared. I thought for sure they were going to tumble over the edge and take you with them."

The tears she had been holding back began to seep out against her will. He murmured her name and pulled her back into his arms. They stood that way for a long time. Long enough for Tori to realize she had been hiding the truth from herself for a long time.

She was in love with Sam.

She certainly could have found a more convenient time to figure that out than right now when they were both in the middle of a crisis.

She still didn't know what she could do about it, but at least she could start by being honest with herself.

"I should get back next door. I just heard your voice and wanted to check on Cristina. And you."

He hugged her again, and she could almost swear she felt his lips press against her the top of her head, but he released her before she could be certain.

"Keep me posted if Em goes into surgery tonight. Cristina will want an update."

"Same. I wouldn't be surprised if they asked to share a room at some point."

His smile warmed all the cold, frightened places still lurking inside her.

36

Liam

He would miss this.

Even at midnight in the pitch darkness, the deck of Seafoam Cottage had become one of his favorite places on earth.

Liam listened to the waves brushing the sand, an owl hooting somewhere to the east, the breeze murmuring in the treetops.

He loved Cape Sanctuary and figured he would be completely at peace right now if he weren't still filled with guilt at his deception and worry for Meredith.

She wasn't home. Her car wasn't parked out front. She and her cousin had raced away several hours earlier, and Liam hadn't seen her return.

Josef had walked Aspen home about an hour ago. After he left, the lights at the cottage next door had been on for maybe twenty minutes before everything went dark again. Still, Meredith hadn't returned.

His imagination was running wild, wondering where she might have gone with Tori.

"Where is she?" he asked Jasper, who gave an unconcerned snuffle and rolled over to his other side.

"Some help you are," Liam muttered.

Had something happened to her? To her cousin? What other reason would they have for rushing away so quickly?

Why the sense of urgency?

Maybe they decided to go gambling at Lake Tahoe. Or they had a friend who broke down and needed a ride.

None of the random scenarios he came up with made sense. Meredith and Tori barely talked. Why would they have driven off together so abruptly late on a Friday night?

It was none of his business, he reminded himself. *She* was none of his business. He was leaving town in a few hours and would likely never come this way again.

He was packed and ready to go at first light, but he knew he wouldn't be able to sleep, filled with unease and no small amount of guilt.

He had handled this entire situation wrong, from beginning to end. What arrogance on his part, what sheer unvarnished gall.

A task force made up of highly skilled agents from multiple agencies had spent two years investigating Meredith and her dealings with her husband.

Still, he had been arrogant enough to think he could solve the mystery of the missing money. That he could waltz in and fix everything for his mother and the others who had lost money in Rowland's shoddy investments.

The idea had been ridiculous to begin with. What had he been thinking?

Simple enough. He hadn't been. He had been so blinded by his own anger and frustration that his mother and so many others had been conned, that innocent people were suffering.

Like the angry woman in the restaurant that evening, he had been looking for a scapegoat. And like her, he had also landed on Meredith.

He had been so convinced she knew more than she was telling anyone. How ridiculous, in hindsight. He hadn't known her at all. If he had simply gone to Meredith and told her who he was, what he did, how his loved ones had been impacted by her husband's financial crimes, she probably would have helped him.

They could have sat down together, and he could have picked through her brain and worked out a joint lifestyle analysis that might have revealed some hidden clue leading straight to the missing funds.

Instead, he had held on to the erroneous belief that he unilaterally had the power to make things right.

He had wasted time and money on a fruitless effort. Worse than that, he had hurt and betrayed a woman who had already been through enough.

He was still castigating himself when he suddenly heard a car pull down the road, and a moment later he saw her old sedan park in front of her cottage.

Instead of going inside, though, she walked past his cottage, moved around behind Tori's, then unlocked the back door. A moment later, a light went on inside and he heard Tori's little dog yipping at her.

Jasper did wake up for that excitement. When Meredith walked across the beach path toward her own cottage, Liam walked out to intercept her.

The little dog yipped ferociously at him and Meredith stiffened, whirling around.

"It's me. Liam," he said before he reached her. She carried pepper spray on her key chain, he had observed one day at the café. He didn't really feel like having to wash out his eyes for an hour before he took off back to LA.

Jasper ambled forward and started sniffing the other dog, who stopped yipping so he could circle around the bigger dog.

"You scared the life out of me. What are you doing out here? It's after midnight."

"I was worried about you," he admitted. "I saw you and your cousin rush out a few hours ago. Is everything okay?"

She continued walking toward her cottage, and he took a

chance and followed her. She didn't look very pleased, and it suddenly occurred to him that she might still decide to pepper spray him, even knowing his identity.

He would probably deserve it for what he had done to her.

"No. Everything is not okay," she answered, voice taut. "In one evening, I've been yelled at by a stranger, found out someone I considered a friend had been lying to me since the moment we met and learned Tori's daughter was in a potentially fatal car accident."

His attention caught on the last part of her list. He pictured the girl, dark-haired and pretty, brimming over with life.

"Oh no. I'm so sorry. Will she be okay?"

Meredith released a heavy breath. "She has a couple of broken bones and plenty of bruises. But she's alive."

"What happened? Do they know yet?"

"She and her cousin sneaked out of a party at a friend's house and apparently went off with some older boys. The car they were in rolled and nearly went off the cliff, until rescuers were able to pull it back to safety."

He had seen a bunch of flashing lights on the cliffs across town and had wondered what had happened.

"I'm so sorry. How terrifying for everyone involved."

"The video rescue has gone viral. If you search for *cliff rescue*, you can probably find it."

Why would he want to look at other people's misfortunes when his own life felt like one giant train wreck right now?

"I drove Tori to the hospital. With the state she was in, I didn't want her to wind up in an accident herself."

She seemed so tired, so disheartened. He hated knowing he played a big part in that.

"I'm so sorry," he said again. "Is there anything I can do?"

She gave him a long look. "I think you've done enough, Liam. Don't you?"

He sighed. "I'm sorry about that too. I've been sitting out

here thinking how I messed this whole thing up, from beginning to end."

She gripped the little dog's leash. "What do you want me to say? That everything is fine, all is forgiven, and now you can go on your merry way back to Los Angeles without giving me a second thought?"

That wasn't likely to happen. He hadn't stopped thinking about Meredith since the day he met her.

"You have every right to be furious. I know you must hate me and I can't blame you."

"I don't hate you." The sea breeze played with her hair, twisting it across her features, and she tucked a strand behind her ear. "You were trying to help your mother and all those other people who lost their savings. I understand."

"I was an overconfident, egotistical jerk. I've been on a roll the past few years, able to break several really big cases for the FBI and the Los Angeles County District Attorney's Office when I temporarily worked with them. When the task force closed the investigation into Carter after his death without finding the missing funds, I couldn't let it rest. I thought I could succeed where everyone else had failed."

"You must be stubborn to be so good at your job."

That was his superpower. When he was on the scent of something that smelled wrong, he couldn't rest until he had tracked it down. He could pick at something for days, coming at it from a dozen different directions until he found the one weak spot that let him in and revealed the truth.

"You say stubborn, my family says bullheaded. I suppose on some level, I've convinced myself that while I may not run into burning buildings like my father did, I can still be a hero. I wanted to swoop in and save the day for all those desperate people."

She looked sad, suddenly, and so weary it was a wonder she was still standing.

"I'm sorry I couldn't help make that happen for you."

"I'll say it again. You have nothing to apologize for, Meredith. Nothing. I am the one completely in the wrong here. I wanted to help my mother regain all she had set aside to protect her and Patrick's future. I didn't really care who I hurt in the process. I'm very sorry."

"Thank you for that."

He couldn't tell if she truly accepted his apology or not. He hoped so, but either way he had expressed what was in his heart.

He took a chance and stepped closer to her. "I didn't want to leave without telling you something else."

In the moonlight, he saw wariness creep over her expression like the morning mist coming off the water.

"What's that?"

"I came to Cape Sanctuary determined to despise you almost as much as I hated your husband. After only a few days in your company, I came to see how very wrong I was. You're nothing like him. You're a good, decent, kind person. You work hard to bring light and joy to those around you. You're humble enough to work busing tables at the café when you're part owner and could surely have a role in management if you wanted."

"Except I still know nothing about running a café. I would probably bankrupt the place in a matter of days."

"The point is, you have a huge heart. I'm amazed that even after everything you've lost, everything you've endured, you still have so much capacity for love."

She made a sound somewhere between a laugh and a sob. He took a chance and pulled her into an embrace. He thought she might push him away. Instead, after a moment, she slid her arms around his waist and held on while the dogs sniffed each other at their feet.

He had come to care about her, Liam realized in that moment. Everything he said was true, but there was so much more he could have told her.

She was beautiful, inside and out. She was kind enough to open her cottage to Aspen, she wanted to bring beauty to the patrons of the café through art and style. She had endured things that would have broken most women, turned them sour and bitter. Instead, Meredith demonstrated endless grace and courage.

He found her nothing short of remarkable.

He didn't want to leave. When he left Cape Sanctuary, a huge part of his heart would stay here.

"Goodbye, Meredith," he said softly. He kissed her forehead in a gentle farewell, then grabbed Jasper and headed back into his cottage and out of her life.

37

Meredith

How could he say those things, hold her so tenderly, and then simply walk away?

Meredith stood in the sand, the night closing in around her. Shark looked sad at losing his new friend. She knew exactly how he felt.

"Come on, bud," she said, taking the dog's leash and heading toward her cottage.

She walked inside, finding comfort from the familiar walls. She turned on the light above the stove and looked around at the home she was creating out of castoffs and secondhand items.

She loved this place. This cottage, this beach, this town. She didn't want to leave.

Her whole plan had been to flip Spindrift Cottage and use the money she made from selling the place to rebuild her life somewhere else.

Why couldn't she rebuild her life *here*?

She wanted to find the person she was during her childhood when she would come here with Frances and Tori. Someone who could go toilet-paper a house simply because her cousin had been hurt by the girl who lived inside.

When she had stayed here with her grandmother, she never had to try to wrap herself inside out to become someone else. The daughter her parents sought, cultured and educated, who never caused them a moment's inconvenience. The perfect corporate wife Carter had wanted, who could throw a dinner party with twenty minutes' notice.

Here, she could build sandcastles on the beach and play Monopoly for hours on rainy afternoons and laugh so hard she snorted milk out her nose.

She had forgotten how much she once liked the person she was in Cape Sanctuary. If she stayed, maybe she could finally like herself again. She could be all those things Liam saw in her.

She pressed a hand to her heart, to the empty place he would leave there.

How silly that they had only shared one earthshaking kiss yet she knew her life would never quite be the same without him in it.

She would always treasure the things he had said to her, especially because he knew more about her than anyone else on earth and seemed to like her anyway.

You have a huge heart. I'm amazed that even after everything you've lost, everything you've endured, you still have so much capacity for love.

She wanted to believe him. She loved her cousin dearly and wanted to work more on repairing their relationship. She was certain she could love Emilia as well, given the chance.

She had hit rock bottom. That didn't mean she had to wallow there. She had a cottage she was coming to love beside the sea, she enjoyed working at the Beach End and her relationship with Tori was on the mend.

That was far more than she thought she would find when she returned to Cape Sanctuary.

38

Tori

Ten days after the accident that had nearly taken her daughter, Tori sat in her in-laws' backyard chatting with Elena and Teresa and doing her best not to let either of them see how her hands trembled whenever Sam came near her.

She couldn't believe she was in this position. No matter how many times she told herself things would never work between them, she couldn't stop thinking about him.

The day after the accident, she had awakened in the cramped, uncomfortable chair at her daughter's bedside filled with gratitude that she was there listening to her daughter sleep with her back aching and her eyes bleary from too little rest.

She had also awakened to the stunning surety that she was head over heels in love with her late husband's older brother.

While she had talked to him several times since then, this was the first time they had spent any significant amount of time together in the presence of the family.

She didn't know how to act around him, which was exactly what she had feared would happen.

He looked so gorgeous, so big and muscled and *dear*. She

wanted to crawl into his lap, wrap her arms around his neck and hold on tight.

"Do you think they've learned anything from this?" Sam was asking her, and Tori had to force herself to focus on the conversation and not that little scar beside his mouth she was longing to taste.

"I hope they've learned not to lie to their parents and go off with older boys."

"Right. They should keep that in mind when they can't swim all summer or go surfing or any of the other fun things they've been looking forward to."

"Yes. But on the flip side, now we have to listen to them complain about it."

"There is that, unfortunately," he said with a laugh.

She stared for a moment too long at his mouth. When she lifted her gaze to his, his expression once more had turned ravenous.

Tori rose abruptly. "Looks like the water pitcher is almost empty," she said, grabbing for any excuse to put some distance between them. "I'll go refill it."

With a sense of desperation, she picked up the pitcher that held a few remaining lemon slices and blueberries for flavor.

She opened the freezer to grab more ice, grateful for the cold air that rushed out, cooling her skin. If Sam continued giving her those sexy smiles, she would have to stand here all night to keep herself under control.

By the time she had scooped out several ice cubes and added them to the pitcher, she thought she had almost cooled sufficiently for her to enjoy the rest of the party without making a fool of herself.

She closed the freezer and turned to carry the pitcher back out to the party when she nearly bumped into something.

Someone.

Sam.

At the intense expression on his face, her heart gave a little lurch and Tori could feel herself panic.

301

She held up the pitcher as a shield. "I just…need to take this back to the party. People will be thirsty."

"I hate that you're uncomfortable around me now," he said, his voice low.

"I told you that would happen, didn't I?"

"You said that would happen if we, er, had an affair. We've only kissed and here you are acting as jumpy as a grasshopper around me. I never wanted that, Tori."

"What did you want?" Her voice came out sharp.

"You. Just you."

She set the pitcher down on the kitchen island so abruptly some of the water sloshed over the side.

"That's not fair," she muttered.

"I'm sorry, but it's true. I have feelings for you, Tori. I have had them for a long time. I would like to see where things can go between us. Isn't there some way we can figure this out?"

His words sent joy spiraling through her. He had feelings for her as well? She wanted to bask in the knowledge, to clutch them tightly to her heart.

She couldn't, though. Not with his family, their daughters, sitting outside.

"Figure out what?" she asked quietly. "We're both part of this family. Neither of us can change that, even if we wanted to."

"So we spend the rest of our life seeing each other at family events, wondering what might have been if we had taken the chance? No. I'm not willing to do that. I care about you, Tori. I think you might care about me too. I can't imagine the people we both love would want to stand in the way of what we could have together."

She gazed at him, miserable and aching for him, wishing she had the courage to take the chance of risking everything.

As he had done when he risked his life to save their daughters, climbing under that teetering vehicle to attach the rope that would lead them to stable ground.

"Sam."

He gazed down at her, his expression both tender and intense. She loved him. She didn't want to spend the rest of her life filled with regret. In that moment, she knew she had to be the one to take on the risk now, no matter how it scared her.

She slid a hand to his mouth, to the tiny scar there. She wondered how he got it. Probably skateboarding, the dangerous, reckless boy he had been.

At her touch, he grew still, hardly moving. She traced that scar with her fingertip and then, gently, slowly, she stood up on tiptoes and brushed her mouth where her finger had been.

He closed his eyes and let her take the lead, touching and tasting.

This was heaven. All she ever wanted.

Why, again, had she been so convinced she shouldn't be doing this? At this moment, she felt like kissing Sam was the only right thing in her world.

He remained still, muscles leashed, for a few more moments of torment. When she licked at the corner of his mouth, he groaned, wrapped her tightly in his arms and kissed her with a fierce, wild hunger that left her breathless.

Oh yes.

This.

She fought a laugh of pure joy as she realized this was the only place she wanted to be.

They kissed for several long, beautiful moments. She was lost to everything but him. Sam, who made her laugh, ache, feel, *live* again.

A sound somehow managed to pierce the haze of emotions pouring through her, of someone clearing his or her throat.

Tori froze. Oh no.

"Sorry to interrupt," came her mother-in-law's voice, "but the kids are done swimming and are coming inside to dry off. I thought you might want a heads-up."

She wrenched her mouth away from Sam and stared at Teresa. What must she think of her?

Tori had been married to one son and was now wrapped in the arms of another. She took a step away from Sam, feeling her face heat.

"I'm so sorry."

Teresa looked genuinely amused. "Why? It's not the first time my kitchen has seen two people kissing. Probably won't be the last, either."

Teresa reached for the water pitcher Tori had filled. She thrust it to her son, who appeared bemused and more than a little uncomfortable.

"Here. Take this out to the party, would you?"

He looked as if he wanted to say something, though Tori wasn't sure if he wanted to say it to her or to his mother.

After a moment, he nodded, reached for the water pitcher and headed stiffly for the door.

Tori waited for the inevitable questions and accusations. Instead, her mother-in-law seemed wholly unconcerned as she pulled another bowl of pasta salad out of the refrigerator.

She set it on the island and started to take off the lid.

Tori couldn't stand it anymore. She cleared her throat.

"Aren't you going to say anything?" she finally said.

"About what? You think I've never seen people kiss before?"

"You've never seen *us* kiss before," Tori muttered.

Teresa studied her briefly, then smiled. "True. But I've been in the same room with the two of you quite a bit since he and Cristina moved back and figured it was only a matter of time."

She sounded so placid, so matter-of-fact, Tori could only stare at her.

"You're not upset at the idea of me and Sam, er, kissing?"

Her eyebrows rose. "Upset? Why would I be upset? Pablo and I were saying just the other day after you came to dinner how wonderful it would be if the two of you got together."

The words took a long moment to penetrate. "But... I was married to Javier."

"And you were a wonderful wife to him. I couldn't have asked for a more loving daughter-in-law."

"You don't think it's weird that now I have...feelings for Sam?"

"I think it's wonderful. My son is a good man, and I can't imagine any woman I would rather see him with than you."

"What would people say if...if Sam and I started dating?"

"What people? Who are these people who matter so much to you?"

There was no one whose opinion she cared about as much as she did that of Teresa and Pablo.

Still, she couldn't quite understand how the other woman could be so casual about this.

"What about Joni?"

Teresa shrugged. "Joni moved on three months after their divorce. She has no right to say anything about anyone Sam might care about, as far as I'm concerned."

Teresa took her hand. "If you care about Sam, that's the only thing that should matter. Not what other people think."

She was exactly right. How lovely, to have such a wise mother-in-law.

"Thank you," she murmured.

"For what?" Teresa smiled.

Tori didn't have the chance to answer before the kitchen was suddenly filled with noise as Elena's children tromped through to change out of their swimming suits for dinner.

Tori's mind whirled through the rest of the family dinner. She wasn't seated near Sam, but she could still feel his gaze on her. Every time, she felt a little answering burst of awareness.

What was she going to do about it?

Take a chance.

"I was thinking," Teresa said as people were enjoying their

desserts. "Why don't we do a Grandma sleepover tonight? It's been a while since our last one."

Elena's kids shrieked with excitement and even Cristina and Emilia looked happy at the prospect of hanging out here overnight.

"Great idea, my dear," Pablo said.

"That new animated movie came out last weekend and everyone is raving about it. Maybe we could all go to Redding tomorrow to see it it. My treat."

Was Teresa only doing this so she and Sam could have a little space away from the girls to explore the possibilities between them?

"We're in. The kids would love it," Elena said. "You can keep them all week, if you want."

Teresa gave a placid smile. "Overnight should be enough. What about you girls?"

"Yay," Em said. "We've been dying to see that movie."

"I heard it's hilarious and sad at the same time. And I love the music already. It's all over YouTube."

"That's settled, then, if your parents have no objection."

Everyone's attention shifted to Tori and Sam.

"What about your pain meds?" Tori finally asked Em.

"I'm down to regular Tylenol and ibuprofen most of the time now," Em said. "I know Grandma has that."

"Same here," Cristina said.

They probably wouldn't sleep much. They would spend the night whispering and talking and be bleary-eyed for the movie. But this was Teresa's gig. If she didn't mind that, Tori didn't.

"It's fine with me," she said.

"Same," Sam answered. "I don't mind. Sounds like fun."

The party broke up shortly after that. Sam didn't say anything about meeting up with her later. Somehow he didn't need to. She knew he would come to the cottage, that they would finally have the chance to talk without fear of interruptions.

When she drove back to Starfish Beach, she found Meredith taking advantage of the last rays of sunlight to work in her little flower garden.

She had a mission, she remembered, so she put the leash on a thrilled Shark and headed that way carrying a small grocery bag.

Her cousin smiled when she approached, though Tori thought her eyes still looked a little sad, as they had since Liam Byrne had left town.

"How was dinner?" Meredith asked.

"Delicious, as usual. My mother-in-law insisted I bring you some of the leftovers."

"Oh. That's sweet of her. She's so kind. That will make a delicious lunch tomorrow. Thanks."

"You're welcome."

They chatted for a few more moments about the café and some of the staff issues for the upcoming week. When an impatient Shark tugged at the leash, Tori had to laugh.

"I had better take him for a walk. He'll bug me all night if I don't."

"Sounds good. Thanks again for the food."

She started to walk the little dog down to the beach when suddenly a familiar SUV pulled up. A moment later, Sam climbed out with Risa, unfolding with athletic grace.

They didn't even really talk about it, only started walking down the beach together. Before she quite realized it, they were holding hands. It felt so natural, so perfect, as if they had done this a hundred times before.

They walked to the edge of the beach, where a peninsula of rocks jutting into the ocean prevented them from going farther unless they wanted to swim.

There, it seemed perfectly natural and right for her to tug him toward her so she could kiss him as the setting sun cast vibrant rays across the waves.

She wasn't afraid, she realized. This felt entirely too right for her to worry about what other people might think.

"I'm really glad you and Cristina moved back to Cape Sanctuary, Sam."

He pressed his forehead to hers. "So am I. You know, when I made the decision to come home, I thought I was coming back to be closer to family. Now I wonder if I was really coming back to be closer to you."

He kissed her again, and as the waves brushed their feet and the dogs played in the sand, she fell further in love.

There might be people who would talk, who would find it odd that she was now with Sam when she had once been married to his brother.

She didn't care. If the people she cared about most were okay with it, what did it matter what others thought? Tori intended to listen to her heart now, which was completely convinced that being right here, in Sam's arms, was exactly where she belonged.

39

Meredith

Two months later

Her cousin was in love.

On a Thursday in early August, Meredith was taking a breakfast order from a family of tourists when she spotted Sam Ayala come into the café, thermos in hand for his daily refill.

He headed straight for Tori, who hadn't seen him yet as she worked on training a new employee who was taking Meredith's old job.

As Meredith headed for the kitchen with the order, she saw Tori's face light up with joy the moment she spotted Sam.

It warmed Meredith's heart. She loved seeing Tori so happy, especially after her cousin had endured so much loss.

She followed Sam out of the restaurant after he refilled his thermos. As Meredith finished taking the table order, she saw Sam press Tori against the wall for one brief, intense kiss that left her cousin flushed and smiling, then he hopped into his unmarked police car and headed off for the day.

Tori stood for a moment, watching after him, hand pressed to her mouth, then she came back into the restaurant. The table of regulars teased her a little, as they did almost every day when Sam came in for a refill and a kiss.

Meredith didn't tease her cousin. She thought it was wonderful to see Tori and Sam in love. The two of them were so sweet together.

There were times, she had to admit, when seeing their joy gave her a sharp ache of longing, but she was too busy working at the café and serving as a volunteer with the local Arts & Hearts on the Cape event to focus on it for long.

Today was no different. The restaurant was packed with hungry people, some of whom, she wanted to think, had come in because of the social media advertising or the new bright, cheerful sign out front that Meredith personally changed out daily with clever sayings or funny line drawings.

After two months of working at the Beach End, Meredith had come to love the rhythm and flow of the café. She wanted to think she was offering a contribution too.

Her idea of hanging art on the wall proved remarkably popular. At least ten works of art had been sold as a direct result, and she wanted to think she had introduced many people to local artists they might not have discovered otherwise.

She was grabbing beverages for her family of tourists when Tori came back to the kitchen, a funny expression on her face Meredith couldn't quite read.

"Hey, can you take care of table six for me?"

"That's Aspen's section," Meredith reminded her.

"I know but she's swamped. Can you help her out, just with that table?"

"Sure." It wasn't an unusual request. The servers often swapped tables. She grabbed her pen and pencil and headed toward the booth in the back, the one she generally tried to avoid.

She still considered that Liam's booth, and it was hard for her to see anyone else there.

As she moved toward the booth, she saw one diner there, his face turned away from her. His coloring, his shape, the angle of his jaw seemed to grow more familiar as she approached.

Her footsteps slowed even as her heart started to pound in her chest.

It couldn't be. Surely Tori would have given her some warning.

Finally he looked up. The sharp burst of joy she felt almost made her stumble.

"Hi, Meredith."

That low voice had haunted her dreams for two months. This wasn't a dream, though. This was real.

"Liam," she gasped. "What are you...why are you here?"

He gave her a slow smile. "The food at the Beach End is so good, I couldn't stay away."

There was something in that smile, something that left her light-headed.

"That's a long way to come for one of Denise's Reubens."

"But they are delicious. Actually, do you have a minute to sit down? I'm here to see you."

She didn't. The morning had already been hectic, and they had more people waiting outside to be seated.

She opened her mouth to apologize and ask if he could come back after the breakfast rush when Aspen rushed over.

"I've got this. I'll cover your tables," she told Meredith. "Can I get you anything, FBI?"

He looked momentarily startled, as if he hadn't expected everyone to know who he was.

Of course she had told Aspen. The young woman had become a dear friend to Meredith over the past two months of living together.

Aspen's paintings had turned out to be among their most popular in their rotating art exhibit at the café. Meredith knew she had sold three that had been hanging in the café as well as several others.

"Thanks," she said to Aspen, then turned back to Liam. "Looks like I'm on break."

She slid into the booth across from him, wildly curious about what he might be doing there. Beneath the table, their knees touched, and the contact assured her this was real. He was here, not just another fleeting dream.

She couldn't quite believe it.

"How's Jasper?"

"He's good. He wasn't happy that I didn't bring him along on this trip. I left him with a friend who has a couple of kids and a nice pool. The only thing Jasper likes better than the ocean is a swimming pool. A couple of kids to play with is always a bonus." He reached out and picked up her hand. The contact, after all these weeks, made her feel slightly dizzy.

"How have you been?" he asked, his long fingers twisting through hers. "Do you have the cottage up for sale yet?"

"No. I'm not selling. Not right now, anyway. I'm happy where I am."

"Good. That's good."

As much as she would like to sit here all morning holding hands, she sensed he hadn't come here only for this. She decided to come straight out and ask him.

"Why are you here, Liam?"

His smile was slightly sheepish. "I have news. I wanted to share it in person, not over the phone or email. I…have something that might interest you."

From the same battered messenger bag he had brought into the café all those times he was pretending to be a writer, he pulled out a file folder. He slid it across the table to her and opened it to a page on top covered in rows of numbers.

Meredith gazed at it, unsure what was happening but sensing it was something important.

"What is it? You're the numbers guy. It looks like gibberish to me."

"Ha. I like that. Two months of work on my part and you're calling it gibberish."

"I mean, it's not the great American novel, right?"

312

He laughed. "No. I'll admit, I still haven't written that yet. Sorry to disappoint you but I think you'll like this better."

She looked at the numbers again and still couldn't make sense of them. "You'll have to explain to me. I work in a café and have a fairly useless degree in art history. I know how to split my tips but that's about it."

He leaned closer and she breathed in the familiar scent.

Oh, she had missed him. She wanted to toss the folder to the floor, grab him by the shirt and kiss him with the same intensity she had seen Sam kiss Tori.

Instead, she folded her hands into her lap. "What is it?" she asked again.

"The column on the left shows dozens of bank accounts in the Caymans. The ones on the right are Swiss. If you do the math, which of course I have, they represent a combined total of four hundred and three million dollars."

She stared at him as the implications washed over her. "You... you found it? You found the missing money? How?"

"Two months of dogged persistence. With your help."

She hadn't talked to him in two months, not since the night before he left town. She hadn't done anything to help him.

"You gave me a clue when you told me about his strong reaction on your wedding day that his parents weren't there. I sensed that was the key. It had to be. I collected all the information I could on them, and after months of research, I found one account in his mother's maiden name. That led to three more linked to that one. And then more linked to those. Three hundred in all."

"You...did that?"

"It's not all of it. We calculate he spent about a hundred million that will likely never be recovered. But at least it's something."

"You...you did that?" she repeated.

She couldn't quite take it all in.

He nodded. "Mostly on my own time. Yes. Though when I started getting closer, all the other agencies involved in the task

313

force were only too happy to give me assistance. The Bureau is holding a press conference in two days where they will be announcing the recovery of a big portion of the stolen funds. I have insisted they include a carefully worded statement that it was found in large part thanks to the full support and assistance of Carter Rowland's ex-wife, Meredith Collins."

Oh. She gripped her hands together as the implications rolled through her. Would that be enough to change the tide of public opinion? Probably not completely. But it would help, so very much.

"But... I had nothing to do with it."

"Not true. You had everything to do with it. I never would have looked in that direction if you hadn't told me that small bit of information. I couldn't get that out of my mind, what he did to you on your wedding day. It ate away at me." He tapped the list of numbers with a finger. "And eventually led to this."

She couldn't quite absorb the impact of everything he had done...and why he had done it.

Yes, she knew he had wanted to find the missing funds for the victims, especially his mother.

But as he looked at her across the table with that warmth in his expression, she realized he had done it for her too, so that she could finally begin to crawl out from under the weight of Carter's crimes.

"I...don't know what to say." Tears began then, tears of gratitude, of relief, of the fragile beginnings of a joy she never expected to feel again. "Thank you."

"You are so welcome, Meredith."

And then, to her shock, he leaned forward and kissed her with fierce, blazing tenderness.

That joy exploded and she wrapped her arms around him, returning his kiss as all the aching loneliness she had battled for two months seemed to drift away in an instant.

"I've missed you," he murmured against her mouth. "I couldn't think of anything else when I left Cape Sanctuary.

Eventually, I decided to channel all that tangle of emotions into something positive."

Was it any wonder she was in love with him? How could she not be? He was kind and honorable. The exact opposite of the man who had hidden away all that money for himself.

"How long can you stay?" she asked. She wanted the chance to tell him of her feelings, but not right here in the middle of a crowded café, with her cousin and all her coworkers watching on with avid interest.

"I have to be back in two days for the press conference." He paused. "I'm supposed to ask if you would consider attending with me. You don't have to, but it might go a long way toward helping people see the truth."

She couldn't possibly do that. She had shrunk away from the public eye after the horror of those first months after Carter was charged. She was building a good life here in Cape Sanctuary. She had friends now, a job she loved, a cottage where she had found peace.

But as she looked at this man she loved, she thought perhaps she was ready to put the past completely in her rearview mirror so that she could be free to focus on the horizon and the joy-filled future she suddenly knew was waiting for her there.

"I'll think about it," she said.

He smiled and kissed her again. "What are the chances you might be able to take a few hours off today while I'm in town?"

She glanced over at Tori, who was beaming at her.

"I think that can probably be arranged. I'm pretty good friends with the owners."

He laughed and reached for her hand. Together, they rose and walked out into the summer sun.

★ ★ ★ ★ ★